Chinese Crossfire

God Walks in China

Stephen L. Thompson

Chinese Crossfire

Books by Stephen L. Thompson

The Crossfire Series

Colorado Crossfire
International Crossfire
Israeli Crossfire
Believer's Crossfire
Spirit Crossfire
Faith Crossfire
Chinese Crossfire
Texas Crossfire
Dark Crossfire
Island Crossfire
Jagged Crossfire
Violent Crossfire
Russian Crossfire
Nuclear Crossfire
End Times Crossfire
Revelation Crossfire
Gates of Hell Crossfire
Assassin's Crossfire
Albatross Crossfire
Global Crossfire
Far East Crossfire

The SFO Series

Station Force One – Onset

Chinese Crossfire

In *"Chinese Crossfire"* The Crossfire Team becomes the target of a demon-controlled Chinese government official that believes he is the next Emperor of China. His purpose is to attain his worldly desires regardless of the people he has to destroy to do it.

The story begins with an attack on Jack and Laura in Washington, D.C. which the official arranges. His demon has convinced the official that he must acquire the holy treasure held by Jack and eliminate the Crossfire Team to get his victory.

The conflict rages between the official and the Team as China and the U.S. Administration try to prevent an all-out war between their countries. The tension increases as the official forces the Crossfire Team's hand to save a hundred hostages.

- Stephen L. Thompson

Chinese Crossfire

Published by
Stephen L. Thompson
Facebook.com/CrossfireNovelSeries

ISBN- 978-1-943879-02-1

Foreword

To my Christian readers –

The Crossfire continuing series of action-adventure novels include depictions of violence which are unusual in Christian literature. It would be nice if there were no conflict or violence in our world. But we live in a time when evil is increasing instead of diminishing, when some men seem to be controlled by selfishness, madness, or evil forces. When the enemies of decent mankind are bent on subjugation of other men and women, righteous men and women must stand against evil. The yoke of oppression is not lifted by prayer alone. God is our Shepherd and we are his sheep. As long as there are wolves about, God will use some of us as sheep dogs to defend the rest of us. These stories are about people like that and the forces they fight against. The stories describe violence because it occurs in the real world and it is active in the lives of all people whether they recognize it or not.

To my non-Christian readers –

The Crossfire series include depictions of spiritual warfare and spiritual activity with which the non-Christian reader may not be familiar. These stories describe the realms and activities of both God and Satan because they're real and active in the lives of all people whether they recognize it or not.

Steve Thompson

CHAPTER ONE

As the Ski-Doo slammed into the passing craft's wake it rode up the wall of water. It started to rapidly roll over to the right as it rose into the air. Jack and Laura hung on for dear life as the watercraft went sideward to the water. As the larger boat passing between them moved out of the way, the Chinese agents opened fire with two sub-machine guns. The fleeing water ski's bottom presented a good target.

Quite a few of the rounds missed the Ski-Doo due to the movement of the two watercraft. Still, some bullets smashed into the bottom of the Ski-Doo and punched through the fiber-glass body without much effort. Pieces of the hull were blown off as the water ski continued to roll and dropped into the lake upside down. The rush of water tore the two riders from the seat.

Jack floated underwater and felt the numbness in his left side and his left leg that told him he had been hit by at least two rounds. He could see Laura floating a few feet away and he could see blood flowing out of her body. He looked up and could see the wake surrounding the hull of the boat with the Chinese agents coming around for another pass. He had taken a big breath just before they hit the water and hoped that Laura had done the same.

He couldn't get his left leg to move but used his hands to pull himself through the water to his wife. She was still conscious but didn't look like she could move under her own power. Her eyes were big and looked at Jack for reassurance. Jack smiled at her but wasn't too sure how much assurance he could give her right at the moment. He silently prayed that God would sustain them.

The need for air was becoming critical for him and he put his left arm around her and used his right leg and hand to push them to the surface. He tried to only get their faces above the surface for air and to present the smallest targets.

Both of them gulped in the fresh air and Jack pushed them under again as far as his damaged body would let him. He looked through the clear water for a sign of the enemy craft. He saw it about thirty feet away but it was going away from them. He stroked to the surface and pulled both of their heads above the water. He could just see the back of the boat as it pulled away. He looked at Laura but she had passed out. He was attempting to keep her head above the water when a shadow fell over him. Twisting his head around, he saw a boat directly above them blocking out the sun. He also saw hands reaching down for them. Before he could do anything, the hands had grabbed Laura's life jacket and arms. They were pulling her up onto the boat. He tried to fight but felt the strength draining out of him. The people above him grabbed his shoulders and he was pulled strongly up out of the water onto a flat surface. When he tried to roll to his left the pain hit him so hard he fell into a large, black, silent pit of nothingness.

Jack came to with a feeling of panic. He didn't know where Laura was and he was tied to a bed. He started to thrash around and try to get loose. Two people rushed over to his bed and restrained him from moving. The person on the right said. "Stop moving or you'll tear out your stitches!"

That command made Jack settle down and look at the two people holding him. The one on his left was a nurse. The other person was a doctor or an intern. Jack relaxed and stopped struggling. He tried to talk but couldn't make much in the way of sound to start with. By the third try he was able to ask. "Where is my wife?"

The doctor looked at the nurse for a few seconds and Jack's heart sank. The man looked seriously at Jack and said, "She's in the next room but she's in a coma. We are monitoring her vitals and they are stronger now then when she came out of the OR.

Jack's mind suddenly pictured the string of events that brought him to this bed.

---------------------------******---------------------------

They had been asked to give a special report to the Secretary of Defense and the Joint Chiefs of Staff regarding their trip to China to rescue kidnapped hostages. The report went well and they were on their way back to the airport with George Holcomb, an Undersecretary of Defense. He was another, born-again Christian in the upper levels of government and was interested in hearing about the spiritual warfare that took place on that trip.

They traveled up Highway 233 on the way to Ronald Regan National Airport in the undersecretary's limousine. They were describing the defeat of the demon that was attacking them, by the angel Caleb. George shook his head in wonderment and a deep desire to see Yahveh's warriors in action.

There was a loud explosion which slammed the occupants around and suddenly smoke and debris littered the back of the vehicle. The heavy limousine went to the right and smashed through the guardrail. The well-built guardrail slowed the limousine enough that it remained upright and slid to a halt on the bank of the Potomac River. All three of the passengers had been shaken by the events. George Holcomb forced open the door on the uphill side and stepped out of the limousine. Five men appeared at the broken guardrail. They were all dressed in black and each one held a handgun. As George held up his hand to block the sunlight from his eyes, all of the enemy agents fired at the undersecretary.

George Holcomb saw the Father even as the bullets snatched away his life. He knew that everything would be well with his family. Full of Yahveh's peace and compassion he was able to say "forgive them" as his life ended.

As George's body fell to the ground, gravity pulled the door shut. Dozens of rounds bounced off the armor-plating of the door and caromed off of the bullet-resistant glass. As he saw the gunmen start down the embankment toward the limo, Jack opened the downhill side door and fell out of the car on his back. He pulled Laura out of the car on top of him. Using the limousine as a shield, they crawled down the slope and slipped into the cold water of the river. The embankment was steep and they were able to submerge and swim downstream away from the killers. Jack saw the tracks of several bullets through the water around them.

They came to the surface of the water to get air. The water's flow had pulled them downstream so that they had passed behind a stand of trees and bushes. This effectively shielded them from the killers. Laura was praying that the Father would protect them and keep the spirits of their new friend and the driver of the limousine. Jack saw several watercraft pulled to the embankment, several hundred yards downstream on their side of the river. He lifted an arm and pointed them out to Laura. They were still shielded by the trees but through the branches Jack could see the killers running around the stand of trees.

There were several people on the shore a few hundred feet away from a boat and two Ski-Doos. Whatever they were doing was keeping them oblivious to the silenced gunfire or the on-rushing danger. Jack yelled a warning to them and they stopped and looked at him. He pointed toward the on-coming killers and yelled, "Look out!"

Two of the killers had come around the stand of trees, on the other side of the three men on the shore, and proceeded to gun down all three men. It happened so quickly they probably died without even knowing that they were in danger.

Jack reached the first Ski-Doo and grabbed on to it. Laura, right behind him, grabbed onto him and was pulled away from the shore by the current. Their combined weight pulled the craft away from the shore and it bounced off of the boat parked next to it and then swung out into the stream. Hiding behind the watercraft, Jack saw that the key was in the ignition of the two-seater craft. As they passed some large rocks they were again shielded from the gunners. He pulled himself up onto the Ski-Doo and reached back and helped Laura aboard.

Familiar with this type of water machine, Jack started it up and cranked the throttle wide open. Laura hung onto him as they curved farther out into the river and headed downstream, away from the men with guns. Laura looked back and saw that several of the killers had jumped into the boat on the shore and were pushing it out into the water. She yelled at Jack and he looked back. He urged as much speed out of the little water jet as possible.

They entered a wider part of the river as the boat began to catch up with them. Jack saw a larger boat coming upstream and veered to the right side of the other craft. The boat with the killers had to veer to the left side to avoid a collision. As the larger boat had passed them,

Jack remembered the Ski-Doo flying up into the air off of the wake of the large boat and the bullets hitting the hull.

------------------------******------------------------

He looked at the doctor and said, "How badly was she wounded?"

The doctor put his hand on Jack's and explained. "She had a wound to the left side of her head which was caused by a bullet striking the side of her skull at an angle and ricocheting off. She had another bullet wound that passed through her right arm. I can't tell yet if the damage to her head is the cause of her coma but the CAT scan didn't show any penetration, just concussion."

The doctor smiled at Jack. "You, on the other hand, took a bullet in your left thigh and another one that tunneled through your left side and out your back. How it missed your vital organs is an absolute mystery, but it did. I even have the x-ray of the bullet path through your body. At one place it should have severed an artery, but didn't. Anyway, we went in and cleaned out the wounds. I don't think that you will have any permanent muscle damage from either bullet wound. To set your mind at ease about your wife, I think her body is in a state of repair and she will come out of this fine."

Jack looked at the young man and said, "Thank you for your efforts Doctor. Can you tell me how we got here? The last thing I remember is being hauled out of the river."

The doctor shook his head. "I really don't know that information, but I think the two policemen waiting outside to talk to you will probably have the answer to your question. You seem strong enough so I will let them talk to you. If you feel weak or faint, push the red button next to your head on the pillow." He left the bedside and walked to the door of the room. Jack looked at the nurse who was adjusting a saline drip on a rack. "Do you know where my cell phone is? I need to warn some other people about our attackers."

She smiled and went to the closet. Coming back, she handed him the cell phone. "I don't think it will work. It was full of water and apparently hit something."

Jack held the phone up in his right hand and looked at it. It had obviously deflected another bullet because it was gouged and deeply dented. He opened the battery compartment and some water drained out of it. He handed it back to the nurse and asked if there was a phone he could use.

Before she could hand him the room phone, two men entered the room and approached his bedside. One look and Jack knew that these weren't Washington, D.C. area policemen.

CHAPTER TWO

Both men were built rock solid with short military haircuts and no-nonsense attitudes.

One of the two men reached inside his dress jacket and Jack braced himself. The hand came out with a miniature tape recorder and Jack relaxed. The man asked, "Mr. Jack Malone?"

Jack nodded. The man switched on the recorder. "I'm Bill Armitage and this is my partner, Jerry Knowles. We're from the Central Intelligence Department of the Army. We are investigating the death of George Holcomb, three other civilians, and the attack on you and your wife. Do you feel up to talking to us for a few minutes?

Jack analyzed how he felt and responded. "I will talk to you, but first I need to make a phone call to warn other people about this attack. Can you wait a couple of minutes?"

The two men shrugged and Jerry said, "All right, go ahead, but please make it brief."

Jack took hold of the phone and then stopped and asked Bill Armitage, "Are you armed?"

When Bill looked around and then opened his jacket to reveal a .40 caliber automatic, Jack said, "Listen carefully, both of you. The men that attacked us may well come here to finish the job. I need someone to protect my wife in the next room."

Bill looked at his partner and smiled. "Don't worry about that Mr. Malone, we have a man outside her room and I doubt that anyone will be foolish enough to attack you here. Please make your call so we can get on with our interview."

They weren't taking this seriously enough. Jack said, "Mr. Armitage, I hold the rank of General in the U.S. Air Force and I'm telling you that the people that had the audacity to attack and kill the Undersecretary will not hesitate to break into this facility to kill us. Now, this is an order. Get some troops here. Now!"

Bill looked doubtful but after considering the tone and delivery of Jack's comments, he took out his cell phone and hit a preset number. He talked to someone for a few minutes and nodded. He hung up and said to his partner, "He is a General and we have been tasked to give him all assistance possible by the brass."

The change in their attitude was remarkable. They both came to attention and Bill saluted. "Yes Sir!" He recalled a number on his cell phone and spoke rapidly to the person on the other end.

Jack picked up the room phone and dialed the number for the Fortress. It was answered on the second ring by Sarah. Jack filled her in and then stopped. He looked at the CID men and asked, "What hospital is this and what address is it located at?"

They told him he was at the George Washington Medical Center and gave him the address information which he relayed to Sarah. She said, "We'll be there in three hours." There was a momentary pause and Mark came on the line. "I called a friend from the SEALs and they will be there in no time. How's Laura?"

Jack said, "I don't know. The doctor said she is in a coma but feels she'll be all right. Listen, I've got two CID investigators here and they are also arranging for military protection, probably from the Army. Let's not get any service rivalries going and take the focus away from the real threat, okay?"

Mark assured him that it would be taken care of before he got there. He hung up.

Jack called Bill Armitage over and explained what Mark said and repeated the warning against clashes over who's in charge. Bill nodded and got back on the phone.

When Bill hung up his phone, Jack asked him, "How did my wife and I get here?"

Bill looked at his note book. "It seems that a small flotilla of boats was coming upstream when your Jet Ski flipped over and sank. They all headed over to the area and found you floating on the water. They hauled you in but said they never saw your Jet Ski again. They saw that you were damaged and immediately started first aid and got a MediVac helicopter to bring you here. You couldn't have found a better group to crash in front of. They were all Firemen and Paramedics on an annual picnic."

The room phone rang and the nurse answered it. She talked for a few seconds and then handed the phone to Jack. She grinned a big beautiful grin, "It's the President!"

Jack smiled back at her and took the phone, "Yes Sir, Mr. President."

The President's voice was agitated and concerned. "Jack, I just got the news of the attack. Are you and Laura all right?"

Jack explained the situation and told the President how sorry he was for the loss of the Undersecretary and the driver. The President said he understood and then asked the big question. "Was this retaliation for that trip your Team just made to China?"

Jack prayed for the right answer. "Yes Sir, I'm sure it was. The attackers were Asian and very efficient. It was only by the grace of God that Laura and I survived."

The President told Jack he would pray for them and to get well as soon as possible. They would talk about the problem when he and Laura were better. He then asked to speak to the Army investigators. Jack motioned Bill over to the bed and handed him the phone. Bill answered and nodded several times. He ended with, "Thank you, Mr. President."

The door was opened by an Army ranger in full battle dress and holding an M-16. He said, "Sir! Army Major Wells and Navy Captain Tallman would like to see you." Jack nodded and the two men walked into the room. They both stopped at the foot of the bed and came to a stiff attention and saluted.

Captain Tallman spoke first. "General Malone, General Connelly ordered my squad to provide protection for you and your wife until he arrives. I have liaisoned with Major Wells here representing the Army Special Forces unit, that is also involved and we need definition as to our mutual roles in this task. Sir!

Jack would have sighed if he had the time. "Thank you both for responding so quickly. I believe that there is a role for both of your units in this situation. I just spoke to the President and he is also concerned that foreign forces on our land have initiated a violent attack against us and have already killed an undersecretary of the Defense department. I am ordering both of you to lose the service attitudes and cooperate for the sake of all of us. Gentlemen, this is not a football game. There are Chinese agents loose in America and they are determined to destroy my wife and I. Now, I want you two to figure out a way that each of your Teams can be the most efficient working together, because if they are coming against us again, it will be with everything from direct assault to a truck bomb. Are we clear on this?"

The gravity of the situation had been brought home to both men. "Yes Sir! They chorused in unison. Major Wells said, "We'll work it out Sir, and no one is going to get to you or your wife."

The SEAL grinned and nodded his agreement. They both saluted again and turned to go. As they left they started figuring out the optimum defensive strategy for their combined forces.

The two CID investigators had been quietly standing in the background, somewhat awed by the involvement of the President and so many officers. Bill said, "Excuse me, General, but the President wanted us to get everything we could on the attack from you so that we can start tracking these people."

Jack nodded and shifted his weight on the bed. A sharp wave of pain flared up from his left side, leg, and back. He took a moment to let it subside before he could talk. Then he gave the investigators everything he could remember. They thanked him, saluted and left.

After the flurry of activity, the sudden quiet and peace seemed strange to Jack as he lay there alone. He tried to think about what was next, but it just didn't seem too important and he drifted off to sleep

CHAPTER THREE

Mark reached the hospital at six p.m. straight up. He stopped and conferred with Captain Tallman of the SEALs and Major Wells of the Army Rangers. He approved of their precautions and told them so. Then he headed for the rooms holding his best friends.

Sarah was already at Laura's bedside, brushing the hair away from her forehead and staring at her sleeping face. She owed such a great debt to this woman that she wished she could have taken the bullets instead. Mark walked into the room and looked at Laura still in her coma. He tipped his head toward the room with Jack in it. Sarah patted Laura's hand, "We'll be right back, Sweetie." she whispered as they left.

Jack was conscious again and working his injured left side as best as he could. He looked up and smiled a wan smile as Mark and Sarah came into the room. Sarah hugged him and kissed his cheek. Mark went around and looked at his damaged left side. "When did the doctor say you could get out of here?"

Jack laughed a quiet laugh. "They are concerned about this and that and have no predictions of less than three days. I personally plan to be up and out of this room in about ten minutes. I have been praying and I'm led to believe that God wants the three of us to lay hands on Laura and pray for her healing."

Sarah nodded, "That's what I felt, too."

Mark looked at his watch, "Let's see, Laura has been in a coma, for what? The last five hours? That's enough R and R." Jack could sense the concern Mark had for Laura underneath the humor.

Mark reached up and shut off the monitoring equipment, detached the electrodes, and took the IV drip tube out of Jack's arm. He then taped a bandage over the small wound. Jack eased his battered body out of the bed and put his feet on the floor. He gasped in the crush of the pain when he tried to stand and would have fallen if Sarah hadn't caught him and held him up. The pain was significant but not debilitating and Jack knew the consequences of being too inactive. He worked on making his left leg hold him up and was rewarded by a shaky stance on his own.

Mark reached into a bag he had brought with him and gave Jack a set of clothes. Jack limped into the bathroom and freshened up. He changed out of his hospital gown and into the clothes. The pants rubbed on the bandages on his leg and his shirt pulled on the ones on his side. He ignored the pain, the discomfort, and prayed that God would strengthen him. He felt the pain recede to a nuisance level and thanked the Father. He came out of the bathroom and sat on the bed. Bending over to put on his socks and shoes proved to be beyond him at the moment. Sarah gently pushed his hands away from his feet and put his socks and shoes on for him. The thought went through Jack's head that Sarah had humbled herself, doing a service similar to the one where the woman had anointed the feet of the Lord. When she was done he stood up gingerly and put his arms around her. "Thank you for being humble Sarah, I can't tell you how that touched my heart."

She stepped back and both men could see the tears in her eyes. She just nodded, patted Jack on the chest, and turned to go to Laura's room.

Right then, the physician on call came into the room and demanded that Jack get back into bed. Jack looked at the man with ice frosting his gray-green eyes. He looked at the chart in the man's hand. "Is that my chart?"

The physician nodded and Jack limped over to the man. Taking the chart he looked for a pen. Mark handed him one and Jack signed himself out on his own authority. He handed the chart back. "Doctor, thank you for the services you've provided me but it is time for me to get moving. I release you and the hospital from any liability in my case." The three of them left the room and went into Laura's room. The doctor followed and smirked. "I take it that your wife will be staying a while longer?"

Mark bumped him aside and told him, "Why don't you hang around and find out?"

The three of them laid hands on Laura and prayed that the Lord would bring her back to them and heal her wounds. The doctor rolled his eyes and shook his head. "As if these people think that would change her condition", he thought smugly.

There was warmth that ran through each of them and out of their hands into Laura's body. Her eyes flickered and opened. She jerked a little and then settled down. Looking up into the faces of her husband and her two best friends on this earth she made a small smile. "Hi" she croaked.

Sarah was smiling at her, "How do you feel?"

Laura looked introspective for a few seconds and then said, "A little worse than I did after your landing in the mountains." Laura was referring to the damaged plane that Sarah had managed to crash land in Zyngola.

Jack asked if she had clear vision. She looked around and nodded slowly. She lifted her right arm and looked at the bandages there. She moved her fingers. "The digits are somewhat numb, but usable."

Jack smiled at his wife and tenderly kissed her forehead. She smiled weakly at him knowing how much he tried to take care of her and how much he loved her.

Sarah took the bag from Mark. "We brought you some new clothes. I'll shoo the men out and you can dress."

The doctor's smirk disappeared and he was becoming really irritated. "You can't move her! We don't know the extent of the injury to her head. Good lord, woman, she was in a coma until just a minute ago and you want her to walk out of here? I won't allow it!"

Mark went to the door and pulled it open. He talked to the Army Ranger standing guard outside the door. "Sergeant, if this physician interferes with us in any way, I want you to apprehend him and place him in custody. Take him to the brig until I can get around to him in the next few days. If he refuses, shoot him!"

The Ranger stepped into the room and brought his rifle up to port arms. "Yes Sir!" It was obvious that he would do exactly what he had been ordered to do. The doctor, three years out of residency, had never seen the military in action before. Shocked, the doctor looked with panic from Mark to the Ranger and then hurriedly left the room without another word.

Everyone but Sarah and Laura stepped outside and in a few minutes the two women joined them. Jack and Laura weren't hurrying too well but they managed to get to the elevator and down to the lobby. There were radio communications going on and soldiers at every corridor. By the time they got to the ground floor, the Rangers watching the lobby formed a human shield around them and they moved to an armored SEAL Humvee. This wasn't an H2 General Motors civilian knockoff. This was the real deal. This was a solid military vehicle with an M-60 machine gun on the roof and a SEAL Team warrior manning it. The four Team members got into the Humvee and it left the hospital in a convoy of three other armed Humvees. The surrounding traffic was careful to defer to the vehicles and kept their distance.

The convoy made its way to the same airport that the Malones had been headed for hours earlier. This time there was no interference and they were able to board their own corporate jet inside a hanger. Jack waved weakly to Su Li in the pilot's seat. She nodded and started her takeoff checklist.

Jack and Laura went back to the sleeping part of the plane and crawled gingerly into the available bunks. Their trip from the hospital had taken a lot out of them. Laura either passed out or went to sleep, right away.

The Navy doctor checked her head wound and arm and declared her in stable condition. He checked Jack's wounds and had to rebind the one in his side and back because it had started leaking. He told Jack that he needed to rest and not move, for the next several hours, then gave him a sedative. Jack felt the sedative start to work and then everything faded out as he felt Su Li gently lift the aircraft from the runway and head west for Denver.

Mark sat down and called all of the military commanders of the Teams sent to safeguard the Malones and thanked them.

Jack had a long series of dreams which he couldn't remember. Some of them were replays of the attack and some were of Caleb and himself. There seemed to be no end to the dreams.

CHAPTER FOUR

Jack awoke to a quiet Jewish melody being sung by Sarah. He slowly looked around and saw that he was in his suite at the Fortress in Denver. Laura was also sitting in a chair reading a book. She looked up and saw that he was awake. She brightened and put her book down. She came over to the bed, leaned down and kissed him on the forehead. "Welcome back, Sweetheart," she said.

Jack felt much better than when he fell asleep in the jet. He noticed that he could move his left side with almost no pain. There was some discomfort, but little pain.

Sarah came over to the bed and sat on the edge. "The Navy doctor apparently knew your type. He gave you a sedative and then continued it in a saline drip to keep you from tearing open your wounds, again."

Jack tasted the inside of his mouth and asked, "How long have I been out?"

Laura smiled, "Three days. I agreed that you needed the rest to let things heal. You normally don't consider your injuries serious, but this time they were and we all knew you wouldn't give them time to get better."

He sighed, "How long have you been up?"

Laura laughed, "About two hours before you. He knocked me out, too."

Mark came into the room and grinned at them. "Good news! I think we have a lead on the guys that tried to whack you. They are definitely Chun's goons and a really elite Team, at that. We've got them on the run at the moment and should have video of the chase in the next few minutes."

Jack lifted the sheet to see what he had on. "I think I need a moment of privacy so that I can get dressed. I'll meet you downstairs. I feel hungry enough I could eat two meals, right now."

After Jack ate his fill, the four of them walked and limped their way into the War Room. After gingerly settling into a seat, Jack told Mark, "Show me the pursuit."

Mark typed on his keyboard and the 54 by 40 inch screen lit up with four separate views. The top view was a panorama, wide-angle shot from a camera in the front of a Humvee. Below it, on the left, was an aerial view of the chase with lit icons, showing the quarry and the pursuing units. The other two views were head and shoulder shots of two Oriental men with their records next to them.

Jack watched for a minute and asked Mark, "Where is the chase taking place?"

Mark pointed at the map view, "Somewhere in the West Virginia hill country. We got a break when they ran a minibus off the road. The driver remembered that they all looked Asian and called it in to the Sheriff. The West Virginia Sheriff had seen our APB and referred it to us. A combined CID and SEAL Team picked them up with chopper coverage and we now have four vehicles closing in on them."

Jack grunted. "Yeah, but will they be taken alive? I doubt it and we don't want to lose any of our men to their suicide tactics."

Mark nodded, "The men are aware of the type of people they're pursuing and their callous lack of concern for human life, including their own. They want to get at least, one alive, but if that doesn't happen, then it doesn't happen."

Laura had been looking at the map and wondering why the killers would be driving into such a dead end area. She asked Yahveh's Spirit, out of habit. She was surprised at the answer she got. She said, "You'd better get some air assets in there besides the helicopter. They're planning to fly out of the country."

Mark didn't even ask how she knew that. He was aware of her closeness to God. He punched in a number on the phone. "This is General Connelly, there is a possibility that your suspects are headed for some form of air travel to get away. Do you have any assets in the air that could be used if that turns out to be the case?"

The answer obviously came from a jet fighter, "That's a Roger, General. This is Blue Cover flight. Five Raptors and we are vectoring in on the Humvee's signal at this time".

Mark gave him a "Roger that" and waited. The Humvees were moving up a dirt road toward where the fleeing car had disappeared. The vehicle commander reported hearing a roaring noise ahead. The Humvee topped the rise in time to see a high-wing, swept-back passenger jet thundering into the air on JATO units from a short grass runway.

Mark hit the microphone switch and said, "That's a Chinese AN-24RV modified reconnaissance aircraft. Blue Cover flight, can you bring it down without destroying it?"

"Roger that, Blue Flight in with guns. Disable the engines, only."

The top view switched suddenly from the Humvee view to an aerial view, from the commander's F-22 Raptor. The Chinese plane was headed for the sea on a direct, low-level flight. The first two F-22s made a pass and you could see the tracers from their guns. The right engine of the two-engine jet exploded and smoke began to pour from the other engine. The AN-24RV slowed and began to drop toward the ground. At first it looked like the pilot was going to try to land on a roadway but then the plane tipped over and dove straight into the ground. The plane exploded on impact and burned furiously. It would have made a great scene in Hollywood but here it just meant a dead end for this part of the investigation.

The flight commander signed off and Mark turned off the video and map portions of the screen, feeling resentment at the loss of the aircraft and the people on board. They could have been interrogated as to the reason for the attack on Jack and Laura. Mark didn't feel any failure or guilt or even any remorse about the end of the chase. He was just frustrated at the sudden loss of headway concerning the attack.

CHAPTER FIVE

Chun Xiaoping listened to the recap of the latest attack on the Crossfire Team in America. A total shambles and exorbitant waste of money! He hung up the telephone and thought for a few minutes. Then he picked up the glass ashtray on his desk and threw it at the wall. Cigarette butts flew everywhere and the glass smashed into dozens of small shards.

Feeling better, Chun got up, and went to the window and looked down on Beijing. His rise to power and eventually, the position of Emperor was being delayed by this accursed group of Americans! He was the legitimate descendent of the last Emperor and had the right to ascend to the throne! He just needed to find a way to remove these last two embarrassments from his life. And, he needed to get their trophy away from them. He didn't understand how a Christian artifact would help his rise to royalty, but he knew intuitively that it was necessary. He knew that he knew, because his inner voice was always right, and it told him it was critical to his future.

As Chun pondered the whys and hows of his problem, the head demon assigned to him; Qualpian, continued to whisper the importance of the crucifixion nail in Chun's ear. Qualpian had been Chun's companion from the day he had been conceived in his mother's womb. Qualpian knew that his voice was more familiar to Chun than Chun's own voice. Actually Qualpian hated all human life. He despised Chun and would be glad when he was no longer necessary. But an assignment is an assignment and Chun was a perfect foil for getting the nail for the master.

Chun sat down at his desk and used the computer to explain away the loss of men and damage to the arena caused by the battle. He was very good at casting all blame on others. He even had his new minister believing that he was the victim of the previous incursion into China, rather than the perpetrator. He embellished and modified orders and directions. He noticed a particular policeman that had spoken to his men before the battle in Hong Kong, who was not following his directions concerning the actual event, and was describing it like it really happened. That would not do. Chun picked up a phone and spoke to one of his agents in Hong Kong. Good! That particular policeman would die tonight in the line of duty and not be a problem any longer.

He used a graphics program to alter some video evidence and doctored it so that his superiors would see what he wanted them to see. They would see that the attack was caused by the Americans and he had been smart enough to try to stop it, but with a failure on his men's part, had been unsuccessful. He sent the document to Li Zhiluan and promptly forgot about it. It was something he had been doing for years. His superiors read the reports and used them to further their own careers. They promoted him and gave him more men and resources to continue his valiant efforts for China. They were all fools and tools.

Chun turned out the light and left his office for his apartment. He had a date this night and was looking forward to the encounter.

The next morning when Li Zhiluan went through the reports of his directors and commanders, he saw the report from Chun Xiaoping and selected it to read more carefully.

Li was a third-generation government minister. He had started low and had worked his way to his position. He believed in China and he hated corruption. That may be a way of life for some countries but not for China. At least, not on his watch. He promoted people on merit and their allegiance to China. Popinjays and yes-men made him ill with their fawning ways and conspiratorial lies. He had just taken over the Ministry of National Security two months ago and he was quite interested in Chun's history and progress. He could well be positioned as a future Minister with the progress he had been achieving.

He read the report on the American debacle and then pulled up the report on the incursion into China, by this same Team of American terrorists. He could not believe that there had been no hue and cry about this business. He thought about it and decided that this needed more exposure and national recognition of Xiaoping's efforts in defending the homeland. He printed out the reports and had an appointment scheduled with the Vice Prime Minister. He continued to think about the affair and his presentation as he completed his other duties.

Three hours after making his decision he was seated in Zhongnanhai, the headquarters of the Chinese government. Across the desk was the Vice Prime Minister who handled National Security, Zhou Tangtao. Zhou was an ex-military man who took threats to China very seriously. He indicated that Li Zhiluan was to proceed with his presentation.

Li Zhiluan used the report and some computer displays to highlight his comments. "Mr. Vice Prime Minister. I have some disturbing news from one of my divisions. Chun Xiaoping has reported two incidents that I believe need attention at your level. From his report of last month, I want to describe the activity. Chun's report reads, "While attempting to track the smuggler, Su Li, I have learned that she has become a member of a foreign terrorist organization called the Crossfire Team. This unrecognized American group has been involved in trouble around the world, from Israel and Libya and several countries near the northern Polar Regions. She was a pilot for the smuggler, Thor, who was killed by our agents in the South China region. She has been involved in attacks against the government of Zyngola for several years and apparently has become quite efficient in all forms of helicopters and aircraft. We have sent agents to capture her in the past and have suffered the loss of those agents. After one such incident, she sent an anonymous E-mail to our agency and threatened us if we didn't leave her alone. These events are several years old and we have attempted to track her activities since then."

Li Zhiluan continued reading, "She apparently convinced this terrorist organization to help her steal one of China's national antiquities. I learned of this plan only an hour before it was to happen in the province of Hong Kong. I dispatched a Team of our agents to stop this. She was meeting with the criminal that had already stolen the artifact. He is also a traitor who used to work in our division named Zhijian Chochun. He is also living in the United States under the name of Charlie Wu. The artifact, one "Golden Spike of the Third Dynasty" had been stolen from the Hong Kong museum earlier in the week. He showed the altered list of antiquities from the museum listing the "Golden Spike of the Third Dynasty".

These traitors were meeting in a concession area of the arena southeast of Hong Kong. My men moved in to arrest them when the smuggler, Su Li, appeared on the scene in a stolen Chinese military Helicopter. The men fought valiantly but were overcome by the superior force of the helicopter. There were also other agents of the Crossfire Team there and they contributed to the killing of our duly authorized agents, and subsequently helped Zhijian and Su Li to escape the country. The helicopter was destroyed in the battle, but apparently Su Li was not injured. "

Li Zhiluan furrowed his brow in anger as he continued reading Chun's report. "My investigation of this violation of Chinese borders has led to the incarceration of several employees of the Hong Kong police and Aviation Authority. I regret to say that there were nineteen National Security agents killed by these terrorists on our soil."

Li Zhiluan shook his head and asked Zhou, "How can we just sit by and allow this type of invasion to occur without striking back?"

Zhou had been involved in the government at the security level for twelve years and had much more experience than Li. "I hate to admit it, Li Zhiluan, but these types of things go on all the time. We do it to them, they do it to us. It is cause for concern but not for war."

Li nodded in comprehension, "All right, let me read you the report I received this morning". He picked up the newer report and started at the top. "After completing my investigation of last month's incursion into our country by the Crossfire Team, I set in motion a plan to retrieve the stolen Chinese artifact. I sent a Team into the United States to achieve this goal with the assistance of a local support group. I received this information early tonight. Our Team that was supposed to capture the two main leaders of this terrorist group came under heavy fire from a military group that is apparently supporting this terrorist group. They escaped from the trap which resulted in the deaths of two Americans, one of them a government official, who was apparently in charge of setting the trap. He had an identity as an Undersecretary of Defense, but was obviously a field agent. During the battle, our valiant agents were able to wound the two leaders of the Crossfire Team.

My troops then attempted to find the leaders again but were rebuffed by a huge military presence at the medical facility where they were taken. After a heroic battle in which a great number of American soldiers were killed or wounded, our outnumbered agents attempted to disengage, but were harried by units of the American military. They were able to reach the aircraft with which they had used to be inserted into the country. In an air battle with U.S. Air Force aircraft, our men accounted for several downed military jets before the plane they were in was hit by several missiles and crashed into the ground with a loss of all aboard. I again regret the loss of noble Chinese lives in combating this terrorist group which is apparently supported by the U.S. Military. - signed, Chun Xiaoping, Director of Internal Affairs, National Security."

After Li Zhiluan finished reading, he sat back to see what the Vice Prime Minister wanted to do about these matters.

Zhou mashed out the American cigarette he had been smoking. "Li, I appreciate your bringing this to my attention. I do believe that we will protest the invasion of our country and the downing of our aircraft. I think it will be done on the highest levels. But, I remind you that my request could well be dismissed because of the high level of occurrences of these types of activities. For example, the U.S. will come right back at us for sending agents into their country, without permission, to seek out the terrorists. Even more so, I believe that they will decry the loss of their "Undersecretary" as a wanton murder by our agents. It could get very dirty with little or no success on our part. Still, I will talk to the Prime Minister and see what he recommends."

CHAPTER SIX

Zhou watched Li Zhiluan leave his office and then called one of his people in Hong Kong. "Cho, Listen to me carefully. I want you to find out what you can about a battle that happened last month at the arena southeast of the city, between enemy agents from America and some of our people. Don't go by surface repetition of the story. I want you to dig and find out what really happened. I smell a rat and, sadly, I think it is a Chinese rat."

Zhou had been an avid student of history for twenty-five years and was pretty sure there never had been any "Golden Spike of the Third Dynasty" in the Hong Kong Museum. Add that to some of the comments he'd heard about Chun's activities and techniques and he knew there was something wrong with his reports. Li Zhiluan was too new to be aware of these things and Zhou was also aware that Li's zeal would blind him to the realities of the situation. Therefore, it would be up to Zhou himself to see that China didn't get a bloody nose over one of Chun's grandstand plays.

Zhou then placed a transatlantic call and talked to one of his most trusted spies in the United States. He suggested that a discrete high-level meeting between Liao Jilong and his counterpart in the FBI could be beneficial in soothing things over in America and could provide more information about this subject.

During the afternoon of the next day in the restaurant in the Ronald Regan airport, Liao and George Miller had a quiet, casual lunch together. Unless you knew the players, you would have thought that it was two engineers eating before catching flights.

Liao finished ordering and waited until the server left the table. Then he turned and looked at his long-time acquaintance and friend, George Miller. He saw a quiet, competent man with a keen sense of authority and control. "George, I have been asked by one of my superiors to inquire as to a certain happening several days ago near this airport. We believe that there was a conflict between some of our people and yours and I want to understand what happened if you can talk about it."

George Miller had studied Liao Jilong for fifteen years and understood him as well as anyone could understand a Chinese spy. He had also traded information with him many times in the interest of national security. It worked both ways and had been significant in both of them getting to where they were in the spy world, today. George knew that everything he said would be known by his superiors as well as Liao's. There was no clandestine sneaking around their roles. This was simply the quickest way to resolve situations that could grow to be unmanageable if not contained. The situation Liao spoke of was definitely one of those matters.

George looked at Liao, "What is the "official" Chinese version of the "incident"?"

Liao told him what he had been given from Chun's report.

George thought about it and shook his head. "You're getting some bad Intel somewhere. Here's how it played out from our investigation of the problem. He then gave Liao the information they had confirmed from many sources, about the initial attack on the limousine, all the way to the destruction of the aircraft. He ended it with, "Our analysis of the crash was confirmed by your own black box from the crash." Listen to this."

George took a micro digital recorder out of his pocket along with an earphone. He handed it to Liao who played the recording several times and then handed it back to George. "Thank you. I can only extend the condolences of my nation and government at the loss of life you have suffered in this incident. We are especially sad at the deaths of your Undersecretary and his driver. I think you know that this incursion was not authorized by my government and the man responsible for it will be dealt with most severely.

George looked at Liao for several seconds to determine the veracity of his words. He decided that he meant them as they were said. "Good, it's about time you put a leash on Chun Xiaoping before he starts world war three."

Liao paid for the meal and they shook hands and left the restaurant in different directions.

It was eight a.m. in the morning in Beijing when Liao called and gave his report to Zhou. Zhou questioned him for a few minutes and ended with, "Do you feel that Mr. Miller was being honest with you?"

Liao laughed quietly, "Minister Tangtao, I have known and studied George Miller for many years. He was being honest with me. In addition, I listened to the last minute of the cockpit recording from our lost aircraft."

Zhou realized that if the Americans had such a recording, denial would be useless in any case, "Are you sure it wasn't fabricated?"

Liao spoke quietly. "I am quite sure, Minister. The tape was in our language, between the pilot and one of Chun's mercenaries, named Jin Xuding. I knew both men. It was them. The pilot said that with one engine shot out and the other one shot up he had to land the airplane. Jin told him that Chun's orders were that they were not to be captured under any circumstances. The pilot told him that after he brought the plane down, Jin and his men could readily die in a hail of gunfire but his responsibility was to land the wounded aircraft. Jin said, "We will not land." There was a shot and then the noise of an aircraft in a dive. The recording ended there. I could see the personalities of both men clearly. It was them. I also offer the fact that the pilot indicated that both of the engines had been "shot" rather than destroyed with missiles as was in the original report."

Zhou said, "Thank you for the speedy information Liao. Now I have to decide what to do with Chun and his loyalists. He has a considerable following in the government and a large number of men who are fanatically loyal to him alone, you know."

Liao said "Yes sir, a sticky situation, especially with his connection to royalty. Isn't Li Zhiluan aware of his activities since he is Chun's supervisor?"

Zhou laughed, "At Li's level, the only investigatory personnel he can use work for Chun." Then he asked, "Did Mr. Miller disclose anything about the arena event of last month in Hong Kong?"

Liao thought for a few seconds, "He told me the Crossfire Team and Su Li went into China in response to something to do with Chun and Su Li's parents. But her parents have been dead for years so I don't know what that is about. But, one thing that is for sure. Chun's involvement with this group involves a Christian artifact, not a Chinese one."

Zhou said, "Then I will ponder this and determine our best course of action. In the meantime I will keep a watch on Chun and his activities."

Liao hesitated for a few seconds and then decided to provide unasked for information. "Minister, in light of the threat Chun said that this group posed to our country, I did some checking up on this Crossfire Team and I don't think they are the terrorists we have been led to believe."

Zhou said, "Give me what you have learned."

Liao reported what he had found about the poisoning in Israel and the U.S., the Believer's Temple nuclear incident, the Jordanian factory making air-borne population destroyers, and most recently, the challenge between religions in Zyngola.

Liao continued, "Although their actions in these events have not been for or against China, I believe that they have acted honorably in each of these cases. I am concerned that Chun's activities are going to prejudice this Team against China. This, I believe, would not be in our great nation's best interest. Please forgive me for sounding like I can determine things like this for China. I just feel we are in danger by Chun's activities."

Liao gave the Minister the information on a web site where he could review public information on the incidents in which the Crossfire Team had been involved. Then he hung up and disappeared into the late afternoon, Washington, D.C. traffic.

Three floors down from the Vice Prime Minister's office a mini-CD was removed from its machine and another one inserted.

CHAPTER SEVEN

Chun finished listening to the tiny CD of the conversation between Zhou and his pet spy and sat back and contemplated what that meant for his future. He knew that his immediate supervisor was completely fooled and in his corner, but, the Vice Prime Minister was going to be a challenge. A challenge that Chun felt could be turned to his advantage. Quite possibly allowing Chun to leapfrog Li's position and move directly into the VPM spot. "Yes! This will be a good thing for my advancement if I can apply the correct pressure", thought Chun.

Unaware that his security had been breached by his own subordinates, Zhou finished his daily load of commitments and relaxed with a cup of tea. He thought about his conversation with Liao and the man's devotion to Zhou and China. It was unlike Liao to endorse a group such as this Crossfire Team from America. Determined to understand this odd behavior, Zhou used his computer and located the web site that Liao had mentioned.

He read the reports of their initial involvement in the poisoning of Israel and America. He was fascinated by the "prayer" that Sarah Cohen had led and the fact that the "poison" had utterly disappeared from the world, after that.

Zhou had been an atheist his entire life. There was no god, no higher being that took control of human history and changed things upon request. But he couldn't find any reason for this plague to have disappeared unless it was all a concoction of Israeli and American intelligence services. The same could be said for the Believer's Temple incident, except for the fact that Zhou had been acutely aware of the Russian weapons purchased by that group.

He also knew about the Jordanian desert plant that was to produce the deadly, air-borne population-killing spores. It was because of his own government's secret orders that the plant had been bombed, out of existence. He gave some credibility to the Crossfire Team for exposing that nest of snakes.

But the most baffling was the incident in the Zyngola. China had dispatched their China News crew to cover the "Challenge" because they felt that the two religions would be shown to be bankrupt concerning this showdown and by covering it they would prove that there was nothing to the Zultar cult or the Judeo-Christian movement. The video coverage was crystal clear and the events recorded and had been analyzed carefully by experts. The witnesses had been debriefed and knew what they had seen and heard.

Zhou watched for the third time, the four members of the Crossfire Team standing proudly in an at-ease position with their hands behind them, in a row facing the Zultarian group across the wire fence. He skipped over the four hour boredom of the Zultarian people praying and nothing happening, as he expected. But he watched in fascination as the God of the Hebrews and Christians precisely froze and then disposed of two thousand of Zultar's greatest advocates. Then the appearance of the twenty-ton statue, its precision accuracy, and its melting went beyond understanding. There was no Chinese method of lifting and dropping such a weight from such a height and he doubted that the Americans or anyone on this earth could accomplish such a feat.

The evidence had been pondered by many in the government and while there was an effort to simply dismiss the entire event, there was no reasonable explanation. Zhou could understand now why Liao expressed himself about this group. This would need to be settled before Zhou would be able to carefully categorize it and file it away in his belief system. To simply ignore it was like leaving an active itch that needed scratching. Also, something very deep inside him was making itself known to him. It was like a knocking on his psyche.

Zhou thought about the resources used to analyze this event, and realized that every one he had access to, had already had a shot at it and failed to explain it within the context of acceptable Communist or atheistic philosophy. So then, Zhou thought that he personally would go to some non-acceptable sources for an explanation. He would have to see his old friend, Shang Zhanjiang.

Shang had been a good childhood friend and an excellent student. He had risen quickly in the government along with Zhou until one day he walked into Zhou's office and told him that he could no longer be a loyal member of the government. He resigned his position and dropped out of sight for several years. Shang reappeared in Zhou's reports as a dissident leader of an underground Christian church in Beijing. Zhou wanted to be mad at him and hate him, but he couldn't. The two of them were too much alike, except for this aberration of Shang's. He had subtly protected Shang and kept his group from being persecuted or destroyed. In return, Shang's group kept a low profile and didn't denounce the government or protest publicly. As Zhou continued to be promoted he kept a private eye on his friend and knew where he lived and worked.

Zhou closed up his office and had his driver take him home. His wife, Mingna, was beautiful and graceful and loved him very much. She was always genuinely glad to see him and enjoyed being together with him and their children. His daughter, Hailu, was quickly becoming a lady like her mother and his two little boys, Rangji and Shi were becoming terrors around the house. His brother, Ziyang kept order in the house because he was a reserve policeman who had been wounded and was on government pension. He enjoyed helping Zhou keep his house in order and preventing anyone from bothering his family. Zhou actually loved his older brother and was glad to have him living with them.

Zhou kissed his wife and played with the boys. He changed into casual clothes and told his daughter to change out of the western-style short skirt she wanted to go out in and put on something decent. Ziyang kidded her that she was going to end up in an arranged marriage if she kept on defying her father and rebelling against solid Chinese customs.

Zhou walked out of the house, through the garden and quickly got lost in the Beijing crowds. He had been a field agent himself and knew how to become invisible if he wanted to. He really wanted to this time. He didn't want anyone in the government to know that he was going to consort with a banned religious group.

He waited quietly until he saw Shang come out of his residence and then approached him from behind as he walked along. He said, "Some people never will learn to dress properly." This was a constant ribbing he had given Shang while they were in the government together. Shang just didn't seem to understand decorum in dress. Never did, and probably never would.

Shang was startled and turned to see Zhou smiling at him. He stepped over and hugged Zhou. "My brother, I never thought I would see you again, especially with you smiling at me."

Zhou clapped Shang on the shoulder and said, "Surprise! Is there somewhere more private we could talk?"

Shang smiled and nodded. He led Zhou to a small tea shop and they got a private booth in the rear. Zhou had borrowed one of the watches from the investigation division that contained a small but effective scanning device for detecting people wearing a wire or hidden microphones. Zhou looked at the watch and determined that there were no active listening devices in here. The tea shop probably was too poor to harbor important spies, so they were free to talk. They were just two friends in their early thirties, enjoying a cup of tea and conversation.

He and Shang caught up on their divided histories and he learned for the first time of Shang's acceptance of the Christian God, Jesus. He wanted to feel resentment but actually could see the happiness in Shang's eyes. There was an honesty there that Zhou saw far too little of any more, anywhere.

Zhou finally breached the issue that had sent him in search of Shang. After he described the incident he asked Shang to tell him what had actually happened, from his perspective.

Shang sat back and seemed to be in thought for a few seconds. Actually, he was praying for the right words from God's Holy Spirit. Then he sat forward and looked Zhou in the eye. "You've run out of human explanations, so you're going to have to accept an inhuman explanation. When the natural doesn't fit, then you have to accept the supernatural. I so wish I had been there." His zeal and happiness were contagious.

Zhou shook his head. "Assuming I can postulate a God or a higher being, what happened?" Zhou was a seeker after truth regardless of the system of belief.

Shang smiled. "You have to understand that God created this entire world and everything in it. He can supernaturally change things whenever he wants to. My understanding is that he diverted the jet stream that flows over the African continent and pushed it downward, so that it touched the earth exactly where the Zultarians were. God didn't have to use lightning or fire and brimstone as when he destroyed a sexually immoral city because it wasn't necessary here. Although I have to admit, this Crossfire Team did portray the contest between religious parties pretty closely on an earlier event. Oh well, the old favorites bear repeating every now and then." He smiled wistfully.

Zhou frowned somewhat; I don't understand.

Shang nodded, "The Jewish Old Testament from the Christian Bible. The book of First Kings, chapter 8, verses 20 to 46. The story is that of an Old Testament Prophet of Yahveh and a time of trial for the Hebrew people. Baal worship was very pervasive at that time and the people were undecided about Yahveh. So Yahveh told His Prophet Elijah to challenge the Prophets of Baal to a contest to show which Elohim, or Mighty Man, was real. The Prophets of Baal put a sacrifice on a wood platform and hundreds of their men prayed for Baal to burn it up. They did everything they thought was worship and prayer, including slashing themselves to offer their own blood. After a half of day and nothing, Elijah called all the people over to his sacrifice and had them cover it with water and even soak the wood and make a trench around it, full of water. Then Elijah prayed and fire came down from Heaven and consumed the sacrifice and even all the water. I kind of like this modern version better; though. God in Heaven took care of the Zultarian prophets with His Strider. He even cleaned up afterward. Elijah had to take the Prophets of Baal to another valley and have them killed."

Shang looked at his friend closely. "Zhou, you need to accept the fact that the things that happened there are beyond human capabilities. It needs an Elohim to do them. So, if it needs an Elohim to do them, then an Elohim is there. End of story."

Zhou was still skeptical. His whole life made him skeptical. But still, there was something involved in this situation that needed resolving. He looked at Shang. "What can I do to bring this to a conclusion? It's going to eat me up if I can't put it in a box and close the box with finality."

Shang said, "You could resolve it easily. If you can assume that there is a God, then pray and ask God to resolve it. If there is no God then you won't get an answer and can say the whole thing is impossible." Shang looked at his long-time friend earnestly. "But, if you don't try, you'll never know."

Zhou wasn't at all comfortable involving himself in religious rites but he wanted an answer and he was pretty sure he wouldn't find it by a simple prayer. So he agreed, but, looking around he decided he didn't want to do it in a tea house. "Don't we have to be in a church?"

Shang smiled, "No, my brother. God is not in a building, He is here with us right now and if we go out into the street, He is there, too. If you want privacy we can go to the place where the believer's meet. There will be no one there but us at this time of day."

So they left and went to the small store-front Shang's flock met in. Shang opened it up and then locked the door behind them. He saw Zhou watching him. "That's not to keep you in; it is just to keep the police out in the event they want to raid us."

Shang and Zhou each sat down on one of the simple chairs and Shang told Zhou to pray as he repeated the following prayer. *"Jesus, I am a skeptic. I don't know if you are there or not, but if you are, please come to me and let me know you and the truth about the challenge in Zyngola"*.

Zhou looked quizzically at Shang. "Don't you have to shake some holy water or perform some mystical rite?"

Shang sighed and shook his head. "Zhou, God is real and he doesn't need magic or our posturing to invoke him. If you see things like that, then you are dealing with Satan, the enemy of all mankind, not God. Remember, God loves you and always has and always will."

Zhou pondered that and then had Shang repeat the prayer and he spoke it truly from his heart. The response was anything but what he expected. Shang and the room he was in faded from sight and Zhou was surrounded by such a great cloud of love his heart broke at the beauty of it all. He was trembling with the power of the experience.

"This God is REAL!" Zhou thought. His tears ran freely down his face as God's Spirit convicted him of his sinful life. He felt so miserable in all, what he now knew, was rebellion against a loving God. Then God forgave him of that sin. For the first time, Zhou found love and acceptance on a scale beyond his capacity to understand.

The really amazing thing to Zhou was that while there was a total commitment required, what God really wanted was for Zhou to love Him in return. Oh, He also wanted piddling little things like giving his life to Christ as his Lord and Master, and doing everything he did as to the Lord. The tears continued to run like rainfall and he realized that he was crying on Shang's shoulder and Shang was holding him and telling him that it was all right. He also realized that he had been given the answer to what happened in Zyngola. God had done it to show his power to the Zyngolans and the rest of the world.

Shang led him in a prayer of salvation and gave him a Bible. He told him where to start reading. Zhou wiped his face clean of the tear stains and straightened himself up. Zhou was ready to leave when Shang stopped him with a caution. "Zhou, you are now truly my brother in Christ. Be careful; remember that our country does not allow Christ to operate here openly. You will be especially vulnerable in your position."

Zhou thought about that and sighed. "Yes, that is true. But I think it is something I will have to live with while I sort this all out." He punched Shang in the shoulder. "You know you've destroyed my whole life!" Then he pulled Shang to him and hugged him. "But, it is to make it better. I have such hope now that I didn't have before. You have done a wonderful thing."

Shang shook his head. "I didn't do anything but know you. The Spirit of God did all the work. Do you know that God knew you were going to give your life to Him before the world was formed?"

Zhou shook his head in wonder, "What do you mean?"

Shang walked him to the door. "God looked down through all eternity and saw you and called you. He then wrote your name in the Book of Life and sealed it. This was before he formed the earth. When Adam sinned in the Garden of Eden and condemned all men to a life of hell on earth, God had already prepared for His Son to walk the earth and die for you so that you could be free and know God's truth. Isn't it great?" Shang was grinning from ear to ear. "And, it is free. There are no strings attached other than you love the God the Father, live for Christ, and walk with Him into eternity."

Zhou took a deep breath. "This is an amazing whole new life I've got to learn about."

Shang frowned, "You need to be baptized and really should find some other Christians to be around so that you can be fed the Word of God, rather than the world. If you can get back here tomorrow night, I can baptize you. You might be surprised who you find are Christians. But, like Saul who became Paul of the Bible, you may have a hard time convincing Christians that you are one of them."

Shang looked at him sternly. "Remember, the devil comes to kill, steal, and destroy. Especially, he comes right after a victory. So, be prepared to weather a storm by also remembering that you are not alone. He who did that work in Zyngola will do a work in you too."

Shang let him out with a fond goodbye. Zhou hid the Bible in his belt in the back, under his jacket and headed for home with a new life, a new paradigm, and a whole new set of concerns.

As he stepped into the street he wondered who Saul and Paul of the Bible were. He'd have to read about that. He was excited! At least he had determined the truth about what had happened in Zyngola.

When he arrived home he secreted the Bible and spent the evening with his wife and children. He felt light and clean and for the first time in a long time loved on his children and smiled continually. They truly had a good time and he realized that he had been ignoring them due to the pressure at work.

One day later that week after his wife and children had retired for the night he was reading his Bible when there was a knock at his door to his study. He slid the book into a drawer and said "Come in."

His brother Ziyang entered and asked to speak to him. Zhou waved at a chair for Ziyang to sit in.

Zhou was suddenly concerned his brother might have ferreted out his new secret and feel it was anti-China.

Ziyang studied his younger brother for a few minutes and then asked, "What has caused the change in you? You have come back alive and know such peace and love. Your children are worried about asking you but they all gush over how much more a daddy you are now. I want the peace I see in your eyes and your smile. How can I have that?"

Zhou was going to come up with a cover story but was quite sure his brother would see right through any false story. He also remembered reading that God sees a liar the same as He sees a murderer. So, for the first time in his life he mentally asked God what he should do. The next hour flew by as he told his brother about the truth of Jesus and the gospel. His brother listened and repeated his request. "I want the peace you have."

Zhou led Ziyang in the sinners prayer and realized the words coming out of his mouth weren't really his. God was talking through him. Ziyang accepted Jesus into his heart and after the tears hugged his brother and promised he would not let on about their new found lives until Zhou told him to say something. Zhou was amazed as his brother left the study because he was actually dancing. His place in Heaven was assured and that made Zhou so very happy.

CHAPTER EIGHT

As they prayed for guidance, Sarah felt the closeness of God and the heaviness she associated with the Holy Spirit. She felt a tremendous peace come over her and a great contentment. Contentment had never been a given in her life. Everything she used to do was based on being skillful enough to reach the next level. And there was no end to the levels she would have to climb. Now that she had surrendered her life to Yahshua she knew that it was only through His power that she would reach new heights. So, she had learned to relax and did her best in everything she did to show her gratitude to a loving Yahveh that had saved her when she was still a sinner.

What started as a soft light became brighter. She sensed a presence, and began to see the angel Rose becoming clearer in her mind. Sarah had met the angel when she had been with Laura on one of their earlier adventures. The mixture of gold and brilliant white seemed to be the angel's signature colors. She was very lovely and Sarah was happy to see her.

"Hello Sarah" said the angel. "God loves your gentle spirit and your warrior mentality. You still do not fully trust God for everything but, you have come a long way. A task is coming that will test both the depth of your faith and your warrior capabilities."

Rose smiled at her. "Stand firm in the face of the human enemy and when the real enemy strikes, stay close to Laura because she will protect you. The rest of the time it will be up to you to protect her. Remember the saying "Let go, and Let God."

Sarah said to the angel, "I don't understand. I feel like I have given everything I have to God and trust Him to provide for me. I need to know if any idols remain in my life so that I can rid myself of them."

Rose deepened in color, shifting from the blinding white into a more golden hue. "You have indeed rid yourself of the idols from your old life and your earlier misconceptions. But, know that the real test will be when your life is on the line and you choose either to handle it your way or do it God's way."

Sarah understood the concept of this. While she knew she was good, she knew God was better and she wouldn't know how real her faith was until it was tried in the fire.

"Sarah, remember and move in this," Rose moved and put her hand over Sara's heart. "God sees a person's heart in everything that they do, say, or think. Regardless of the perceptions of other people, God knows what the person really means. God knows their heart. A person can even fool themselves and think that their motives are true and noble, when the truth is, that they are serving their own desires and have wrongly convinced themselves that God is in agreement with them. The Most High has a plan for you that He wants you to discern and follow. Men tend to have desires and expect the Father to agree with them. You must guard against this form of idol worship, where your desires are presented as God's." The angel lowered her hand back down to her side.

Sarah thought about that and realized that she would have to be careful not to sin in this fashion. "What other things do I need to do to truly give Yahshua everything and be an empty vessel for Him?"

Rose laughed, "You will discover that your desire to truly follow the Lord must be renewed every day. Remember the Most High said; *"If anyone would come after me, he must deny himself and take up his cross and follow me. For whoever wants to save his life will lose it, but whoever loses his life for me will find it."* He meant that you needed to pick up your cross and follow him every day. This is the road you must follow. I think a recent saying says it well. Your walk with God is a process, not an event."

Rose slowly circled around Sarah. "You have come a long way and still have a long way to go. You will have opportunities to become a servant and allow God to direct your path every day. You have learned to listen to His voice and to prefer to do His will rather than your own. He is proud of you. You are a warrior of honor and God needs warriors, especially now."

Rose shifted into the brilliant white color and gave Sarah one last reminder. "Sarah, you must tell the rest of the Crossfire Team this; *"In your upcoming battle in China,* the whole world shall know that God does not save with sword and spear; for the battle is God's, and He will give your enemy into your hands."

It will take many warriors with true faith and stout hearts to face the enemy and to walk in the promise that the battle is the Master's. God is about to use your husband to gather this battle force of Christ's people. Be ready to lead them!" Rose faded from sight and Sarah thought over the entire sequence she had heard.

Opening her eyes she saw the other three members of the Core Team still in prayer. She rested until everyone sat back and then quietly said, "I have a message from Rose." That got everyone's attention.

Sarah repeated what she had been told about herself and the Team. Then she discussed the impact with the others to see if they could add anything.

Mark nodded, "The leading I got was to speak to the Chairman of the Joint Chiefs of Staff about a group to help us. I believe that Chun is going to find some way to make us come into China to fight him. In that case we might need more guns than we can carry."

Jack agreed, "If you're going to speak to the JCS I want to be there, too. I also want to clear this with the President before we get in over our heads in international politics and start a world war."

Laura sighed, "Good point."

CHAPTER NINE

The Chairman of the Joint Chiefs of Staff, General Howard Miles, welcomed Mark and Jack into his office personally. His estimation of their capabilities had gone off the scale as he had watched the showdown in Zyngola. He was more than happy to listen to their proposition concerning the latest in the subtle war of nerves with the Chinese. "Please, be seated. Can we get you anything to drink?"

Both men deferred and Mark opened the discussion. "General Miles, you know that I'm a military man, God's supernatural involvement is still pretty much unknown territory to me. Usually in these matters I defer to my friend Jack here and his wife. But, I am learning to hear God's voice and use his planning rather than mine. Two days ago, during prayer I got a leading from God to put together a Special Operations Group (SOG) for an upcoming sortie into China."

Mark nodded, seeing the concerned look on the CJCS's face. "Yes sir, I realize the international implications of such an act. I have to believe that the God of the Universe can work it out without it resulting in World War three, us against two billion Chinese. In fact, that is what the leading I received told me."

Jack interjected, "I asked the President if he would bless this and he agreed, pending your decision. He said to tell you that this was your decision."

The CJCS thought long and hard for a bit, and then he took a deep breath and exhaled. "Okay, maybe. Go ahead with your briefing."

Mark continued, "What I'm asking you to do is to set up a SOG and to let me command it, personally. There is a built-in test or a Biblical fleece involved with this concept."

The CJCS wrinkled his forehead, "Fleece! What in the Sam Hill is a fleece?"

Jack offered a quick explanation of Gideon and his testing of the truth of God's assignment for him through the use of a fleece or lamb's wool, as told in Judges

Chapter 6. "First, he asked God to make the fleece wet from the dew when everything else was dry. After that happened he asked God one more time, to show him the truth of the assignment, that he would be the man God would work through to save Israel. The second time he asked for the fleece to be dry while everything else would be wet. It happened as he asked so that he knew that the commission was from God."

The CJCS nodded his head, "Yes, I remember that now from my Sunday School days. That stuff is real?. What "fleece" is in this operation?"

Mark smiled. "We need to post the new SOG but do no recruiting. God told me that He would bring the personnel He wanted, to be part of it. If it is Yahveh then the people He will bring to fill it will be spirit-filled Christians who are willing to trust in God during battle."

The CJCS considered that and decided it was a good fleece. He grinned, "I wonder if I will get to be a part of it?"

Jack had been listening to the Spirit and received a word of wisdom. He said, "Sir, you are a part of it. In fact, that is the reason that God led us to you. You will be directly in charge of this group and they will report only to you. God's Spirit already has a name for the group, "Miles Marauders".

The CJCS smiled and told the men, "How could I refuse to charter a group named after me? All right," He slapped his hand on his desk. "I'll set it up and post it tomorrow. You will be the officer in charge and I'll have the senior officer or non-com that responds to the posting, report to you as soon as he requests the duty. Good enough?"

Jack and Mark nodded and got up, stood at attention and saluted the CJCS and then left the office.

On the flight back to Denver, Mark talked to Sarah and told her that the group was being set up. She laughed and said, "Okay, General, I want to be the first to sign up for the group."

Mark stopped for a second. He hadn't thought about his wife being part of the SOG. "I'll have to think about that for a bit. Is that all right with you?"

Sarah laughed at Mark, "Yes, of course. Just remember, it is Yahveh who is bringing in the recruits and I think He is telling me that I need to be a member and I'll tell you why. I think this is going to be a co-ed group and you're going to need a dis-staff leader."

Mark looked at Jack and rang off. "Do you think we will get female operatives for the SOG?"

Jack laughed, "Why not? Yahveh is no respecter of persons. Since He is bringing in the troops, then, why not?"

Mark started revising his operational plans to include women. This was a thought that was foreign to normal SOG operations. After he thought about it for a few minutes he could see many advantages to having women in the group. He called Sarah back and agreed to take her as the first recruit, but as a member of the SOG only when the Crossfire Team and the SOG worked together. "You're too valuable to this operation to lose you to the SOG if they have a different operation going on."

Militarily, Sarah could understand that, but she also knew that Mark wanted to keep her close to himself. That gave her a warm feeling inside.

CHAPTER TEN

The SOG operations phone at the Fortress was busy over the next four days. General Miles had encountered a crisis and passed the formation of the SOG to Mark. Exactly thirty-five recruits called and asked for inclusion in the new SOG.

Mark and Laura flew to the Marine base at 29 Palms in Southern California, to hold the interviews. They left it to each prospective member to find their own way there on time. First round interviews started promptly at seven a.m.

Two days later there were no second round interviews because each candidate had been accepted for service in the SOG during their first interview. Mark looked at the thirty-five service folders in front of him and shook his head. God did not fool around, that was for sure. Each man or woman that applied was a rock-solid Christian or Judeo-Christian and tops in their particular branch of the service. Some could have run their own groups but were humble enough to serve as a member of the Crossfire SOG. Intelligence ran to the high end of the scale and they were totally dedicated to their job.

Laura had sat as an instrument of God's Spirit on the interviews and had been assured each person was the right person to join. No one came that wasn't exactly right. Under close questioning as to why they had volunteered for this particular assignment, each one had a vision, a dream, or a leading of the Spirit that led them to call.

As Mark and Laura flew back to Colorado, they compared notes on the new group's members. There were eleven women counting Sarah and twenty-five men between the ages of 24 and 31. Experience ran to the extreme in SpecOps and elite groups. There were eight Navy SEALs, none with less than four years service, two Team leaders, two squad leaders and twelve top Army Rangers, of which six were women. The Rangers are an all male force as far as the public was concerned. A special operation of the Rangers recruited women and trained them covertly along with the men. There were also nine

Force Recon Marines, all with extensive combat service. Mark was not surprised to see both Craig and Kevin Steel in that group. The two Marines had fought alongside the Crossfire Team in Israel against the ASF.

The last five members were U.S. Air Force Special Operations personnel, three of them were women from the Psychological Operations or PysOps group. This could be a distinct advantage for the Crossfire Team as they dealt with Chun and his Chinese conspirators.

Mark split the SOG into four sub Teams; three were primary combat specialists and reported directly to him. The other one was a clandestine warfare group that reported to Sarah.

Mark asked for a remote base in Arizona for the SOG training grounds and for unique weapons development and testing. It was to be set up by the SEALs under direct orders from General Miles. The base and the equipment were to be brand new, best quality, and of sufficient quantity that there would be no shortage problems. These people had already had enough combat and SpecOps training that they only needed honing and a game plan. Mark wanted two weeks to weld them into a Team that worked together like they had always been a single unit.

Laura watched the Rocky Mountains out of the aircraft window as the plane began to settle down for a landing at Denver International Airport. She thought about all the battles they had already taken part in and how she had seen God's hand in every one. This one was even more of God's doing. He organized it and had told Sarah that He would do the fighting for them. The whole thing was simply amazing.

CHAPTER ELEVEN

Chun had carefully researched his target and knew where his weaknesses were. He arranged his scheme carefully, sliding his operatives past his fellow government agents without a hint of his intent. All was now in readiness. He listened to his inner voice again and was assured that what he wanted to do was the right thing to do. He picked up the phone and dialed a number. He let the phone on the other end ring three times and hung up. He waited exactly two minutes and repeated the call. It was now done. He closed up his office and went to be seen with other managers and ministers.

At the home of Zhou Tangtao there were three guards, supplied by the government. Money had changed hands and two of the three simply walked away from their posts that afternoon. The third one could not be bought. He fell to the ground never having heard the silenced round that killed him.

The five black robed and masked raiders had studied the layout of the house and used a purchased key to gain unannounced entry, at five o'clock in the afternoon. They slipped through the halls and killed anyone who discovered them and weren't their targets. Two of them found the boys playing in their room. The man was on Rangji and Shi before they could yell out. A stun gun rendered each child unable to move or speak. Both boys were picked up and taken back toward the outside.

Minga and Hailu were working in the kitchen when the men surprised them. Both of them were quickly subdued by the stun guns. They were being carried out when the raiders were confronted by Ziyang, Zhou's older brother. He had a sword and blocked the men's path. The third man shot Ziyang with his silenced automatic four times. Ziyang still tried to advance on the men even with blood running down his shirt from his wounds. A fifth shot to the head killed him and cleared their way. They rushed from the house and joined the men with the boys. They carried the four hostages to a moving van that had backed up to the gate. Loading the four inert bodies into the back they pulled down the tarp and the truck pulled away, quickly merging and disappearing into the traffic at that hour.

Ten minutes later, Zhou's driver dropped him off at his house and started to drive off when he saw Zhou's signal to stop. He braked and backed up. Zhou told him to call for the police and to give him a gun. The driver gave the Vice Prime Minister his own gun and called on the radio for assistance. He then got out a reserve pistol and joined the VPM as he entered the grounds to the house.

They found the guard murdered outside and three servants dead inside. Zhou moved carefully through the silent house until he found his brother lying on his back, his sword still gripped tightly in his hand. The five bullet holes testified to his loyalty and bravery. Zhou bent down and fell to his knees. He closed Ziyang's eyes and took his already cool hand. Looking at his brother he sadly shook his head. Softly he whispered, "I'm glad that I had time to tell you about Jesus. I am so sorry. Ziyang, my brother, I will avenge your death. I promise. He put his brother's hand back on his chest and said goodbye to Ziyang.

Zhou stood up with anger mounting right along with fear for his family. He stormed through the house with the pistol in his hand, but couldn't find his wife or children. He walked back into the living room just as the Police arrived and started their investigation. He didn't need an investigation to determine who had killed his brother and kidnapped his family. He knew it was Chun. The slimy creature obviously knew of Zhou's interest in his activities. There would be a phone call soon. Terms and conditions would be dictated and he would have to make decisions. He wasn't going to give up his wife and children.

He walked over to the undamaged bar and made himself a drink. He understood the situation all too well. His brand new conversion to Christianity was going to be severely tested. His friend Shang had been right. The enemy hadn't wasted any time striking back at him for leaving Satan's camp. What he needed was some effective help but couldn't think of anyone that could help.

Zhou saw his driver talking to a policeman and motioned to him. The man came over and it was obvious that he was truly sorry for what had happened to Zhou.

The Vice Prime Minister told the man to get him a secure phone. Ten minutes later he had people looking for the other two guards. They may have been killed or they may have been paid to look the other way. He figured that if their bodies weren't outside, then they had been bought off. He hoped that was the case because he would like to "talk" to them personally and find out if what he thought was true.

Now that the police had their pictures, people from the ministry came in and bowed to him and started cleaning up his house. He felt nothing but cold. The house didn't mean anything without Minga and the children. What could he do? His mind whirled in circles. Every resource he had available was probably contaminated by Chun and his money.

He excused himself and went to his bedroom. He sat in the chair and stared at the bed he had shared with his wife just hours ago. Now she was gone and Zhou didn't know if he would ever see her again. He thought of Shang and what he had said about Jesus walking side-by-side with one through every problem in life. This was a major problem for him but it was his time to depend on the thought that this shouldn't be too big for God. He walked over and locked the door. He got down on his knees and prayed that God would protect his wife and children and would give him wisdom as to what he should do.

As he wound down and rested in his communion with God a thought came to him. He knew it wasn't his and it was radical. But he thanked God for it and got up and paced the room trying to figure the angles. He finally nodded and smiled a wan smile. He'd use some of Chun's own tactics. He unlocked the door and went back to the secure phone. He called several people and made an overseas call. Then he spent a restless night with little sleep. He got up and cleaned up for work at dawn's first light.

After he got to his office he continued to make his plans and occasionally had time for a silent prayer for protection of his family and for further guidance.

At ten minutes until noon he got the call he had been expecting from Chun. Although it wasn't Chun himself, there were plenty of clues that implicated him. It came down to his agreeing to supply a division of crack Chinese commandos to help repel a foreign penetration of China. If he did as asked he would get what he had lost back, unharmed. The alternative wasn't even mentioned. It would be at least a week before the troops were needed so he would have time to accomplish his own plans first. He told the toady on the phone that if he didn't have acceptable proof of the safety of his family by noon the next day he would bring the entire weight of the Chinese government down on Chun and all his operations. Then he hung up and cut off the protestations that the man didn't know who this Chun was. It was just bad acting.

His office staff brought him his papers and his updated passport, plus tickets. He placed them carefully into his thin briefcase and put on his coat and headed for the waiting car. Four hours later he was airborne.

CHAPTER TWELVE

Jack took the call from the FBI early in the morning. He did not know George Miller but his credentials were impeccable and had the backing of the President, so it was important. Jack flipped on the recorder and answered the phone. "Hello Mr. Miller, this is Jack Malone, what can I do for you?"

George Miller hadn't met Jack Malone either but had read the FBI files on him and his organization very carefully. He liked what he had seen. "Jack, call me George. I see that this line is secure on my end, is it the same on yours?"

Jack grinned, "Yes, George, it is secure on this end, also."

George started the ball rolling, "Jack, I have an extremely sensitive matter that involves you and your organization that has to be resolved in..." George looked at his watch. "...the next two hours. How are you set for time?"

Jack said, "Go ahead."

George sighed, "I've had a business relationship with Liao Jilong for the last fifteen years or so. Liao is a top flight spy for China, living here in the U.S. The FBI and CIA have known about him and his connection with the Chinese government for as long as he has been here. Sometimes our two governments use us to handle communications that can't be done at a higher level without causing ramifications we don't want. He and I discussed the recent attack on you and your wife. I, for one am sure the Chinese government was not behind the attack. In other words, it wasn't a sanctioned hit."

Jack thought for a few seconds. "George, if the Chinese government knows that Chun was behind the attack, why don't they stop him?"

George sighed again and ran his fingers through his hair before answering. "Believe me that it is very complicated but we believe that they are attempting to put a collar on him. But, he doesn't seem to be the problem here. Two hours ago Liao called me and asked me to arrange a meeting between you and Zhou Tangtao. Tangtao is the Vice Prime Minister of National Security for China. Pretty close to what our Homeland Security Chief would be over there."

Jack was at a loss for words. A very, very senior level Chinese official from an Atheistic dictatorship wanted to talk with him. This needed some prayer. "When does Mr. Tangtao want to meet with me?"

"Tomorrow morning around nine a.m. somewhere in Denver, I believe." George wasn't still sure of the place because Zhou's group didn't have the information. Zhou was playing this one really close to the vest. Not even his trusted advisors knew what was going on. "It is to be a one-on-one meeting without listening devices or cameras. Frankly, I don't have a clue as to what he wants to talk to you about."

George was slightly exasperated and it showed in his voice. "He is high-level enough that we can't demand anything from him. He is above cabinet-level caliber. If he was making an official state-sponsored meeting it would be with the President or, at the least, the Vice President. You should be flattered to have such attention. But, the FBI is still concerned that a figure like this would want private talks to what essentially, is a citizen who could be representing the entire nation."

Jack thought about that for a few minutes. "George, I realize that it was a Presidential order and probably unmerited, but I do carry the responsibilities and rank of a one-star General in the U.S. Air Force. I did swear the oath to defend the country and the constitution to my death. In the last year I have put my life and that of my wife and friends on the line for America several times. Don't have any concerns about my loyalty. Unless it is strictly Crossfire business, I will tell you what we've discussed. Most likely it concerns that little excursion we made into Hong Kong two months ago. But I can't see why such a heavyweight would be involved."

Mollified somewhat, George said, "Okay Jack, I will contact you as soon as I get information as to where he wants to meet."

Jack said, "Instead, tell him I will meet him in room 110 of the Loews Denver Hotel in Cherry Creek. I will insure that the room is bug-free and my people will keep it that way."

George winched, "I hope he agrees."

Jack had a feeling of assurance from the Spirit of Yahveh. "He will agree. I will be there at 9 a.m. sharp. Do us both the favor and stay away. I'm quite sure he will have his people checking everything and I will have Mark Connelly making sure that we're not interrupted. Is that all right with you?"

George was silent for a while. "General Connelly? Okay then, we'll be hands off and wait for your report." He hung up and thought for a few seconds. Mark Connelly was right up there on the leading edge of intelligence, counter-intelligence, and spy-stuff in general, no pun intended. They would be better off not trying to slide anything by him. Connelly had Presidential pull and a group of gung-ho Navy SEALs that took a dim view of things that General Connelly didn't like. He hoped that Zhou's group knew the same things.

Liao Jilong sat there on the executive jet for ten minutes and didn't blink. He was going over in his head the information he had just received from George Miller. Liao knew about Mark Connelly and his abilities and it concerned him that his own surveillance plans had just become useless. Mark knew about all the latest Chinese spy toys, and if he didn't, Liao was sure that Charlie Wu did. Maybe George was right on this one. Hands off and let his boss do whatever he was going to do in private. There were few men or situations that Liao didn't feel he could out-spy. This was one that he wasn't sure of and that was enough to go with caution, rather than rashness.

Cleared through the State Department on a diplomatic visa, the Chinese executive jet touched down in Denver at the Arapahoe County Air Field and taxied out. Zhou was met by a private car belonging to a friend of Liao's in Denver. The car took Zhou to a private residence of a friend for the evening.

The next morning the same vehicle took Zhou to the Loews Denver Hotel and dropped him off at the front entrance. He walked in alone and was directed to room

110. Zhou knocked at the door and Jack opened it. They sized each other up for a few seconds and then Zhou held out his hand and Jack shook it. They walked into the sitting room and Jack closed the door.

Zhou was about to say something when Jack held his finger up to his lips and shook his head. He led Zhou to the connecting door to the next suite and then out a sliding glass door onto the ground level patio. Walking off the patio they walked to a luxury vehicle and climbed in. The vehicle left the hotel grounds and headed south on 1st Avenue. Jack opened up a laptop computer and typed a command. After several seconds the display showed a green light. Jack turned to Zhou and said in flawless Chinese Mandarin, "Minister Tangtao, you do me a great honor by your visit. I apologize for the run-around at the hotel but the security there is not very good. In here we are secure and I assure you that my people will not record us in any way or listen in. I can also assure you that as long as that screen stays green, nobody else is listening in either."

Zhou was pleased that Jack spoke such good Chinese. He detected a variation that indicated Jack's Chinese was probably learned in the northern districts. He responded in his native language saying, "I too feel honored to meet you Mister Malone, or should I say, General Malone?"

Jack smiled at the trim figure of the Chinese official. "You can call me Jack if you please."

"And you can call me Zhou which is my familiar name. Jack, my time here must be brief to prevent people I work with from determining what I am doing."

Jack nodded, "And, what is it you are doing?"

Zhou knew this was a leap of faith. "Two weeks ago, in secret, I gave my life to Jesus and became a Christian."

Jack was startled by the revelation. "That is an automatic death sentence in your position, isn't it?"

Zhou nodded. "Yes, but the Lords love is overwhelming and I am not worried about death or dishonor any more and have come here for your help. Actually, you are the cause of my conversion and several times, the reason for my needing help. We have a mutual enemy and his name is Chun Xiaoping."

Jack assimilated the information as it came to him. Shocking, unusual, but honest as confirmed by his spirit. "What is it that I have done, to do all these things?" Zhou looked at him. "Zyngola, Hong Kong, and now, me. Let me explain."

Zhou filled Jack in on his search for truth, his conversion, his distrust and determination about the faulty reports by Chun and his decision to do something about the loose cannon in the Chinese government."

Jack listened and asked if that was all of it. Zhou shook his head. "Two days ago, Chun's men broke into my house, killed my brother, my servants, one of my guards and kidnapped my wife and three children. He is using them as pawns in a game he is playing with your Team. He has arranged through a middleman, to trade my family's safety for a division of Chinese commandos to be used sometime in the next several weeks."

Jack thought and prayed and Yahveh's Spirit confirmed Zhou's words. Jack sensed that he and the Team were committed to this course.

Jack looked at the Minister. "What can I or the Team do to help you?"

Zhou said, "I don't know for sure as yet. But, and I am new at this, the Spirit of God led me to you to save my family and I have obeyed. I am sure that things will take more shape in the next ten to fifteen days and we can discuss it then." Zhou took a deep breath, "Jack, I am scared for my Minga and the children. I want to take Chun and flay him alive to find them. But I am now in the clutches of Christ and I know in my heart that to do that will only result in their deaths. I don't know what to do." He looked at Jack expecting pity but instead saw the love of Christ in his eyes. It was the same look that had been in his friend Shang's eyes. "More wonders!" he thought.

Jack said, "Let's pray and see if God will tell us what to do."

The two men prayed as the car drove slowly through the Cherry Hills suburb. After a few minutes Jack got a leading that was positive. He tested the spirit and was assured that this was from God and not the enemy. He put his hand on Zhou's shoulder. "I believe that God will guide us to your loved ones and He will protect them until we find them." Jack reached into a compartment in the back seat and took out a cell phone. He handed it to Zhou. "Here, use this to contact me when you need to. It will not be traceable nor will anyone be able to eavesdrop on our conversations. If you lose it don't worry. It will quit working and there won't be anything for anyone to reverse engineer. It is as secure as we can make it."

Jack knocked on the sliding glass window between them and the driver. As the window went down Zhou saw the computer screen change from green to red. Jack spoke to the driver. Take us back to the hotel, please."

As soon as the window went back up the computer reverted to the green secure color. Zhou thought, "Interesting."

Jack reversed their path and when they entered room 110 there was classical music playing over the conversation between two men. It was all nonsense but it would give any listening devices something to lock into without revealing anything. Zhou liked the circumlocution and false leads. Very Chinese. They shook hands and went their own ways.

CHAPTER THIRTEEN

The Commander of the American USAF Orion P3 reconnaissance plane had a sick feeling of history repeating itself, when the Chinese fighter disabled his plane over international waters off the southern coast of China. The unarmed, slower propeller aircraft didn't stand a chance against the Mach 3 fighter. As the pilot struggled to keep the Orion in the air he received a direct communication from the jet fighter, in English. "You will descend to 2,000 feet and will land sixty miles inland at a field I lead you to. Any attempt to change direction will result in a complete loss of your aircraft with all crew on board. Do you understand this?"

Another fighter was off his starboard wing with missiles in plain sight. The pilot responded in the affirmative while the communications officer continued to try and raise their base and inform them of the unwarranted attack against their aircraft. All frequencies were being blocked and the direct satellite link was unresponsive.

As the aircraft dropped below the radar altitude of the carrier it had come from, it disappeared from its last link to the American military.

Four hundred miles to the north in the East China Sea the sudden and unexpected attack on a U.S. Navy Spruance-Class Destroyer had been extremely well-planned and executed. Three Chinese SU-27 fighters broke off from a routine fly-by of the destroyer and each fired five missiles.

The Su-27 "Flanker" aircraft then used their 23mm cannons to destroy any of the superstructures that held command and control, including all antennas and radars. At the same time five torpedoes raced through the water and struck the ship at the water line, breaking the back of the ship and causing it to list almost twenty-five degrees to port. The abandon ship alarm was sounded within two minutes of the torpedo attack and the Sailors and Marines on the decks, launched rafts or simply jumped into the sea and swam away, to escape the rapidly sinking ship.

The combined missile and torpedo attack killed eighteen of the Officers and 136 of the enlisted crew. There were over two hundred crewmen and eleven Officers that survived the initial attacks. The ship suddenly rolled over to its port side, smashing many men under the water, as it turned turtle and sank in a matter of minutes. When the survivors did a head count there was only 96 enlisted men and three Officers left. Two Chinese warships arrived and collected all the survivors.

North of that, fifteen U.S. Army troops were captured on the South Korean side of the DMZ. These troops were herded back to the north and disappeared completely into the Chinese mainland.

Any one of these attacks would have sent up the alarm in Washington but great care had been taken to see that each of the events went without any notice in the form of electronic messages or calls for help. The analysts in the Pentagon were somewhat concerned that a reconnaissance aircraft and a destroyer both went missing around the same time, but had no hard evidence that there was any foul play involved.

Efforts to find the ship and the aircraft were fruitless and the Chinese professed to know nothing about the two craft. A few eyebrows were raised but ships had gone missing for days due to electronics failures and aircraft had the bad habit of falling out of the air without any help. The search was broadened for the destroyer and the alphabet organizations were asked for their assistance by the Navy.

Three days after the attacks, a series of ultra-sharp black and white photos were given to COMPACFLT. What Admiral Wall saw in the photos sent him to the DOD on the run. Within five hours, the President of the United States listened, while the photographs were explained to him.

The Captain handling the technical briefing pointed out the picture showing the Destroyer as it sailed normally. The second photo included the flyby of the Chinese MIGs. The third picture showed the explosions of the superstructure and the impacts of the torpedoes. The fourth picture showed the bottom of the hull and the survivors in the water. The last picture showed the Chinese ships picking up the survivors. A detailed close-up showed the survivors being held at gunpoint.

The President conferred with the Admiral and the Chairman of the JCS. After some protests by the Admiral, the CJCS was able to convince the President to open direct talks with the Chinese Premier.

None of this was to get to the press or people were going to be put in prison for more years than they had left to live.

Alone in his office, General Miles placed a call to Mark Connelly. "Mark, this is General Miles. There has been a terrible incident off the Chinese coast and I need to know if this has any bearing on your SOG. The Chinese, without provocation attacked and sank a U.S. Navy Spruance-class destroyer. If the NSA is right, they outright killed two hundred and eighty-two Sailors and Marines and captured the survivors."

Mark thought for a few seconds, stunned by the audacity and evil involved in such an attack. "General, I can't tell you if this is connected to Chun and his operations or not, but I think I can find out for you in the next ten hours."

General Miles laughed harshly, "Do the best you can. We may be at war in the next ten hours. Get back to me as quickly as you can."

Mark hung up and then dialed Jack's cell phone number.

Jack was jogging on a trail near the Fortress when the cell phone chirped at him. He swung it up without breaking stride. The injuries he had sustained were mostly painless now and only scars remained to show the bullet wounds. His constant exercise helped to bring his leg and side back to full functionality much quicker than any other medicine. The caller-ID gave him Mark's identification. He said, "Hello Mark."

Mark relayed what the General had told him. Jack slowed down to a walk as the loss of so many men struck him. "What do you want to do?"

Mark explained his idea and Jack agreed. Hanging up, Jack dialed the number of the cell phone he had given Zhou. Zhou answered it on the second ring. Jack realized that it would be around twelve-thirty in the morning in Beijing at this time. The Vice Prime Minister quietly said, "Yes?"

Jack repeated the information about the attack and asked if this was a government affair or something Chun had worked up. He heard Zhou sigh.

Zhou was saddened by the savage attack by his country against the U.S. warship. He told Jack, "This hasn't come to my attention as yet. Are you sure it was Chinese aircraft and Naval units involved?"

Jack took a deep breath and exhaled, "I wish I didn't have to tell you this, but the NSA has photos of the attack and the ships that picked up the survivors. I don't have to tell you how good the photographs are from a K-11 Keyhole satellite, do I?"

Zhou said, "No, I've seen them Jack. I will tell you this, I am in charge of National Security for the nation of China and I authorized no attack, haven't heard of any attack, and am very afraid that Chun is going to propel our two countries into all out war. I will go to my office early this morning and see what I can find out." He paused. "But, I do know this; if your President confronts our Premier with this attack, he will deny it and the ball will start rolling toward a conflict." Zhou's voice was heavy. "My new spirit is very saddened by the death of all those men. Please help me keep it from being in the hundreds of millions."

Jack said, "I'll do what I can but it won't be long before someone in the Navy wants answers or retribution. Our people are as proud as yours and the probability of more incidents will get higher as time goes by. Find out what you can and have an answer for our government as to why yours isn't putting a stop to Chun's evil."

CHAPTER FOURTEEN

Hui Cheng, Chun's closest political ally, bowed into Chun's office and closed the door. Hui was the military attaché for the Internal Security Ministry. He was the only one who could have cut the clandestine orders that Chun needed without upper level approval. Hui had done so at Chun's request in the hopes of being able to rise on Chun's coattails as he ascended the political ladder. He raised an eyebrow at Chun who nodded. The office was secure and their conversation would not be overheard. Of course that didn't mean that Chun was above recording the meeting for his own purposes.

Hui sat down and looked at his contemporary with a mixture of excitement and fear. "Chun, what have you done? I thought you said you were going to "threaten" the Americans, not kill them! How can you so underhandedly use the military with my compliance but without permission and threaten China with war?"

Chun had been expecting Hui's visit ever since he initiated his strikes. "Hui, you don't have enough vision. I had to engage the enemy ship because they would have found out about our little arrangement if I hadn't."

Although this didn't make much sense to Hui, he wanted to listen to all of what Chun was going to reveal before he complained.

Chun continued, "These little incidents will not cause a major riff between Beijing and Washington. I have "borrowed" some of the American military to give me the leverage in an operation I am conducting. I don't think that the Premier will lose any sleep over a few American deaths and come down on me. Anyway, I have an "ace in the hole" which should deflect any criticism that could be forthcoming." Chun chuckled at his Americanism.

Chun sat upright suddenly and became very animated, "Hui, I am on the verge of the greatest political leap of my career! I will become the most feared and famous Chinese hero ever, simply because of these unique and unilateral moves. I recommend that you openly ally yourself to me and I will see that you have an honorable position in the new order."

Chun sat back and affected a nonchalant attitude. "Or, if you are too afraid to walk in the big world, scurry back to your office and act like you don't know anything. You can say I forged your signature on the orders."

Hui was scared, right down to his patent leather shoes. But part of his fear was that if he did not agree with Chun, he could miss out on the best thing he would ever have a chance at, and earn himself a probable death sentence at the same time. He nodded his head and temporized by sagely saying, "This is a major thing you're proposing. I will have to think on all the ramifications and the correct timing. How are you going to use these foreign military assets you've acquired?"

Chun did not want to discuss his plans to lure the Crossfire Team into China to get acquisition of their Treasure and destroy them. It would not make sense to Hui because he was not privy to Chun's internal voice. A major failing of his that would, probably lead to his early demise after Chun became Emperor. "You think on it and realize that time is rapidly flying by and your window of opportunity is very short."

Hui got up and bowed to Chun and hurried from the office.

Chun dismissed Hui from his thoughts and concentrated on maintaining his planned order of events. He had his middle man call Zhou and threaten the man's wife and family, if Zhou didn't smooth over the events of the aircraft and naval ship. Chun doubted that Zhou had any inkling of the capture of the soldiers in Korea, or their introduction into China.

Now he was ready to make an offer to the Americans that would make his dreams come true. His demon, Qualpian, turned up the heat and gut-level desire in Chun, to acquire the Crucifixion nail regardless of the danger to his nation or the world. He whispered dreams of truly epic proportions concerning Chun's ascension to the throne of China. He let Chun fantasize about what he would do to each of the people, in his way, when he was considered a god. Those people would regret the day they offended the Emperor.

He re-read his message that he wanted delivered to the President of the United States. Yes! He had done a magnificent job in crafting the paper so that he would be seen as the benevolent savior of the conflict and the Crossfire Team as the villains. He smiled wistfully, knowing the American President would be envious that China had Chun working for them rather than the U.S.A.

Qualpian chuckled to himself as he watched the delusional deception that he had nurtured in the prideful man.

CHAPTER FIFTEEN

The Chinese Ambassador to the United States delivered the message to the American President and bowed and left.

The President opened the message and read:

Dear Mr. President,

My name is Chun Xiaoping and I am writing you today to advise you of a serious situation. There is a terrorist group operating in your country with the assistance of the U. S. Military. This group is called the "Crossfire Team". While I am sure that they are represented to you as patriotic and helpful, they are actually fermenting a clash of world powers.

Mr. President, this group has in its possession a rare and valuable Chinese artifact that they arranged to have stolen from our country. This is unacceptable and we demand its immediate return. The Crossfire Team needs to bring this artifact back to China in the next four days or it could well result in the escalation of hostilities between our nations.

To insure that the entire Crossfire Team brings this item to us we have captured one hundred and thirty five of your Army, Navy, and Marine Corp personnel who were spying on our country. I am authorized to return these individuals only if the Crossfire Team brings back our artifact within the time allotted. If they fail to meet the date then these people's lives will be forfeited.

I await your response.

Chun Xiaoping

President Bollen was livid, "Just who does this idiot think he is jerking around? Somebody needs to clue the Chinese Premier in about this megalomaniac!" He shoved the paper he had received from the Chinese Ambassador into General Miles' hands.

The General read the message twice and looked up at the Commander-in-Chief of the Armed Forces. "Normally, I would suggest that we strap a nuclear weapon onto this message and give it to the Chinese Premier with the option to get our people back, execute this character, and make reparations to us for the loss of life and property or we bomb them back into the stone age!"

The General had a concern that the President might think he was loosing his edge and therefore he looked somewhat distressed, but he forged on, regardless. "But, Sir, I think that there is more going on here than we are able to see. This could quickly escalate and become something no one can control." He leaned toward the President and lowered the tone of his voice. "Mr. President, I've never said this to anyone before, but I have the feeling that we need to pray about this before we make any decisions."

The President looked at the man that ran the Military for him, thought for a few seconds considering the implications and nodded. "You're right Miles, you're absolutely right."

The President pushed his intercom button and told the Secret Service agent that he and the CJCS were not to be interrupted for any reason for the next thirty minutes. Then he walked over to a couch and got down on his knees next to the General and they started asking God what to do.

An hour later in the War Room in the Fortress, Jack, Laura, Mark, and Sarah were staring at the television images of the President and the CJCS in an Ultimate Flash secured teleconference.

Jack read the message Chun had sent to the President and looked up at the man that ran the country. "Mr. President, I want to extend our deepest regrets at the loss of life on the destroyer and the captives Chun is holding. Satan doesn't care how many good men and women he kills to achieve his goals and that through his demons he is the one that is pushing Chun's buttons." Laura nodded her head and concurred with Jack's assessment of the spiritual forces involved, and said so.

"Jack," General Miles asked, "Pardon me if I don't use the right words here, because I'm in unfamiliar territory. But, the President and I believe God is leading us to cool our reactions to this incident and let you and your Team handle Comrade Chun. What I need right now is something to tell the relatives of the men killed on the destroyer."

Jack listened to Yahveh's Spirit and he felt the message was uplifting and helpful rather than destructive like the enemy's thoughts. "General, can you paint this as a terrible accident at sea and be looking for the survivors rather than the result of hostile enemy action?"

The President sighed, "There is a possibility that we can do that. But there is also a possibility that someone in the NSA might leak these pictures to the press." He leaned back quickly in his chair. "Also, because this atrocity happened on their watch, I want the Chinese vice Prime Minister that you mentioned, to make sure this type of action can never be done again." He paused. "I can do that privately and not stir up a national flap. I need to see that they feel genuinely sorry that it happened and they are willing to see the relatives are financially compensated at China's expense.

Jack responded to the two men. "Sir, I agree with your course of action but feel that any remedial response may have to wait until Yahveh has dealt with Chun. Otherwise, it might not continue to be effective. Also, I need to make it very clear that Zhou Tangtao has a lot on the line. One reason is because he has become a Christian."

That was news to both the President and the CJCS. President Bollen asked, "How can the man function in his position as a Christian?"

Jack thought about that, "I really don't know how he can do it, Mr. President. He has just recently become a Christian and I don't know that his new faith and his job have reached an unbearable level of conflict as yet. I believe that this event will be a real opportunity for us to see if his faith is real.

General Miles asked, "Jack, do you think his conversion is real? And, do you think he will deal fairly with us concerning these events?"

Jack didn't have to think about it, "General, the Spirit of Yahveh confirmed his conversion to me and led me to believe that his involvement is Yahveh's doing. Also, I doubt that you are aware of it yet." He looked down at his clasped hands and then back at the General. "Chun has kidnapped Zhou's wife and three children. Chun is using them to force Zhou to do his bidding which makes the situation doubly dangerous for the man".

"Mark" The President asked. "What are you going to do about his "invitation" for the Crossfire Team to walk into his trap?"

Mark was rather grim. "Mr. President, we are going to do what he has asked because God asked us to do it several weeks ago. Yahveh also told us that He will do the battle for us. The new SOG will stand with us on this one."

The General agreed with Mark and told him, "Well, then you'd better get the ball rolling."

Mark said, "Yes sir. Mr. President, General, Thank you both. Goodbye." The President and the General wished them the best of luck. Mark disconnected the call and turned to the others in the room with a somber look.

In the White House, the President looked at General Miles, "New Special Operations Group?"

The CJCS nodded his head and said, "Miles Marauders, Let me tell you about it."

CHAPTER SIXTEEN

Chun surveyed the prisoners with a hatred that he lived with but seldom admitted. These were the enemy's troops and they should be made to bow and scrape before the next Emperor of China.

He told the head of his guards to make sure each man got at least a single session of torture to break their spirits. As he was talking to the head guard, one of the Marines being held shouted an insult. Chun smiled at him and told the guard to take him first. He was beaten until he was unconscious. The guard quietly noted that the prisoner never broke and pleading for mercy was obviously far from the man's mind. The guard could see the prisoner's thoughts in his eyes. Those eyes said, "Just let me get a chance at you."

One by one they were dragged into the "confession" room. One by one they were whipped, beaten, shocked, and other ingenious, painful things to make them humble and willing to be obedient. None of the men broke. Some cried, some screamed, but none of them were less defiant than when they started. The guard knew that it could take months of daily beatings to break their spirit. But he wasn't about say that to Chun. He would become a prisoner, too.

Chun rode quietly during the four-hour drive back as he contemplated his plans. He imagined himself taking his rightful place on his ancestral throne, seating himself slowly, savoring the precious moment. He snapped back to reality and watched the scenery as they drove to Beijing. He made a feeble try to do his regular job. He generated more phony reports to keep his overseers happy. He couldn't really concentrate because he knew that this was the beginning of his time and within the next week he would have the power to wipe away the competition and ascend to the throne. Everyone would then hope that they were on his good side. He carefully made a mental list of those who weren't and what he wanted done to them.

While the Emperor Wannabe was reveling in his expected glory in Beijing, the prisoners were whispering among themselves, back at the encampment set up to hold them.

A young seaman asked an older Marine if he thought that they would be tortured tomorrow, like today. The Marine had compassion for the new sailor and told him. "Naw, I don't think their heart is in it. At least not the guards. That Chun fellow would have us chewed up and spit out if he dared." He looked at the bruises on the kid's face. "Keep the faith, buddy. There's no way the service is going to leave us here. It may take a couple of weeks but we are going to get out of this okay. Did you notice that no one got anything too serious? Heck," He spit in defiance. "I've been in bar brawls worse than this. I really don't think they intend to maim or kill us. I think they just wanted to soften us up a bit."

The sailor nodded. "I think they did that."

The Marine growled a low chuckle. "Don't give them the satisfaction. Spit in their eye if you get the chance. I will. And, you can bet that if I get the chance I'll send every slanted-eyed freak in this group straight to hell." The sailor didn't doubt for a second that the Marine meant every word he said. After thinking about it for a bit the sailor decided he would emulate the Marine's attitude and not give in to the enemy regardless of what they did.

The Orion aircraft commander was talking quietly to the ranking naval officer that had survived the onslaught on the destroyer. "Let's do what we can to keep the morale up. That beating today seems to have focused the anger of our little intra service group rather than subdue them."

The Lieutenant nodded, "I wouldn't want to be any of these Chinese guards if the men get a chance at them; that is for sure. Listen, did you have a chance to get a Mayday off before they got you down?"

The Air Force Major shrugged his shoulders. "Don't know if they got it or not. The Chinese Air Force was jamming the frequencies and we didn't get a reply on the sat system. They may just think we are lost at sea."

The Lieutenant nodded. "The slime balls blew away every comm system we had on ship before we had a chance to yell for help. If they are looking for us, I don't know how they're going to find us."

The Major looked with compassion on the young Lieutenant knowing that he had been on some remote duty when the Chinese struck. All the regular officers that ran the ship from the Captain down to the deck officers had been killed in the operations rooms when the aircraft blew the top off the ship. "How many officers do you have left?"

Sadness showed in the face of the young man. "Three and the other two are junior to me. I just came on board the ship two months ago."

About that time there was a commotion and the men got to their feet. The communal cell door was pulled open and twenty more people were herded into the cell and the door swung shut with a clang. The new people were all Chinese rather than American and they weren't military either.

One man looked at the American service men and looked around until he spotted the Major and the Lieutenant. Walking over he introduced himself as Shang Zhanjiang. "I am the pastor of an underground Christian church in Beijing. I understand why they arrested us." He swept his arm around to indicate the other Chinese in the cell. "We are an illegal, banned operation in China. But, why are all you Americans here?"

Major Banning held out his hand and shook Shang's as he introduced the Lieutenant and himself. "We aren't sure of that, ourselves. All I can tell you is that we are from several different places and were attacked and forced here by some strange guy named Chun."

The light went on in Shang's eyes. "Ahhh, Comrade Chun. I had heard that he was angling to get some kind of leverage on an American group. I guess all of us are the bait. Who, I don't know, but, if this is a typical Chun Xiaoping operation, we will find out before too long. He isn't known for his patience or mercy. We need to pray that the Lord will grant us His mercy."

The Major saw the guards approaching the cell. "Shang, each one of us was beaten or tortured when we got here. You might tell your people if they come for them, that it won't be too bad."

Shang nodded and talked to the small Chinese group in Mandarin. Then he led a prayer which was interrupted by the guards who dragged the Pastor out of the cell.

CHAPTER SEVENTEEN

Su Li sat quietly in her room in the Fortress. She concentrated all of her mind on the major discrepancy in her belief system. She had gotten to the belief that God didn't exist and wasn't real regardless of the beliefs of others. She knew that God hadn't done anything to spare her parents when they had been taken by Chun's goons. Despite almost non-stop praying to the spirits of her elders and to the gods, it hadn't saved them.

That, plus her benefactor, Thor, had convinced her that today was all there was and there wasn't any "All-knowing Being" looking over their lives.

Her problem with that was the things that she had seen and experienced on this trip. She couldn't find an acceptable explanation for what had happened.

She knew that in Hong Kong she had seen, with her own eyes, a demonic form appear and brush past her. Knocking her down without even noticing her had been bad enough. But the feeling of sheer evil that emanated from the demon had shocked her to her core.

Su Li remembered that she had shot the demon and the bullets had no effect whatsoever. Then, first one, and then two, angelic beings had popped into her world and fought with the demon until they had destroyed it. She had even watched Laura change into a golden armored warrior and battle with smaller demons. Su Li had felt a surge of victory when Laura had dispatched one of the smaller demons and made the others run for their lives. The two angels, who she had learned were named Rose and Caleb, then, disappeared chasing other demons.

This was very unsettling for Su Li. She had seen, felt, smelled, and fought with forces her belief system said didn't exist. One of the two inputs was wrong. She had racked her mind to see if she could find some way to confirm or deny what she had seen in Hong Kong. There was the explanation from her new friends about their Christian God and she was beginning to think that they may be right.

She watched the tapes of the challenge in Zyngola over and over again and was still amazed by the pin-point accuracy of the "Strider" in destroying the enemies of the Crossfire Team. She watched the earnest prayer of four people she was learning to respect very much. The response had been awe-inspiring and didn't leave any room for argument. Unless one wanted to simply deny those results.

There was a deep yearning in her that needed to know the truth. She made her mind up and spoke to the phone. This impressed her every time she used it. She said, "Intercom, Laura." And the system found Laura and connected the two of them.

Laura's voice said, "Yes Su Li, what can I do for you?" To Su Li she sounded friendly but business like.

Su Li spoke into the air, "Laura, I want to talk to you for a while, when will you have some time?"

Laura was quiet for a few seconds. "Why don't you meet me in the garden in about twenty minutes?"

Su Li said, "Okay, see you then. Phone end."

As she rested in the luxury of her suite she imagined all of the people in the world that would want to change places with her. Most of them would, she thought. Fantastic training, luxury accommodations, any thing you wanted, and all just for a few hair-raising minutes each month where your life was on the line along with everyone else. She hoped there was a God so she could be thankful to something other than fate.

When Laura walked into the underground garden a few minutes early she found Su Li already there. Yahveh's Spirit had given Laura foreknowledge of what the conversation was going to be about.

Su Li was dressed in a pretty, light green summer dress that gave her a coy, almost innocent image. Laura knew that Su Li was an accomplished warrior, superb pilot, and a highly effective martial artist who was willing to take on superior odds. The contrast between what Su Li looked like and what she was capable of was intriguing. Laura walked up and hugged the smaller woman. Because of Laura's six-foot height, Su Li's black hair stood eight inches closer to the ground than Laura's blonde locks.

Laura sat down and watched Su Li gracefully sit down across from her. "What is on your mind, Su Li?"

Su Li had carefully thought this conversation through. "I am concerned about my fitting in with the group here."

Laura, knowing what this was really about, acted like she was in the dark. "What do you mean? I feel like you're fitting in very well. You get along with everyone and your talents are a great asset. What is the problem?"

Su Li looked directly in her eyes, "It's the spirituality of everyone else while I am very unspiritual."

Laura was praying for the right words. "Su Li, you need to understand something. We, the others in the Crossfire Team, serve a real Elohim or God. This is not spiritualism as you may have understood it."

Su Li looked at her somewhat confused. "What do you mean it is different than what I understand?"

Laura smiled at the young woman. "Su Li, you are a brilliant woman. You have innate talents that let you fight and fly with an excellence that most people only wish they had. You are not stupid either. Some brilliant people are pretty stupid you know." Laura tilted her head as she looked at Su Li. "They get so puffed up on their wonderfulness they lose sight of the fact that they got those talents from someone other than themselves or their parents. You have been directly involved in a world you say doesn't exist. I'm referring to the battle in Hong Kong. If demons don't exist, then why did you shoot it?"

Su Li rolled her eyes, "Because it was going to hurt Charlie Wu and his wife. I will never allow that to happen on my watch!"

Laura laughed, "I believe you. But that wasn't my question. Why did you fire your pistol at something that you say doesn't exist?"

Su Li looked somewhat ashamed. "This is what I want to talk to you about."

Laura sighed, "Su Li, you either have to admit that the supernatural world is real or ignore what you saw. Which is it?"

Su Li took a deep breath. She knew that a world other than the natural one existed but; it was like a fable to her up until now. "All right, Laura. I must admit to myself as well as to you; that it was real. It knocked me down without even noticing me. What exactly was that thing?"

Laura started with a simple explanation of fallen angels, giants before the flood, and Satan and his mission. This led to a talk about how Yahveh and Satan operated and then how one could avoid or defeat a demon. Eventually Su Li got to the root of her real question. "If Yahveh is real, then He wouldn't have anything to do with me. My whole life is what you call sin and defiance and I feel so..." She searched for the right word. Her shoulders slumped slightly..." alone." Her voice trailed off.

Laura leaned toward Su Li, "None of us are worthy of God 's love. He gives it as a free gift that He bestows on us because we are his children and he loves us. You don't have to ever be alone again. I was just like you before Jesus saved me. God's only Begotten Son, Jesus Christ, was born of a virgin and lived two thousand years ago. He died for you to erase your sins and let you know God in a deeply personal way."

Su LI knew that this was the truth and she felt the conviction of God's Spirit. Seeing how sinful her life had been, she despaired of ever measuring up to what God wanted. But, she also sensed the love of what Laura called the Messiah as she thought about Him forgiving her sins. "How can I get to know Jesus?"

Laura led her in a prayer of salvation. She sat there and prayed for Jesus to forgive her for her pride and arrogance. She felt His great compassion and His forgiveness as he forgave her and she started crying, which was something she rarely did. The tears freely ran down her face as she felt the powerful cleansing and purifying mercy of God Almighty flooding through her whole being. She felt a healing of the pain she had felt ever since she lost her parents. She was so happy that she couldn't talk. As she sat there with her face uplifted to God, she knew beyond any doubt that she had finally found the love and security and freedom she thought she had lost when her parents were killed.

She started laughing with a happiness she had never known. Many tears later, Laura took Su Li to the living room and left her there looking at God's creation out of the windows. She made a phone call and then she called Jack,

Mark, and Sarah. She had them all meet in the living room where Jack anointed all of them with oil and then they laid hands on Su Li and prayed over her for the infilling of God's Spirit. Then they had a small celebration with Su Li thanking Jesus for her becoming a saint in God's Kingdom.

Laura took her hand. "There is a member of the Team that is going to meet us tomorrow at Minister Throman's church in Denver. His name is Gary Eisenthal and he is a Christian with a mission from Elohim in the area of deliverance. Also, you need to get baptized."

Su Li remembered what she had learned from Laura about Yahshua and the Christian life. She understood about the requirement for a public confession of faith. She also knew that immersion during water baptism was a symbolic dying to the old self and coming up to life in Jesus. She looked forward to this event.

That evening as she lay in bed, she thought about the change she had felt ever since this morning. She felt a calmness and peace flowing through her and she wondered "Could this be that peace they all talk about?" She said a heartfelt prayer of thanksgiving to a God who listened to her every word and treasured every one of her tears.

The next day they travelled to southeast Denver to the Christian church ministered to by Alan Throman. Jack had related what had happened at their baptism with the Minister. Su Li's baptism was a quiet, blessed event compared to the Malones. Su Li came up out of the baptismal water with both fists raised in victory. The whole group got a watery hug.

After she completely dried off and redressed she was introduced to Gary Eisenthal. She saw a thin, nondescript man with a fading hairline of light brown hair and a mustache of the same color. The main thing she noticed was the flame of intensity, love, and the high intelligence that showed in his eyes. He smiled at her and she felt the confirmation of God's Spirit that he was one of God's people that she could trust.

Laura stayed with her in the event she needed any help in filling out the questionnaire Gary gave her. While they were at that task, Jack, Mark, and Sarah brought Gary up to date on events. Jack showed Gary the challenge in Zyngola on a DVD player he had brought with him. Gary watched the power of Elohim and shouted, "Yes!" Then he realized he was in church and settled down somewhat. "Boy!, I wish I had been there. Next time, invite me, will you?"

Mark laughed a deep laugh. "Sure Gary, no problem. Remember though, that we were fairly certain that we would see Yahveh's power but weren't sure it was in His will that we left there in this dimension. It was dicey for sure. But we could have used you there for support and your insight."

Gary had sobered up somewhat listening to Mark's description of the event from their human standpoint. "I don't care guys; call me when you need to."

Mark said, "Okay then, how about you go back to the Fortress with us. We have another sticky situation that we could use your help on right now."

As the other men talked about events, Gary decided he may have jumped in over his head but he felt that it was Yahveh's doing that he was here and he'd look forward to whatever came. He decided that he'd contact his secretary and tell her he was going to be on an extended leave so that she'd delay any appointments he was facing for the next few weeks.

Mark and Sarah went to a remote part of the sanctuary and returned to their busy phone arrangements for the upcoming attack in China.

Su Li brought back her form and she and Gary went to sit in a pew. Su Li asked him, "Gary, I don't understand one thing. I thought when I gave my life to Jesus I couldn't have any demons. Why do I need cleansing? I mean, Laura told me I did, and I'm willing, but I am confused."

Gary smiled at the young woman. This was a common misunderstanding in the Christian community. "Su Li, once you gave your heart and life to Jesus, it is His forever. The problem is that you are made up of three components, spirit, soul, and body. Your spirit belongs to Jesus now, but your soul, which is your mind, intellect, and will, and your physical body are still subject to demonic influence. A believer, can be oppressed but never possessed. But, if you have any broken parts that need the Lord, which is one place the enemy could come in. This is a type of cleansing and that is what we will do."

Gary referred to the paper and started Su Li's cleansing. Su Li's background of Confucianism and other Chinese beliefs had allowed for many open doors, but Gary was an expert. He knew that the old will pass away but Jesus' words would last forever and with her choices she would keep the enemy at bay.

After a rather short time Su Li was set free from years of enemy control and misdirection. Su Li had been greatly surprised to learn that demons had tried to kill her several times and had almost succeeded twice. All at once she could see the hand of God in each of the events, preventing her destruction. It was a wonderful day. She noticed a lightness of being that she'd never known before. In her mind and heart she joyfully thanked the Creator of the Universe for his loving mercy.

CHAPTER EIGHTEEN

Zhou took Jack's phone call in the quiet loneliness of his lunch hour in his empty home. He made sure he was away from the office at this time so that they could talk more freely.

"Minister Zhou, how is everyone holding up?" Jack's question was more about the kidnapped family members than the Minister's complications with Chun and his attacks on the American military.

"It is very hard for my wife and children and they don't have Jesus to call on as I do. I also suffer because of their situation. I have done what I could to make amends for Chun's actions and believe that your President and his people are satisfied for the moment." Zhou took a deep breath, almost trembling with emotion, "Do you have any more information about my family?"

Jack recognized the pain behind the question. Laura and Jack had been seeking God concerning the Minister's family and had come to some knowledge and conclusions. "We feel that God will protect them during their captivity and that the Crossfire Team is responsible to walk out God's will to free them."

That was wonderful news to the Chinese minister. "Thank God. What can I do to help?"

Jack had been expecting this question. "We will need a window of opportunity on the day after tomorrow, for about six hours. We need to be able to enter the country, confront Chun, and leave. There will be about forty people coming in and hopefully one hundred and seventy five leaving. When your family is freed, then we need someone to handle them and bring them back to you. According to the plan we will arrive in the area of Hohhot near the Huang River around eight in the morning."

The Minister asked, "What is your plan to enter our country?"

Jack said, "We will come in over Mongolia which will require the least amount of time, in Chinese airspace. We will be in a single, unarmed C-5 Galaxy aircraft. We will be bringing in several vehicles and medical equipment for any wounded or injured prisoners."

The Minister thought about the incursion and felt that forces he could not control were now in charge. "I regret that I have had to send a division of our commandos to protect Chun's operation. I only did so that he would not hurt my family. If you can get my family out of his grasp quickly enough I can possibly change that situation."

Jack agreed with the man caught in the middle of the event. "Minister, we want to keep this conflict between Chun's men and ourselves. We don't want to have to fight your people.

Zhou agreed with that. "There is a new development but it shouldn't impact your mission."

Jack wondered about that, "What is it?"

Zhou sighed, "Chun has arrested a number of underground Chinese Christians, and we believe there are about twenty members who have been taken to the same prison near Hohhot. If you can release them they will be subject to re-arrest by our people because the church is banned. The Pastor of the church is a friend of mine who led me to Christ.

Jack told him that they would add that to the planning and thanked him for his help. Jack then told him that they would be in contact just before they entered Chinese airspace."

Vice Prime Minister Zhou was smart enough to realize that he couldn't contain the effects of both Chun's duplicity and this short invasion of the country without the possibilities of terrible complications. He made a short call and left his house.

Twenty minutes later he was at his regularly scheduled staff meeting with the Premier. He waited while the routine business was handled and then asked to speak to the Premier alone.

When they were alone, Zhou gave the Premier a short summary of what was going on and how Chun had brought them to the brink of war with the Americans without permission. He explained the kidnapping of his family and the plan to release both the captives and his family.

The Premier looked calmly at his Vice Prime Minister of Security and asked two questions. "Can we allow this incursion of American military into our country with confidence that they will only attend to Chun and the prisoners?" Zhou assured them that they could allow the incursion in complete confidence that the Americans would attend to business and then depart immediately. The Premier then asked his second question. "What will we do with Chun if he survives? He has a formidable power base and many friends that could even threaten my position as Premier. You know he wants to re-establish the throne of Emperors don't you?"

Zhou nodded to show his understanding. He felt confidence from the Holy Spirit of Yahveh and answered confidently. "Chun will not survive this meeting and if we can arrange it, only he and his troops will face the wrath of the Americans, as it should be."

The Premier gazed at Zhou, "You realize that if anything goes wrong with these operations you will be held responsible?"

Zhou nodded again. "Premier, I will gladly accept the responsibility for these events if it can eliminate the cancer that Chun represents for our country. I also will resign after this is successfully concluded because you will need someone on which to place the anger of Chun's allies after he is gone. I have had a successful career and would be leaving the service in a few years anyway."

The Premier admired Zhou's willingness to give up what he had to protect the government and the Premier himself from internal strife. "I will regret your loss and see that you are held in honor in your retirement. You have my tacit permission for this little war between Chun and the Americans."

That was the end of the meeting.

CHAPTER NINETEEN

The War Room at the Fortress had finally settled down to be a quiet place. Input from Zhou had been correlated with satellite photos from NSA and third-person reports from in-place CIA covert operatives. The general plan of battle had been beaten into shape and the logistics for the insertion and extraction of the Team and the hostages had been arranged for, down to the last bullet.

Laura's warning that the enemy would do what he could to disrupt the operation was being taken seriously and there was continual prayer being interceded for the Team and the operation. There were twelve groups in the Denver area that had offered to man twenty-four hour prayer Teams until the operation was completed.

Many attempts at sabotage had been found and defeated. The enemy of all mankind wanted the Team to go to China to get the Crucifixion nail into Chun's hands. He wouldn't have it long. Anything that could be affected was being affected and had to be countered by the prayer chains and the Team itself.

As an enlightened strategist, Mark had taken the natural and the supernatural into consideration. He conferred with Laura, Jack, and Gary Eisenthal to determine the best way to confuse and mislead the agents of the darkness. On the morning of the day before their departure date for China the entire Team was meeting in the living room for mutual prayer to protect the mission and to seek Yahveh's will and leading.

As they prayed in the living room of the Fortress, heaviness settled on them that signified the presence of Yahveh's Holy Spirit. As they felt the peace of Yahveh flow through them, a brightness in the room caused them to open their eyes to see the angel Rose floating in their midst. The fierce gold and white colors that accompanied Rose were streaming around the angel's body and flaring into bursts of high intensity.

Rose looked at the Team by slowly rotating where she floated. Jack and Laura were on one couch, Mark and Sarah on another. Su Li and Gary were in individual chairs. The excitement on Su Li's face matched the confirmation of faith shown on Gary's.

Rose seemed to grow in dimension somehow, and the golden glow surrounded everyone there. Rose spoke in a beautiful contralto voice, "I want to welcome Su Li and Gary to the Crossfire Team in my own way." Rose made a motion and white light flowed from her to both of the new members. The light flowed through them and around them. From the look on Su Li's face, it was wonderful in a way for which there are no human words. The white light faded out and Rose rotated slowly as she talked.

"God is about to show his might in the land of China. Satan is using Chun Xiaoping as a tool to acquire the Crucifixion nail from you. Yahveh is going to fight this battle for you but each of you and your new military group must stand and fight for God. It will be the expression of your wills, submitted to Yahveh's will that causes the power of God to flow on earth in this battle."

Rose seemed to grow larger and darker as the gold overshadowed the white light. "Each of your faiths will be tested over the next few days, and if you do not waver then you will overcome the enemies, both human and demonic. If you lose faith you will fall. I urge you to stand strong in the Father and believe like you have never believed before. There will be individual battles on both the physical and on the spiritual planes with enemies coming from different dimensions to attack you."

Rose focused on Laura, "Laura, you and your sisters in Christ will be challenged to a new level, right to the edge of your talents and gifts. Stay true to what you know is Yahveh's truth and you will be victorious. You must b..."

In the middle of the sentence, Rose stopped speaking and, in a motion that looked like a blur, drew a sword that gleamed with the white light of Yahveh's Glory. She spun in place to her left. The sword went into middle guard position across her chest with the point slightly upward. There was urgent power in the movements and the people all reacted to the sudden change. Laura's armor and sword appeared as she stood up and stepped nearer to Rose.

With a thunderous "crack" that shook the room, a gust of foul-smelling smoke blew in, immediately followed by four demons. The first two had black swords that they swung at Rose. Rose angled her sword and blocked both of the ebony blades.

The other two demons didn't have swords. They had assault rifles and they turned them toward the people in the room. A demon's appearance usually gave them an advantage of fear and shock that petrified normal people. This wasn't so for the Crossfire Team. As the demons raised their weapons, Mark, Jack, and Su Li were already firing with handguns, which each person had instinctively drawn as Rose armed herself.

Normally, bullets don't affect demons. But in this case they had a devastating effect. Both of the smaller demons were struck multiple times and the bullets tore gaping holes through their black skin. Gray smoke rolled out of the holes as the two demons lost focus, dropped their weapons to the floor, and then both demons disappeared completely, one by one.

Mark fired on the two demons attacking Rose but to no effect. One of the rounds hit Rose's sword and ricocheted back into the room. Laura intercepted it with a flick of her sword and caromed it into the ceiling.

Laura then stepped into the battle that was being waged before her. Rose was totally on the defense against the two demons. Laura was praying in tongues as she swung her sword at the leg of the closer demon. To her surprise she severed the leg completely and the demon yowled and fell toward her. Reacting quickly, Laura stepped to her right while turning to her left. She struck at the demon's head as it came at her. Her brightly gleaming sword hit the demon at the neck and severed its head from the body. Both the body and the head turned into noisome black smoke that dissipated quickly to somewhere else.

Rose went on the attack and though she had suffered several cuts and gashes, she was aflame with the power of Yahveh and struck the last demon down by deflecting the black sword to her left and thrusting her sword through its chest. That one also disappeared into black smoke.

Rose kept her sword in her right hand and raised her left hand, palm outward. She spoke a dozen words in a flowing language that no one there understood and there was a flare of white light throughout the room. She resheathed her sword and turned to the people of the Team. She noticed that Laura's armor had faded from sight and the young woman had sagged to the floor. Everyone else was standing up without injury. Rose floated over to Laura and the gold light flowed over Laura for a few seconds and then faded.

Laura got to her feet and smiled at Jack. She gave the thumbs-up signal to the others that she was all right.

Rose surveyed the Team with satisfaction. "I am terribly sorry that happened. I have arranged a barrier that will prevent them from using me as an access into your world. As I was saying, the enemy is on the attack. I commend you on your efficient response. Laura, I would not have survived that battle without your assistance. I am in your debt. You all know what to do in the battle to come. Stand firm in your faith in Yahveh."

It was obvious that Rose was hurting and weary. Her colors faded from their normal brightness but her countenance was still fierce and strong. "I need Yahveh's healing touch, so I must go." The angel faded from sight.

Jack started a prayer for the angel's strength and healing and everyone else joined in. Laura felt the pleasure of the Father that they would sincerely pray for the angel. The Team then prayed for protection and invisibility from the agents of darkness.

When they had finished praying, Jack looked around and saw some damage from stray bullets but nothing that serious. He smiled and said, "I think the last few minutes might be a little hard to explain to people that weren't here."

Mark shrugged, "So what? We know what happened and so does Yahveh. Who else counts? What do we do with these?" He walked over to the two unfamiliar assault rifles lying on the floor of the living room.

Urgently, Laura said, "Don't touch them! Close your eyes and see if you can see them with your spiritual eyes instead."

Each person tried to do that. Three of the others, Sarah, Gary, and Su Li could see the rifles in the spirit. Laura said to Su Li, "Describe what you see."

Su Li's voice was somber, "I see two poisonous black snakes coiled and ready to strike."

Laura said, "Close enough. Father Yahveh, we ask in your Son's name that these weapons of the enemy be destroyed in the fire of Your Holy Spirit and that all curses, spells, and assignments and anything else that remains, be sent to the abyss to never return."

There was a flare of light in both the spiritual and physical dimensions and the two guns were gone as if they had never existed. Mark looked with relief at Laura. "Thanks. I would have picked one of them up if you hadn't been here."

Laura looked at her friend. "Mark, we need to work on your discernment skills and Jack's too. God has moved us up to a level of spiritual battle which means that you absolutely must be able to see the enemy's snares. I wouldn't doubt that those two demons weren't supposed to shoot at us. They were just being used to bring those weapons into our realm. To get these "snares" into our world they had to step "into" our dimension and therefore became vulnerable to our weapons. That is also why our bullets were able to hit them and not the other demons. I think that entire attack by the enemy was simply to get these "snares" into our world. Is that right, Gary?"

"Definitely so, we have to be careful not to fall for Satan's booby traps. I can only assume that those things were physical extensions of demonic forces designed to curse, disable, or kill whoever handled them."

Gary had been reviewing the battle in his mind. He hadn't been able to do anything but observe. He could have been wounded or killed but it hadn't happened and he determined that he still wanted to be part of the battle with the Crossfire Team. He realized that since Rose had filled him with God's power and grace he had a new eagerness to fight the enemy.

Gary looked at the others in the group. "Jack, why don't you and Mark sit here with Laura and me. I think we can ask the Holy Spirit to open your spiritual eyes and enlarge your discernment." He stopped talking as the urging of the Holy Spirit came over him. He nodded his head. "And, Laura, God says you handle your sword fairly well but you could use some real training. Jack, I've seen you demonstrate your weapons skills and after we work on your discernment, will you show all of us how to handle a sword properly? I think we are going to need it very soon."

Jack nodded. Su Li's opinion of the group just went up two more notches. Not only could they draw on talents within the group to improve spiritual effectiveness, they could do the same for physical warrior talents. There seemed to be no end of the possibilities with the Team. She commented to Laura, "I look forward to both lessons."

Jack and Mark laughed at the same time. Jack explained to Su Li. "To learn instinctive sword fighting may take as much as two years. This won't be a single lesson class." He turned to Gary, "I assume that God instructed you to tell us this?"

Gary nodded, "Oh yeah! Each one of us needs to be an expert swords person as well as an expert with a pistol and rifle. These talents need to be learned as quickly as possible."

Jack thought for a few seconds. "I will be able to give everyone some good basic swordsmanship before we reach China, but for instinctive swordplay it will take considerably longer. Actually, Gary, you will take the longest because Laura and Su Li have studied martial arts and can adopt the correct body control quickly from their existing training."

Mark added, "I can test and then add to everyone's skill with guns and rifles but when we get back I want Debbie Hargrove to train all of us in sniper school. I'm very sure I will learn a lot there." It wasn't often that Mark could have learned anything about fighting, but after watching her in action, he had a high regard of Debbie's capabilities.

CHAPTER TWENTY

Word of the arrest of Shang and nineteen of his church members spread quickly throughout the underground Christian church in China. Many of the groups started prayer chains to pray constantly, until those arrested had been freed.

The amount of prayers reaching Heaven, concerning the arrest grew daily until Yahveh's realm reacted. One by one the groups were led to start a secret outreach to as many people as they could, concerning the arrests. There was no work stoppages or open defiance. These actions would be quickly and brutally crushed by the government. It became more like children in class that were in on a secret and only the teacher didn't know what was going on. They were gaining a huge following without inciting the government to crack down on them. The goal was not civil disobedience but a subtle social distaste for the government because of the arrests.

The government had its agents and spies as well as informers, so it wasn't in the dark about the vast movement. It was at a loss as to how to strike back because there were no leaders that could be arrested and made an example of. While the government could ignore the entire thing and it would probably blow over and be forgotten in the daily press of life for the citizens, the problem was that it was a breeding ground focal point for any other rebellion. It created a social fabric that any dissident could use to propel their cause to national proportions. The arrests were done at Chun's orders and would not be a hard thing to correct, but the next thing might be much worse.

Zhou was the top level official involved in the investigation into the causes and cures for the spreading dislike affecting the country. He knew the cause and felt sure the cure was coming in less than twenty four hours. He reported to the Premier and outlined his thoughts on the matter.

The Premier wondered how far this infection was going to spread and how much impact the proposed intrusion by the Americans would have on things. He looked at Zhou and cautioned him. "You realize that Chun has now made this a national inflammation? If things don't go precisely correct with the Americans, this could topple the government? If you hadn't come to me and laid everything out before, I would be tempted to ...Well, you know."

Zhou did know and knew that his family would be dead long before Chun would, if the government waded in with the army to take out Chun and his followers. He prayed silently that Yahveh would set the Premier's heart on the course that Yahveh wanted. He nodded at the Premier and took out a piece of paper he then slid across the desk. The leader of China took the paper and looked carefully at it for several minutes. He took off his glasses, sighed and asked his Internal Security Chief. "Are you sure of everyone on this list?"

Zhou nodded again. "I had that list crosschecked by three other Vice Prime Ministers and the Prime Minister himself. They all agree that the breakdown on that list is correct."

The Premier put his glasses back on and stared at the list again. It detailed who was absolutely loyal to Chun, who was not in his camp, and who were unknown but unreliable in this incident. Three of the Premier's top people were in the definite column for Chun. He looked at Zhou. "How do you want to handle this?"

Zhou stared at the leader of the country. "Sir, I believe the Russians had an operation called a Pogrom which was an organized massacre of dissidents. They used it to clean house and it could be a model for what we need to do here. As we see it, Chun is on the verge of starting a rebellion with the goal of destroying the present government and making himself a new Emperor. We also feel that it has a good chance of working in the present social climate."

While he let that sink in, Zhou prayed that Yahveh would guide his next words so that events could transpire to achieve Yahveh's goals and save his family, too. "Mr. Premier, I believe that if we let the Americans come in and take care of Chun, we can show that we had nothing to do with his demise. Also, if we move swiftly after Chun is disposed of, we can "clean house" and by the time word of his untimely death reaches the rest of the government, there won't be an Emperor or any of his revolutionary support staff to take over the government."

The Premier liked the sound of that because it served his position and eliminated a threat to himself and the country without him having to lift a finger. "I tell you what Zhou, I am going on vacation this afternoon and won't be back until next week. I expect a full report on any events that occur during my absence."

Zhou stood up and bowed, "Yes Premier."

CHAPTER TWENTY ONE

Zhou returned to his office and began to use his computer to set up the assassinations that the Premier had recently agreed to by not refusing them. The Premier's absence would look good politically and would also serve to take him out of reach of any of his "friends" who were marked for removal. As he completed the list of personnel and assignments, his phone rang. This was his personal desk phone, not the "normal" government line.

He picked it up and said, "Zhou here."

The excited words of Liao Jilong rang in Zhou's ears. "Sir, I found your family. I know where Chun is keeping them!"

Zhou asked where. Liao answered back "They are in a remote village near Hohhot. It is called Shingla and only has ten or twenty families living there. Chun has them in the village main building. As far as I can tell, all four of them are all right. Do you want me to get them out?"

Zhou thought for a few seconds. "No, not yet. Call me back at my home in exactly one hour."

After hanging up, Zhou left for the day and got home in plenty of time to make an unofficial call to Jack Malone. Jack answered on the first ring. "Hello?"

Zhou related what he had heard from his top agent. "Should he go in and get them?"

Jack quietly said, "Ask the Master, and then call me back." The line went dead.

Zhou was taken back by the comment. He thought to himself, "I almost reverted to the old way of doing things." He knelt on the floor and petitioned Yahveh for directions. He got up after five minutes and called Jack back.

Zhou said, "I think I have a direction from God on this. I need a confirmation if possible."

Laura came on the line. After a quick introduction she told the Vice Prime Minister of China's Internal Security what God had told her. "Zhou, the Father says that you should not attempt to rescue your family because they will all die if you do. The enemy has a satanic strongman guarding your wife and children. His intent is to kill them regardless of what happens with Chun, but God will defeat him through us. I don't think your men can overcome the spirit."

Zhou sat there and sent a heartfelt "Thank you" winging its way to Yahveh. "I asked God what I should do and my spirit told me to let the Crossfire Team get them out, not my men. Thank you for the confirmation Mrs. Malone, and I look forward to thanking you in person."

Laura laughed and told him, "Please call me Laura, and I too am looking forward to seeing your family reunited with you."

Zhou hung up and waited until Liao called back. "Liao, keep a watch to make sure they don't move them. I have a special Team coming in to get them out tomorrow. Do not interfere or allow anyone else to interfere with these people. Understand?"

Liao agreed and told his friend and boss that he would do the best he could. Zhou thanked him and told him that after this assignment was completed Liao would be assigned at home in China.

Laura took off the headset and shook her head. "I am glad he is willing to work with us in this matter." she told Jack and Mark. "The Father showed me the strongman that the enemy has guarding the family. He is formidable and has great strength. The Father showed me that only He can win the freedom for Zhou's family."

Jack nodded as the pieces came together and fit correctly in his spirit. "Then it will happen because Christ's mission, in part, was to set the captives free. Since Zhou has given his life to the Master, his whole family will be saved."

Mark finished cleaning his .45 caliber pistol and reloaded it. "Let's start the sword practice."

The three of them got up from their seats and swayed with the motion of the C-5 Galaxy aircraft as they made their way between the members of the SOG. Most of these were sleeping because they knew that it could be a long time until they got to rest again. The three Team members made their way down to the lower level. Jack motioned to Sarah, Su Li, and Gary who were sitting in the seats there.

He went to a locker and took out six wooden practice swords from the rack. He handed one to each of the others. Then he took them into the well-lit open area behind the seats and had them stand in a semi-circle around him as he explained the sword and its capabilities.

After showing them how to hold the two-handed hilt correctly, he then went through the positions from high guard to rear guard. In each position he showed them the way to stand, kneel, or turn. After they had learned the basics, he drilled them by calling out a position and having them move into the position. He guided them by doing the same thing in front of them.

After they had a good grip on the basics he started them on a simple kata that allowed them to move from position to position. Gary had some trouble with his feet until Su Li took him aside and worked with him for a few minutes. She showed him how to move on the ball of the foot rather than the heel. Then she showed him the balancing of the body as she moved from one position to the other. He admired Su Li's graceful ways and the power inherent in her motions. Gary was a quick study and was able to do a good imitation in a short time. Then they returned to the group and drilled some more.

After a break and a bite to eat they started again. After two hours Jack felt they had the movements down fairly well. He then started them working in pairs with one attacking and the other defending. He wouldn't have the time to show them all the possibilities but he could get them tuned up on the basics. He worked with each person and rotated the pairs so each person got used to working against a variety of different sizes and capabilities.

Jack told them to keep working as he went up to talk to Major Mike White, their pilot for this little jaunt into Communist China.

Mike had a crew of five working with him for the flight and was in the process of entering Zhou's information into the Internal Guidance System when Jack came into the cockpit. He finished his job and gave control to the co-pilot. The huge plane was droning over the North Pacific Ocean and just passed the International Date Line, moving them into the next day. The aircraft commander got up and stretched. He moved back in the cockpit to talk to Jack.

Jack asked Mike if there would be any trouble in getting across the stretch of Russia and the part of Mongolia they had to travel over.

Mike raised an eyebrow and then smiled. "I have it on good assurances that we will be totally ignored in both countries as long as we stick to our flight path in and out."

Jack smiled back. "Good, I was praying that would be the case. How's the plane handling?"

Mike shrugged his shoulders, "Like an overweight bear with an attitude. Its fine and we have all the equipment to get the people out. Even if we have fifty wounded, we have the capability to litter them and the doctor on-board to help them. I think we're going to be all right. But aren't we going in six hours earlier than we planned?"

Jack nodded, "Yeah, that's Mark's plan." Mike nodded and headed back to the command seat.

Mike thought as he took the control back from the co-pilot that the C-5 was actually quite a sweet plane. She could carry fleets of helicopters, tanks, even mobile bridges. The cargo hold was so big the Wright Brothers first flight could have been made inside. True, he liked things that went so fast his hair was on fire, but if you had to haul something, this was the way to do it.

Their flight path took them over the infamous Sakhalin Island where Flight 007 had been shot down with a complete loss of life. The civilian airliner was reportedly downed by a Russian air-to-air missile, from a fighter. Mike had heard rumors that it was actually lost due to the Shadow War between the United States and Russia, during the Cold War. There was a good chance that the U.S. Air Force was probing the Russian air defenses that night, with ongoing air battles. Flight 007 wandered through the area and was lost because it was mistaken by a third country, as being a threat, from the conflict going on that night.

It didn't matter now because of the changes in the world social order. These changes didn't really make Russia any less dangerous, just not in a nose-to-nose confrontation with the U.S. on a daily basis.

Mike considered the new threat arising out of the post-Iraq invasion world, and the war on terror. NATO had expanded its mandate, authorizing it to go into any country that was considered harboring weapons of mass destruction. That was strengthening Europe and their one-world currency, the Euro, against the dollar. The European Union was building its own army now and it would soon rival any standing army in size. You don't support such a large group of fighting people and not use them. It didn't make economic sense. They would be a world power pushing a one-world government and a one-world currency on the rest of the world, including the U.S. in the future. Jack had talked with Mike and showed him the parallels between the situation and Bible Prophesy.

Many of the events of the last days were becoming reality. The U.S. led the "Coalition of the Willing Nations" into Iraq to preemptively stop the country from providing WMDs to terrorists to use on the world. How long would it be before a coalition of Arab Muslim states allied themselves with Russia and marched into Israel citing the same rationale for their view of the world? That would be the war of Gog and Magog, the first of three battles called the last battle in the Bible. Mike understood that most prophesies in the Bible had been fulfilled exactly as they had been written between five hundred to five thousand years before.

But, right now he was involved in trying to stop a world war from starting between China and the U.S. That was enough on his plate at this time. He was about to violate three hostile nation's air space in a cargo plane with no weapons. True, there was tacit support for the flight in, and hopefully for the flight out. They would see pretty quickly. They were less than twenty minutes away from Russian airspace over Sakhalin Island and approaching it at four hundred knots.

CHAPTER TWENTY TWO

As the giant aircraft winged its way across Russia on a looping curve through Mongolia, Laura got together with the three dozen special operations group personnel. Each one had been handpicked by Yahveh Himself to be able to fight in both the physical world and the spiritual world, simultaneously. She wasn't surprised to find a great deal of humility in such an elite group of Christian warriors.

She spelled out the upcoming battle as far as she understood it. "In the real world we will be confronting Chun's army of thugs and at least a division of the best commandos that the Chinese can field. The commandos apparently don't know that they are being used through a combination of deceit and foul play. All they know is that a foreign invader, that's us, are coming to attack a Chinese base. Needless to say, they will fight for their homeland with all the ferocity that we would if the tables were reversed."

She walked into the middle of the area where the troops were sitting. "I know that Mark and Sarah have briefed you on the combat situation, I'm not trying to improve on that. What I want to do is to prepare you for the spiritual combat that is coming along with the physical battle. There are at least two strongmen coordinating the efforts of Satan to accomplish two goals. The first is to acquire one of the Lord's Treasures from the Crossfire Team. The second, and incidental, goal is to create an international incident that can be amplified into a direct war between the United States and China. Chun's goal is to use this as a power play for control of the country. The devil's intent is to kill as many as possible while they still don't know Yahshua and his love."

Laura saw understanding in the eyes of each of the troops she looked at. This was so different than a normal group of warriors that had no comprehension of the spiritual warfare involved. "On the battlefield, God has commanded us to be brave and extend our belief in Him, our trust in Him, our faith to levels we have not reached before. Now, I'm not sure exactly what that will require of us. We will be battling in the natural, but, He has said that He will battle for us. Does this mean we will suffer no losses? I don't know. I just know that Yahveh has decreed that we go into this battle for Him and stand for Him the best we can. As born-again believers you know that death is just the doorway to being with Yahshua and that will eventually be our reward, anyway. But, until He calls us home we will fight for him. Now, I want us all to pray, in agreement, our service and obedience to God and His Son. We will also pray for protection for each person here and all the hostages. Lastly, we will pray for the opposing force. Our prayer will be that they will yield to the will of the Yahveh without having to die to do it."

The prayers were heartfelt and sincere. The training had been thorough and the warriors felt that they were ready on all levels.

The plane left Mongolian airspace and entered Chinese airspace for the final leg of the flight.

Mike White set his GPS sights on a small, little-used runway in the northern Chinese countryside. The satellite photos showed this to be technically feasible for him to land and take off. On the C-5 the main landing gear is equipped with twenty-four wheels, and the nose gear has four wheels. To adapt the aircraft to the rural runway-bearing capabilities, the co-pilot decreased the pressure in the tires before the aircraft landed. Mike also set the landing gear bogies to an angle from the center line of the aircraft to accommodate the landing operation in the prevailing crosswind conditions. The huge plane landed softly and ran out its speed on the short runway. The twenty-eight wheels kept the weight of the plane from sinking into the dirt surface.

As soon as the plane rolled to a stop, the heavily armed troops disembarked into the warm Chinese landscape. They were accompanied by four Humvees. They formed up into the assault formations and waited for the word to go.

Laura was praying that God would grant them success in freeing all the hostages when she saw in her mind the location of the main hall where Zhou's family was being held and the strongman waiting there. She felt the urging of the Holy Spirit to lead Sarah's group of the SOG against the forces holding the VPM's family. She spoke to Mark and then called Sarah and the other nine women warriors to accompany her.

The loadmaster pulled the Black Hawk helicopter out of the cargo bay and Su Li helped set it up and get it operational. The women loaded on board and Su Li took them toward the village of Shingla at almost ground level to avoid being seen on Chinese air defense radar. Shingla and Hohhot were close to the border and the Chinese air defense was strong there. They had been granted access for the C-5 flight but they didn't know if the Chinese would be happy about an American combat helio flying around their country.

As they approached Shingla, Su Li angled their flight so as to approach the village from behind a small mesa near the town. This would mask the sound of the rotors and give the troops a shorter walk. She brought the heavy chopper into a hover position and then set it down carefully. Laura and the rest off-loaded and quickly helped Su Li put camouflage over the chopper. America wasn't the only nation with satellites. Su Li stayed with the helicopter in the event the ground troops needed some heavier firepower. She could ditch the camouflage quickly and be airborne in minutes.

The eleven women checked their weapons and slipped through the early morning dew toward the small village. Successfully reaching the edge of town without being seen, Sarah sent the women into a circle around the main hall. Carefully checking the remaining huts and buildings convinced the group that there were no non-combatants to get into the way.

Laura was concentrating on the Holy Spirit's leading and the upcoming battle with the strongman. Close up, her spiritual eyes could see him and he was even larger, uglier, and stronger than she had seen before. He was more arrogant, too. He was enjoying demeaning and bossing around a large group of demons that were guiding Chun's men. Laura started praying that God would do the battle with this major spiritual force. She felt the urging of the Holy Spirit to confront the demon and call him out to battle. Laura trusted God completely and had no fear despite the obvious difference in size and power. She felt the incongruous thought flit through her mind that this was a lot like David and Goliath.

Sarah's troops had moved near to the structure when Laura told her what God wanted her to do. Sarah's combat training in the natural momentarily warred with her obedience to God the Father. After several seconds she bowed to God's leading and told her people to back Laura up.

Laura laid down her assault rifle and walked boldly up the street toward the building. Several of the guards saw her and aimed their rifles at her. They were perplexed when she stopped walking and called out in English to the strongman. "Hey, pit-dweller, did you know that this was your last assignment?"

The strongman, whose name was "Fearsome", stepped through the front wall of the building and into the physical world. He stood in the street facing Laura. In a roaring bass voice he yelled at her. "You are exceptionally stupid for a human being to challenge me. Get on your knees and beg for your life!"

Laura shook her head. "My life is not yours to take, slime ball, I belong to Yahshua, Messiah of Nazareth, who came in the flesh, and I don't bow to anyone but Him."

Fearsome took a step backward at the mention of the name. His eyes blinked several times because he knew he was not just facing a mere human woman but a messenger of the Son of Elohim. But, he was arrogant and aggressive and he wasn't going to lose face, regardless. He started for the woman and at each step his weight caused his feet to sink into the earth several inches. He began to vent red smoke from his nostrils as he raised his mighty fists to crush the puny woman. He saw her armor and sword appear but that didn't bother him. Fearsome had defeated many of Yahveh's angels who had been more powerful than this one.

Laura knew what was happening in the physical. A much stronger, much larger force was bearing down on her with murder in his heart. She could be turned into goo in the next few seconds. But, her faith told her that Yahveh would protect her and she let her faith override her "common sense" and stood fast against the rush of the strongman.

Repeating the twenty-third psalm as she prepared to defend against the rushing power, she reached the verse that said, *"Yea, though I walk through the valley of the shadow of death, I will fear no evil: for thou art with me; thy rod and thy staff they comfort me."*

As the giant reached her and swung his massive fists down to smash her, she swung her sword from its high guard position above her right shoulder through an arc, first down and then upward toward the strongman. She knew that she would only strike his hands but that was what she had available.

As her sword came around in the comparatively feeble counterstrike it felt like the sword grew to a hundred times its normal size and power. The glory of Yahveh was streaming off of the blade and it cut through the entire strongman like he was whipped cream. The force of her blow slammed the separated body to her left with so much power that he literally flew away like he had been swatted by a mountain. He dissolved into black greasy smoke as he flew.

Laura brought her sword back into guard position and watched with interest as the remaining demons flew in any direction to escape the power of the light coming off of the blade. Many didn't make it. They were obliterated by the light while they fled.

The guards had quailed when they saw the strongman appear. They were afraid for their lives when they saw the footprints and the red smoke. Even though the guards were in Satan's camp as are all unsaved people, they were terrified by the giant demon. They had watched as Laura's armor and sword appeared and watched as she fought against the seemingly impossible odds. But she had been powerfully victorious and they knew they couldn't face the power she represented. They all decided the best course of action was to leave the area quickly.

The SOG personnel flowed past Laura with looks of admiration and smiles or grins of conviction that Yahveh was with them. They entered the building and quickly rounded up the six remaining guards without firing a shot.

Sarah and Laura, accompanied by Captain Walthers carefully opened the door to the inner room.

Minga stood in front of her children. Fear of death or injury had been ignored by the mother in her. No one was going to get to her kids as long as she could stop them. To the women of the Crossfire Team this was the ultimate bravery. Minga didn't have God or any weapons, but was still willing to impose herself between her children and possible death.

Captain Walthers was an accomplished linguist and spoke Chinese Mandarin fluently. She calmed the family and explained that even though they were Americans, they had come at Zhou's request to reunite them with their father.

Suspicious but hopeful, Minga and her three children went with the larger, heavily-armed and combat-dressed women out of the building. When Minga saw the remaining guards with their hands on their heads under the guns of the American soldiers, she turned to Captain Walthers. Rather formally she asked if they would not be harsh with these guards because they had been courteous and even respectful during their confinement. When Sarah heard the request she ordered her troops to release the guards and sent them out of the village, unarmed and unharmed.

Using her radio, Sarah had Su Li bring the Black Hawk into the town and land on the street. The children became excited as none of them had ever flown in a helicopter before.

One of the troops watching the perimeter called out a warning and Sarah and Laura moved to place themselves between the freed captives and the source of the concern. A single man, wearing civilian clothing, and with his hands raised, was walking up to the group. Since it wouldn't take a genius to figure out that these weren't Chinese troops or a Chinese helicopter, the man's calmness and assurance were surprising. He was searched and a pistol was taken from him. Then he was led up to the little group next to the chopper. The rotors were still turning and the wind was buffeting everything, making hearing difficult as he spoke.

He introduced himself to Sarah as Liao Jilong, an associate of Zhou Tangtao. Minga stepped forward and bowed to him. She asked him how he had been. Sarah interrupted the conversation and asked, through Captain Walthers, if Minga was familiar with the new addition to the group. The answer confirmed and was what she thought. Liao was the Chinese spy that she had heard about when she worked for the Mossad. His reputation was one of class and efficiency but with high marks for mercy and understanding. He had always been attached to the VPM. Sarah felt that he probably was the source of the Intel as to the location of the family. She realized that he would have been here at Zhou's request to defend the family if possible.

Sarah laughed silently to herself. It must have been a real shock for him to see Americans freeing the Tangtao family.

Liao requested that he be allowed to accompany the family until they were safely reunited with Vice Prime Minister Tangtao. Sarah asked the Holy Spirit for advice and had a peace in her spirit about his request. But they were still going to keep his weapon until they released him.

Everyone boarded the helicopter and it flew back to the C-5 near Hohhot.

When they disembarked, Jack and Mark greeted the family and Liao. They listened to Sarah describe the action, especially Laura's confrontation. Jack called Zhou on his satellite cell phone. After talking to him for several minutes he handed the phone to Minga. She talked and cried at the same time. The boys were hugging her and her daughter was hanging onto her free hand. She handed the phone to Liao who spoke for several minutes to the VPM. Then he handed the phone back to Jack.

Zhou told him, "I will send a pre-arranged signal to the commandos to withdraw from Chun's group. Give me ten minutes to accomplish a series of tasks I must do. Praise the Father for you and your people. I thank you from the bottom of my heart for the lives of my family. You will always be welcome in my home."

Jack said, "Thank you, and you and yours are always welcome in our home also. I am going to get Su Li and some of the troops to fly with Liao and your family back toward Beijing, about ten miles. If you can have someone meet them there it would be easier than if we were to appear near the capital."

Zhou agreed, "I already have a helicopter in route. I will give you a secure channel your pilot can talk to our pilot on to coordinate. And, don't worry about being seen. I have prepared everyone as to your presence and purpose. I myself have some things I must do before I can join you. But, you should know that Chun Xiaoping is not at the prisoner camp right now. He is apparently in the air this morning running his operations from there. I pray that the hostages are all right. Thank you again for my family." He hung up and Jack told Su Li what the arrangements were and the frequency to use.

Su Li and five of the women soldiers boarded the helicopter with the freed hostages and Liao Jilong for the short ten-mile hop while everyone else rejoined their groups. The Crossfire Team and the squad leaders went over their attack plans to free the hostages, for a final time.

CHAPTER TWENTY THREE

Jack turned back to the C-5 as the helicopter left and received a call from one of the SOG troops. "What's the problem?"

The Sergeant reported, "Sir, This is Sergeant Franklin, we have detected a force of thirty troops attempting to flank the aircraft to the west."

Jack nodded, "Thank you, Sergeant," He ran over to Mark and relayed the information. Mark pulled up the overview screen on his laptop and studied the situation. Keying his microphone he told the Team leaders to have teams two and three move out to intercept the flanking force while the rest of the Teams stayed put and made sure it wasn't just a diversion.

Jack, Laura, and Mark grabbed their weapons and ran to the two columns of soldiers running toward the indicated coordinates. Sarah stayed with the rest of the troops while they reformed to provide the best fire patterns they could with their reduced numbers.

As Mark jogged with the troops he directed traffic from his combat Pocket PC. He had an unmanned drone aircraft launched that would give them much better video than the satellite pictures he was now using. The drone would be directed from the C-5 by Major White.

The weapons the SOG troopers carried were the latest prototype versions of the IWS or Individual Weapons System. Electronic sensors were linked to the rifle's aiming system and to the computers carried by each soldier. All of these reported directly to the main command computer for instant updates and visuals. The commander could communicate with a man, a squad, or a division if necessary to provide instant reaction to enemy tactics.

The latest version of light-weight body armor was protection against anything except artillery, tanks, or rifles, within ten feet. This involved a new method of taking the inertial energy of the bullet or fragment and redistributing it so that it didn't penetrate. The light-weight allowed for more all-inclusive armor, protecting everything the helmet and visor didn't.

In his helmet, the combined combat infrared/optical system allowed the individual soldier to detect any enemy combatants out to five hundred yards in day or night, good weather or not. The caseless ammunition allowed each one of the troops to carry over two thousand rounds and have over two hundred rounds instantly available.

Mark watched the enemy as they moved toward them. He repositioned his troops and had them settle down three hundred yards before the enemy appeared. As the thirty enemy soldiers came forward it was obvious that these were not the highly efficient Chinese commandos that were originally to fight them. These troops didn't have good command or control and their individual field craft was crude and not very silent.

Mark waited until the enemy was well within range before he had a Sergeant who spoke Chinese call out for them to drop their weapons and surrender. The enemy answered with a fusillade of rounds which crashed into the trees above him. Mark gave the order to open fire. The SOG returned the rifle fire with precision and accuracy that reduced the enemy troops quickly. The cross fire of hundreds of rounds shredding every tree and bush and smacking into bodies and body armor was deafening. Mark calmly shot three of the enemy that tried to charge his position and took note that the SOG personnel were being very calm and efficient in their sight selection and firing.

Jack and Laura were about thirty feet apart, flanked to the right and were advancing with some of the other troopers when a rifle-propelled grenade hit just to Laura's right side. The grenade detonated with tremendous force. At that range the fragments of the grenade were more than sufficient to penetrate Laura's body armor.

As the grenade detonated Laura saw a brief instant of gold and white light between her and the blast. The fragments tore trees on either side of her to pieces but none touched Laura. She heard in her mind the quiet tones of Rose, "It's not your time yet." Laura dropped to the earth and aimed her rifle toward the enemy because Mark had drilled into them that a soldier would always follow a barrage.

Two Chinese soldiers were running her way, firing as they ran. Laura sighted through the electronic scope and knocked both men off their feet with a sustained burst that tracked across both men's chests and back across their heads.

Jack dropped to the ground next to her and fired several rounds at another soldier who threw his hands up and fell back. He looked at her and said, "What happened with that grenade?"

She grinned, "Rose." That was all she had to say.

The shooting died out and the American troops cautiously went forward and checked the enemy troops. None of the thirty lived through the battle. Only one of the SOG personnel was wounded and that was a through and through wound to the wrist that had passed through between his armor and his glove. He had stopped the bleeding and it didn't look like an artery was hit. Laura wrapped it and sent him back with two other soldiers for medical treatment. The men and women of the SOG checked each other and found that their armor had stopped over thirty-two direct hits.

Mark had his troops check them for papers or anything else of importance. There wasn't anything they could use. Mark formed up the troops and headed them back to the C-5.

As Laura jogged back with Jack she told him. "I'm not sure how I'm going to relate this to our children. Should I say that I stopped being a housewife and became a soldier for a time being, or should I tell them that you dragged me into this high-pressure life?"

Jack thought about that and gave her an answer she could use. "Tell them that Yahveh wanted you to participate in His plans for His glory and you obeyed."

Laura nodded. "That's true but, you know it seems like only a few days ago I was more worried about our being able to get along as husband and wife in the suburbs because we held two jobs. Now, that doesn't even seem possible anymore. We have become more warriors for Christ than members of the country club, and guess what. I'm glad". Laura shook her head as she ran, "I never thought I'd say that."

Jack thought about how he wanted to protect her from the danger when this all began and then pictures of her shooting, fighting demons with her armor flaring golden and her sword gleaming with the light of Yahveh, and riding in the back seat of an F-22 Raptor. He realized that he had never been her protector; Yahveh was in that role and doing a much better job of it than he could.

Jack looked over at the body armor, rifle and all the other trappings of a soldier, including the blood stains and mud and realized that his wife meant more to him than he had ever guessed she could. He moved closer and put his arm around her under her back pack and gave her a squeeze.

As they continued to jog she leaned her helmet against his chest and told him, "I love you." Jack smiled and replied, "I know, and I love you, too."

They broke the clinch and finished their run as they reached the C-5. They both knew that the skirmish was over as a decided victory. But, now, the real battle would come.

CHAPTER TWENTY FOUR

After the conflict with Chun's men, Mark explained his battle plan. Since the family had been freed and Zhou was recalling the division of commandos, their objective was clear and they had already reduced the number of troops that Chun could field.

On a map he indicated the shallow valley the camp was located in. It was roughly a one mile long oval with the camp at the northern end. They were near the middle of the oval, which was about a half-mile wide at the middle.

They had four different satellite inputs that showed where the people were, what weapons they had and how active they were. In the event there were any tanks involved on the Chinese side, the anti-armor weapons on the Humvees were capable of stopping them. Two unmanned aircraft would give them a close-up view of the action and prevent surprises.

The plan was a classic pinscher movement with troops advancing up the middle and two squads going around the flanks of the defenders to attack from the sides and the back, if possible. The advanced electronics and body armor had proven themselves and they were all ready to get to it.

Sergeant Tom Bally approached the Command team. He was one of the SEALs that had signed onto the SOG at Yahveh's urging. He came up to the group and saluted. Returning the salute, Mark asked him what he needed.

Tom calmly matched Mark's gaze. "Sir, you said that we should let you know if we were given anything from God. I got some specific information that you definitely need to hear."

Mark nodded, "That was my instruction." He turned and called Laura over to the group. Then he asked Tom to describe his information.

Tom looked at each one of his officers in turn and then spoke. "God normally gives me dreams and visions. This time it was words. Clear and unmistakable words of direction. I tested the spirit and it was true."

Tom was repeating what he had been given. He was surprised that he hadn't forgotten a single word, but then, the message was from Yahveh. "First you must know that what is at stake here is far greater than the release of the hostages. The whole world could live or die depending on what is done here today. Yahveh wants us to know that there is no strongman defending Satan's realm here. You are in direct conflict with a principality. The Prince of Asia is the power behind Chun and his troops. His power and authority are here to insure the capture of the crucifixion nail and the death of as many Americans and Chinese as possible. Father Yahveh does not want this to happen. The message was this. *"You can not win this battle in the natural. Have all the warriors remove their armor and lay down their arms. Walk totally in trust of my protection and walk boldly proclaiming the truth of the Good News. If you believe and trust in Me, I will do the battle for you and you will free the captives who will see that I am God."*

Tom stopped and looked at Mark. "Sir, all these men and women have trained hard since we joined the service to be the best soldiers we could be and this advice goes against everything we've learned, but, it is from the Master."

Mark thanked the Sergeant and told him to return to his group. The leaders discussed his message amongst themselves. Laura spoke up and suggested that they inquire of God as to this leading because every report should be confirmed by two or three other witnesses.

As they began to pray for guidance, Chun's aircraft orbited the site of the valley at a range of several miles. He had no problem seeing the C-5 Galaxy as it sat on the ground. He could even make out some of the American troops gathering in the middle of the valley. He had gotten the message that Zhou's family had been freed but that didn't concern him. The time for that subterfuge was over. He had also heard of the defeat of his small group of men. He was glad that they were dead. They had taken it on themselves to outflank the enemy without his permission. Serves them right to die.

All of his plans were in motion right now. The cameras were running on this impromptu invasion. Zhou would be very surprised to find out that he was impotent and that his message to the commandos would not be received. The Chinese government would be reorganized by his people as he flew above the impending battle. There were messages being sent to the American President denouncing the invasion and demanding that America apologize and make reparations for the damages. This was something they would have to do after he made the well-doctored films available to the world.

He smiled as he thought of the overwhelming force hidden in the valley to destroy the Americans. The division of tanks that no one knew was there. The inability of Zhou to recall the commandos. Commandos who were now going to fight for China to the death. Chun was sure that the pitched battle would result in many Chinese deaths and public outcries for retaliation against America.

In the confusion and turmoil he would hold all the reins of power and be seen as the savior of his country. It would be easy after he had the talisman of power that he would personally take off the body of the dead Mr. Malone.

Chun could see it now in his mind's eye. He would be the hero of the battle. He would be acclaimed far and wide as the wisest and most capable leader the country every had. It would only be a small step to establishing the rule of the Emperor, again. He chuckled slightly as it all went his direction.

Jack was praying for God's guidance when he got a verse from the Bible. Deuteronomy 20:1-4. He pulled out his Pocket PC and brought up the unfamiliar verse. He was stunned as he read.

1"When thou goest out to battle against thine enemies, and seest horses, and chariots, and a people more than thou, be not afraid of them: for the Father thy Yahveh is with thee, which brought thee up out of the land of Egypt. 2And it shall be, when ye are come nigh unto the battle, that the priest shall approach and speak unto the people, 3And shall say unto them, Hear, O Israel, ye approach this day unto battle against your enemies: let not your hearts faint, fear not, and do not tremble, neither be ye terrified because of them; 4For the Father your Yahveh is he that goeth with you, to fight for you against your enemies, to save you."

Jack told the group of leaders what he had received. Laura nodded and said, "He gave me 1 Chronicles 5:20. Jack looked that one up:

> [20]"And they were helped against them, and the Hagarites were delivered into their hand, and all that were with them: for they cried to Yahveh in the battle, and he was entreated of them; because they put their trust in him."

Mark continued to pray because the decision as to what to do fell on him as the commander of the troops. He knew Yahveh was in charge but could he rely on these messages? If he was wrong everyone here would be dead or captured. It went totally against everything he had ever learned. He felt his heart was going to explode with the choice. In his stress he called out, "Dear Yahveh, what am I to do? These warriors depend on me to make the right choice. I am nothing but a mere man. I can not make this choice. You must make it for me."

Mark felt a peace come over his mind and his heart. He clearly heard in his mind, *"Go in my peace, and let me deal with the Prince of Asia and the hearts of the men opposing you. Go boldly as my humble servants and do not fear. I am with you."*

Mark looked into the eyes of his friends and the other leaders and saw conviction, obedience, and more bravery than he had every seen in his life. In his mind he said, "Okay Father Yahveh, we're with you." He signaled the other troops to come back to him. He had something momentous to say to them.

CHAPTER TWENTY FIVE

The seasoned commander of Chun's loyal troops finished talking to Chun on his phone and turned to his lieutenants and gave the order of battle. The plan was simply to draw the Americans in and then overwhelm them. To achieve this, Chun wanted the Commandos to skirmish with the advance troops of the Americans and then move back toward the camp. When the Americans, feeling victorious, chased them and were fully in the trap, the tanks and the other troops would surge out of their hidden places and enfilade the few American troops. The battle would be short and bloody, at least on their side.

Word came that the enemy was advancing up the middle of the valley without sending troops to either side. The Commander of the Commandos, Han Le, thought that the Americans were very stupid to do that. He told the Commandos to move out and harass the enemy with sniping and small battles while falling back.

The first two squads of the commandos slid professionally forward until they could hear the Americans. It was strange for the commandos to hear them before they saw them. The enemy was actually singing as they came. Did they think that they could just stroll in and take over?

As the snipers lined up their first shots, they stopped and stared. The word flashed back to Han Le that the Americans weren't armed and they had no body armor on either. They were just walking up the valley singing, six people across. Even stranger was the man leading the Americans.

Commander Le expected a trick and warned his troops to stay on high alert. He wanted to see this for himself. Chun was calling on him to have his troops fire on the enemy but Le wasn't worried about the timing. If they didn't have any weapons to fight back with against his troops, there was no hurry.

He came to the front of the lines and saw and heard the Americans as they joyfully sang and walked. This was strange. The man at the head of the column was dressed in a simple white cloth. In Le's binoculars he could see that the man was about six feet tall and had long black hair and penetrating brown eyes. The face was serene it was so peaceful. Le realized that somehow he knew this man. He was trying to determine what to do when an even stranger thing happened. The Commander could almost see a distortion start from where the man in white was walking and flow outward like ripple in a pond. The strange thing was that this ripple was moving quickly outward throughout the valley. As the line of the expanding distortion passed through him he was shocked to his core. He suddenly knew the man he was looking at was an incarnation of the one true God of the universe. Commander Le knew the terrible conviction of his sinful life before God. He had been imbued with a full knowledge of who Messiah was and what He commanded all people on the earth to do. Le fell to his knees crying out his sorrow and asking Yahshua to forgive him. Peace flooded his mind and body as he knew that the Messiah did love him, forgave his sins, and welcomed him. Le asked Yahshua to be with him forever. The Commander didn't notice that all of his troops were doing the same thing.

Because the Chinese warriors had never known the good news of Yahshua they had never had an opportunity to make an educated choice. In an instant, Yahveh's Spirit had convicted every person in the valley of the reality of Yahshua and his love for them. They all realized their shabbiness next to the beauty and righteousness of God. They cried out to Yahveh regardless of their previous lives, beliefs, philosophy, or religious training. His love freed them of all their sins and fears. They unanimously chose to love and serve the Son of the Creator of the Universe for the rest of their lives.

Weapons were abandoned and tanks forgotten. Soldiers and officers alike celebrated in their new freedom. In the midst of all the celebration, the SOG walked along singing of an Elohim they loved. The man in white continued to walk before them. The converted guards released the prisoners and led them to the main group of people celebrating their new-found freedom.

Mark talked to the commanders and officers of the prisoners. He had them take a head count and when that was done he told them to take their people to the C-5 for extraction from China. The prisoners had received the good news at the same time as the enemy.

The powerful Prince of Asia had ruled over billions of humans for centuries. His slightest command could cause millions of deaths. But he had been sent to get the crucifixion nail for his Father. He had arranged everything so that it would destabilize the balance of power between Asia and the West. He was always in command. As he looked at the man in white he quaked. He knew he was facing Yahshua the Messiah who had already beaten all the forces of darkness. He turned and fled at a speed to rival light. But, suddenly he found himself chained to the wall in the pit of the abyss, where he would remain until Judgment Day. His roaring and screaming was ignored by all. He yelled at the fallen angel that had gone with Satan in the battle of Heaven. "I should not be here now! Get me out of here!"

The demon stared at him in the semi-darkness of the abyss. "I've been here for thousands of years. Here I have to remain until the Day of Judgment. I'm glad that it won't be much longer in coming."

Chun was furious and screaming into his microphone. "Why haven't you started shooting? Fire on the enemy! Do it now! Do you hear me? He thought, "This isn't how it is supposed to be!" But now, he couldn't remember how it was supposed to be. He tried to hear the voice in his head but it wasn't there any more to goad him on and tell him what to do. Qualpian had seen the defeat of the principality and had fled from Chun only to find that Chun had been his last assignment. He too, was chained to the wall of the pit awaiting final judgment.

Chun's voice came out of the headset which was lying ignored, on the ground, as his men celebrated with the freed prisoners. Regular Chinese troops, tank drivers, and commandos were standing alongside the Americans and they were all singing, albeit in different languages, the same song of love for a merciful Yahveh.

Many of the Chinese troops were attempting to ask the Americans how they could know God. The Chinese-speaking troops helped hundreds of their old enemies to know Yahshua and then celebrated with them in the love of the Messiah.

Jack talked to Commander Le of the Commandos and led him in a prayer of salvation. Jack spoke fluent Chinese and the two of them watched the former enemy troops celebrate and sing together. The Commander was twice as old as Jack but he looked to his new younger American friend and asked him how he would be able to carry on after he returned to "normal" China. He had known nothing but Atheism his whole life and now he was an on-fire believer.

Jack thought about that and realized that only Yahveh could give them the answer so he suggested they pray about it. As they prayed the Commander had a revelation. After they finished praying he shook Jack's hand and gathered his troops. He told them that they would be persecuted, jailed, or killed if they tried to return to their barracks. He was going to start a new life. With that he took off his rank and identifiable parts of his uniform. He converted the coat so that it looked like a non-military coat. Then he was ready to travel. He wasn't surprised to see most of his men ready to go with him. God had given him a plan to disappear into the general populace, but it would require speed and daring, something commandos had in large quantities.

Laura had been praying for all the new converts because she knew they had the knowledge of the Savior but not much else. She was praying that they would find people to disciple them until they could function as Christians on their own. Otherwise their conversion would only last until the first real challenge. The Father dropped a small bombshell into her spirit. She blinked several times as she thought it through again.

Tapping Jack on the shoulder she motioned him to the side of the building away from the enthusiastically milling crowd of baby Christians. Jack knew something was up as he looked at the expression on his wife's face. "What?"

She took his hands in hers and looked up into his eyes. "Sweetheart, God hasn't completed his work here yet. These "baby" Christians won't last long without mentoring in the faith, deliverance from the demonic backgrounds they've had, and an understanding of the Scriptures."

Jack looked at the soldiers as they prepared to give up everything they had to follow Yahveh when they were so woefully unprepared. He had a good idea of where Laura was going with this. "So, God wants us to stay and help them over their infancy and get them planted in a Bible-teaching underground church, right?"

Laura nodded, "The whole Crossfire Team."

Jack made a small face at that but called Mark, Sarah, Gary, and Su Li over to them. He then let Laura explain what the Father had told her. He knew it was confirmed in his spirit but wanted them to do it willingly. This would not be a cake walk. They were deliberately jumping off of their free ride home and into a fiercely aggressive social order that once would have condemned them to death for following Yahshua, let alone preaching the Word. These days the Chinese Government had softened their stance due to the huge size of the underground Christian movement in China. Still, they weren't Chinese and they would be charged with trying to proselytize and that wasn't permitted. They didn't want to test the new attitude and be the first to see if there were any exceptions.

Mark leaned over and talked quietly with his wife. She made a comment and then Mark smiled and said to Jack and Laura, "We've always wanted to vacation in China, you know, see the people, run from the police, all that. Count us in." Su LI smiled and gave Jack a nod.

Gary also nodded. This was a chance in a lifetime for him to help hundreds of people find and keep their new faith in Yahveh. This was blessed work.

Jack walked over to Commander Le and asked if he would mind if six of them and several of the Chinese Christian prisoners tagged along for a while. Le realized immediately what they were asking for. These warriors were offering up their lives to help him and his men. It so fit the image of a believer that Yahveh had dropped into his mind. They would have a much harder time blending in or staying out of sight because of their definite Caucasian looks. Their height would be only a slight handicap because many of the Chinese were tall these days. The odds of their being arrested, jailed, and executed were stacked heavily against them, yet they were still willing to risk it all to help him and his men. Tears came to his eyes and a lump formed in his throat. He nodded as he met Jack's eyes. The communication in that glance told both men that they were willing to risk all for the sake of the Master.

CHAPTER TWENTY SIX

Jack and Mark made arrangements for the SOG to stow all the weapons and high tech gear aboard the C-5 and return to the U.S. Jack went to the pilot and gave him the crucifixion nail in its wooden box. Major White knew the importance of the little box and promised to return it to the Fortress and get it replaced in its outer vault. He looked at the six members of the Team and felt great concern in his heart. This could be the last time he saw them. But they were serving Yahveh and there could be no greater protector. He hugged all six of them and got back on the C-5.

Su Li would have no trouble blending in, but if she was caught, there was a probable death sentence waiting for her. She didn't care at this point. God was leading her to stay with the Team and she knew she would be of use because she spoke the language and knew the country.

Jack and his group scrounged clothes from the civilians and military alike. Some things like the pants would have to stay because they didn't have anything big enough for Jack or Mark. When they were suitably disguised they joined the group of ex-Commandos and watched as the C-5 roared off into the blue Chinese sky. They had left almost all of their high-tech stuff on the plane but Jack had held out the solar powered cell phone that would let him talk to Zhou or the President of the U.S. with equal ease.

As the sound of the plane faded away, the enormity of the Asian mainland made itself clear to the members of the Team. The hundred or so troops left with their new friends, walking out of the valley. The commander kept his hand in his coat pocket where he had a secret weapon. Jack had given him a spare Pocket PC version of the Bible that displayed the scriptures in Chinese.

Chun sat in his aircraft in disbelief. He watched the big plane fly away to the north and there wasn't anything he could do to it. His aircraft didn't have any offensive weapons other than pistols. The Chinese Air Force had orders from the Premier not to bother the American Plane and Chun had not been able to override that order.

CHAPTER TWENTY SEVEN

As his plane landed in Beijing, Chun realized that it didn't matter to him about the Christian artifact he had not secured. It somehow wasn't important to him anymore. He realized that even though the battle hadn't happened, he could still solidify his power now that certain individuals were no longer in power.

As he walked to his limousine he heard engines racing up to him. He stopped and saw three security cars braking hard. Expecting them to honor him, he was completely taken off guard when the security troops drew their weapons and held them on him. He demanded to know what they thought they were doing.

Zhou Tangtao stepped forward and told him, "Chun Xiaoping, you are under arrest for treason, kidnapping, inciting revolution, murder, and a host of lesser charges. Do not resist or we will be forced to kill you."

Chun was shocked to see the man he had issued an order to have killed was still alive. His shock turned to rage. "You imbecile, I am going to be the next Emperor of China, how dare you try to charge me? ME? Two of the security men stepped up behind him, disarmed him and put handcuffs on him. They frog marched him to the back seat of a car and put him in it. They carefully locked the handcuffs to a stanchion so he could not attempt an escape.

Zhou walked over to the window and looked at the man. "You know, your plans were brilliant except for one thing."

Chun looked at his tormentor and asked, "And what was that one thing?"

Zhou smiled, "You went up against Yahveh. You were bound to lose." Zhou slapped the roof of the car and it drove away, bearing an utterly confused Chun to a cell in the prison he had ruled over for so long. Zhou doubted that the man would live to see the inside of a court room. Too many of the people he had imprisoned and tortured were still there. They had long memories and absolutely no mercy.

As Chun rode in the car, he tried to figure out how to make this situation one that would work for him. He spoke commandingly to the two guards in the front of the car. "I am going to be the next Emperor of China, release me immediately." The guard not driving the vehicle turned to Chun and smiled, "My brother sends his regards, and as you wish, I will release you." As Chun sat there more confused than ever, the guard fired two bullets into his head. Chun died instantly and things suddenly got eternally worse for him.

Not knowing about the death of Chun, Zhou thought that Chun would also be surprised to see that the entire group of his hand-picked elite staff of guards had been replaced by military personnel, with which he had no favor.

Zhou went back to his car and looked at Minga seated in the back. "He is now under arrest and will face many challenges to even get to court. He will not hurt you again." His phone rang and he answered it quickly. He sighed, answered with an order, and hung up. Looking at Minga again he shook his head. "I just heard that Chun was killed by unknown people on the way to jail. I insisted on them providing us with his body to make sure it really is him."

Minga smiled and took her husband's hand. "I am glad that he is dead, he was a horrible person. But what will stop the next maniac from doing what he did?" She wanted assurances that Zhou knew he couldn't give her. But he knew someone who could.

He got into the car and told the driver to take them home. He missed his brother but would not lose the rest of his family. He pushed the button that rolled up the window between the driver and them. He put his arm around his wife. "Let me tell you about the group that just rescued you and the children. They are called the Crossfire Team and you will be excited about what they did in Zyngola."

Most members of Chun's take over grab were already in the prison when word came of his death. Zhou's men had made a clean sweep as soon as Zhou had given them the signal. There were many in the government and the military that would never be heard of again. They just disappeared, forever.

When the Premier returned on Monday, he asked Zhou to attend him and give him a report about what had happened while he was vacationing.

Zhou detailed the management changes he had instituted in the government and the military. He then gave the Premier a carefully thought-out description of the action near Hohhot. The Premier listened to everything and then questioned his VPM of Security. "I don't understand what happened to our troops. Most of them have disappeared from their barracks and no one knows where they have gone. The ones that returned don't know what happened, only that they were "changed" somehow. Is this a new weapon the Americans have?"

Zhou had prayed about this report for quite a while over the weekend. "No sir. It isn't a weapon at all. Contrary to our atheistic beliefs, there appears to be a higher power at work here. I have looked at this from all angles and have had both scientists and philosophers review it. There is no explanation that can serve if we discount the supernatural. If you like, we can simply label it as "unknown forces".

The Premier was grateful that Chun Xiaoping was no longer a threat to his future so the loss of a few troops to unknown causes wasn't a major concern. The concept that there might be a higher power didn't interest him. "Make it so. Now, Zhou, about your resignation. I have refused it. I need men like you to help administer this great nation. I am nominating you to replace the present Prime Minister in two years when he retires. You need to start working with him so that the transition is smooth. Do you have someone you can trust to take over your position as VPM of Security?"

This was a bit of a shock but Zhou took it calmly. He had learned that he was going to be where Yahveh wanted him to be regardless of anybody's ideas. "Yes sir. My second in command is trustworthy and very capable. In fact, I have lately endeavored to bring him up to speed in my position because I thought that I was retiring."

The Premier smiled, "Good, good. Why don't you let him run the office while you take a vacation and then start working in the Prime Minister's office when you get back? I will see that your pay and benefits are changed to that level immediately. I really want to thank you for defusing this Chun thing with the Americans. This was hardly the time to go nose to nose with them. It may come to that in the future, but thankfully, not today."

Zhou agreed and expressed his concern on continuing to smooth things over with the U.S. government. This would require many meetings and trips to accomplish China's goals without looking bad to the Americans. Zhou felt that during the interim period while he was being groomed to be the next Prime Minister would be an excellent time to accomplish this and hone his skills in diplomacy. The Premier agreed.

As Zhou headed back to start his vacation he thought, "Well, well, Jack Malone, it looks like my family and I will get to take you up on your invitation to visit your home much sooner than either of us expected."

CHAPTER TWENTY EIGHT

The C-5 had returned to Edwards AFB in southern California. Shang and his people were given priority visas to remain in the U.S. while they worked out their plans to stay or return to China. Shang had often described his flock as being made up of men and women with no ties to anyone else in China, so many would stay for the freedoms granted to Americans.

The members of the SOG were given a week's leave and took flights to wherever home was with the exception of Craig and Kevin Steele. They decided to visit their sister, Christi, in Denver and flew there in the Crossfire Team corporate jet.

Mark, Jack, Laura, and Sarah had spent a little time before the flight left, putting together a quick report for General Miles and the President. Mark put together an action report that covered the deployment and the fire fight. Jack covered the flight and the portion Yahveh handled. Laura and Sarah described the action to free Zhou Tangtao's family and the battle with the strongman. They had all agreed to indent the supernatural events of the report to allow for easy removal if the reports were to be seen by persons other than those two people. The reports read concisely, either way.

Jack explained the major non-battle in non-supernatural terms. "Our forces used our technical and military advantages to convince the enemy that combat would be useless. Instead, they were convinced to come together with us and to release the hostages in a show of good will by the Chinese military that were not happy with Chun Xiaoping's seizures of the American military personnel in the first place. During this phase of the encounter there were no casualties on either side, since hostilities were prevented and cooler heads prevailed."

Jack's indented portion read: "Yahshua walked with us through the valley after we obeyed his command to disarm and remove our body armor. Each man and woman in the SOG is to be highly commended for bravery above and beyond the call of duty. As we moved up the valley we sang songs of praise to the Father. His Son was with us and dealt with the supernatural forces arrayed against us. He also converted approximately two hundred Chinese soldiers and commandos into Christians in an instant. The glory all belongs to God for this bloodless victory.

To walk unprotected and unarmed into the guns of the enemy takes far more courage than even that necessary to fight. General Miles, I would also like to report that there are approximately one hundred and twenty-five highly trained Chinese commandos that have just become members of God's church here on earth. That brings me to a point that I need to advise you both on. The six members of the Team feel that we are being led of God to stay in China for a while to disciple these baby Christians. We feel that the society and the political system will cause them to backslide and lose the freedom that the Father has given them if they don't have anyone to teach them Yahveh's way. By now you realize that God knew we would stay for a time to help them when he gave them the revelation of Himself through the Holy Spirit."

I will attempt to stay in touch with you and VPM Zhou during our time here. You might be able to reach me on my secure cell phone. I must keep this to a minimum because while I don't think they can break the encryption, they can surely track it while I'm talking on it. The professionalism of the encryption might make them very curious."

After their reports were combined, Mark had sent them to their respective places.

President Bollen was upbeat about the outcome of the battle. He looked at General Miles and said, "Congratulations on your mission. The freed hostages have been debriefed and given the cover story about their ship going down at sea. We did let them tell the truth about being interred by the Chinese. I read their report with interest. By the way, I just spoke with Zhou Tangtao on a secure line and he had nothing but great praise for your Team and the results of the mission. He explained that DNA testing has confirmed that Chun was killed by acute lead poisoning on his way to prison."

"Zhou also asked me to tell Jack that he and his family will be here next month for a cultural visit and they would like to spend a couple of nights at his place in Denver. It looks like I'd better let him know not to count on it as yet. Miles, the country will never hear of this action, but they will benefit greatly from it. Do what you can to back them up over there, okay?"

The Chairman of the Joint Chiefs of Staff simply nodded. He didn't really agree with the key people of the Crossfire Team staying in a foreign and hostile country, but knew well enough that he couldn't change their minds. So, he'd make the best he could of the situation.

CHAPTER TWENTY NINE

Han Le, the ex-commander of the Chinese commandos was a shrewd man. He knew how to disperse his men so that it didn't look like a flood of strong, young men all coming into the small northwestern suburb of Beijing at the same time. They had taken various routes in groups of five or eight. They arrived at the village over a two day span and didn't seek each other out. Even though it was only a small suburb, it housed over eighty thousand souls and the additions were such a small increase it went unnoticed, except by the locals. Many of the men found work since it was tourist season and the "Waibin" needed their trinkets. Many of the commandos were well schooled and very intelligent. Not so for the tank and army troops who had been conscripted to serve. Many of these were able to find some kind of menial work in a ten mile circle of their "base camp" in the northwestern suburb.

The income allowed them to rent rooms and eat. Han Le used his contacts with the less desirable elements of the area to obtain papers for all the men including the Crossfire Team. Being outsiders, they weren't able to determine if there were any Christians in the area to help them. Laura passed the word through their word-of-mouth communications system to relax and ask the Spirit of Yahveh to identify other believers. Things improved markedly after that and the group was able to blend into the society through the influence of the local Christians. There was no church in the area though, so the Team set one up under the cover of a martial arts class. They would work all day and late into the night teaching the Word and helping the new believers get free of old habits, old strongholds, and old spirits. At the same time they were learning new techniques and training the ex-commandos in what they knew.

Gary walked into the room the Team was using as a base of operations and flopped down on the futon with a bone-tired attitude. He looked over at Laura and Mark who were resting there at the moment. "I have never seen such generational curses as the ones they have here. I mean, these things go back for hundreds, if not thousands, of years. I just finished working with a young man who had two demons that had been passed down over the ages from his eighteenth generational forefathers. Man, were those demons out of it. One of them asked me how he would go about getting another assignment. I explained to him that if he cooperated with me, I would send him to the abyss and he could seek his information there.

Mark smiled at the thinner man. "If you'd put on some more weight you'd get through these sessions in better shape."

Gary rolled his eyes, "If I put on more weight it would all just pool around my waist and then I'd have to lug that around and I'd be even more tired. No thank you."

While they were talking, Jack was walking back to the building after going out into the country to use his cell phone. Going that far away would help throw off the tracking somewhat, but not completely. If the Chinese had detected the signal then they would know it came from this vicinity and a second call would result in the government bringing in local tracking units to triangulate his position and close on it quickly. But, this call had to be made. He had to let Zhou know that they were still in-country after four weeks.

The country side was pleasant enough, even though it was warm and the smell of the honey pots was ripe on the air. Jack shook his head in wonder at people who would still use human waste to fertilize their crops.

Han Le and several of the locals had worked on Jack sufficiently, that he looked like a really tall Chinese man. His hair was black; he had used a paste they made to force his eyelids to look more Chinese. His skin was darkened by oils as much as by the weather. His clothing was now completely authentic down to his silk pants. He affected a slow gait so that he wouldn't seem like a westerner who was always in a hurry.

He was about a mile away from the village when he spotted trouble. Three Chinese toughs were extorting money out of each person coming down the trail. Jack wasn't worried about fighting them. He knew he could take them but didn't want to draw attention to himself. He looked for another way to go but there were fences on both sides of the road and the only way was forward or backward. He had gotten too close to the hoodlums to backtrack without drawing their attention. "Ah well" he thought, "There was nothing to do, but to go by them."

The leader of the three men stepped into his path and demanded toll for him to pass. Jack studied the man carefully like a Chinese man would. While he was standing there, one of the others said to the leader. "Woy, he's a big one. Sure you want to hassle him?"

The leader had far more bravado than sense. "I can take him." He pointed his stubby finger at Jack. "Hey, man, give me the money or I will have to work you over." He made a clumsy karate movement to show his skill. Jack said quietly, "You would be better served if you let me pass." He didn't show any fear or cowardliness but he didn't insult the punk either. There was always hope.

As normal, the punk decided that Jack was afraid to fight. But shrewdly he called the other two young men to move in on either side of Jack. Jack was about to move when a newcomer joined the little group. A Chinese woman with a black pants suit and a coolie hat pulled low over her face was walking up to the group from the way Jack wanted to go. Three things were instantly noticeable. She was fairly young, she was well built, and she wasn't shying away from the thugs.

All three of the thugs were frozen in position with their eyes locked on her. She walked and swayed right up to the little group. Without warning she struck out with both fists and the two thugs on the side flew away in opposite directions. She then did a really fast spinning heel kick and the leader lost some of his teeth as he fell backward without a care in the world, at that point.

Jack hadn't moved but he knew that style. "Hello, Su Li, fancy meeting you here."

Su Li pushed her hat back so she could look up at the tall American. "I've been waiting for you to return. When I saw these vermin blocking your way I thought I would impress you with my ability. Did I?"

Jack laughed quietly, "It was excellent. I assume that you donned that particular blouse for its mesmerizing effect on the other gender?"

"I did, of course. You taught me to use every weapon I possessed." Su Li turned around and walked back with Jack.

Su Li said, "Don't look back, but the locals these hoods have robbed are drifting back to return the favor. If you, as a man, had taken them out then the locals would have called the police. When it is a woman the local men assume, wrongly, that they can handle a simple woman themselves. That is one great failing of our people. Many of them believe their own press that they are a fighting machine. Most aren't."

They reached the home they were staying at and went in. Jack regaled the Team with a description of Su Li's prowess and then they had a bite to eat. Laura was happy because she had lost twelve pounds in the last four weeks. In truth, they had all lost weight because of the restrictive diet they were on.

Han Le knocked on the door and came into the room. He greeted his new brothers and sisters in Christ. He put his hand on Jack's shoulder. "My friend, the efforts of your Team have helped to made us one of the strongest underground churches in China. Gary has been instructing three of the men on how to move in the prayer of deliverance and they are now praying for others for their deliverances. We have learned so much while you have been here that pastors of other underground churches come to our Bible studies and share the word of Yahveh."

Han turned serious. "But, I am afraid that our time here is running out and we may need to scatter. Each of our members has been well versed and edified and will try to start other churches wherever they settle.

Jack and Mark said that they would consider what they would do if they had to disperse, soon.

Everything kept going well until the night of Thursday in the sixth week. Laura had been given a black wig and with her face darkened and rearranged by reversible techniques, she looked almost like a Chinese woman. She had been helping several of the soldiers with their Bible studies, through a translator. The session had run late and she knew she shouldn't be out this late by herself. But it was only five blocks to the Team's digs and she figured she would be all right this one night.

Two blocks from home she was stopped by a pair of police who wanted to see her papers. She took them out and handed them to the officer. The papers were quite good and she wasn't worried about them. The police man handed them back to her and then sized her up in a leering manner. He said something she couldn't understand and then he stepped forward and put his hand on her chest.

Knowing that she should simply ignore it she still didn't want it to seem like she wanted this kind of attention. She stepped back and slapped at the man's hand. The officer swung his nightstick and caught the side of her head. Although she was able to block most of the blow it still stunned her. The policeman grabbed her right hand and twisted it up behind her back. He made some more comments she couldn't understand. She ignored him and tried to keep the pain in her arm to a minimum.

The two police talked back and forth for a few minutes and then the first one let her arm go and shoved her forward. She stumbled but managed to stay upright. She used her left hand to rub her right arm as she walked away from them.

She was twenty feet away when one of them yelled a command at her. She thought of running but then that would result in their knowing something wasn't right with her. So, instead, she turned around and marched back toward the two cops. She didn't know what the command had been but assumed that the cop wanted to see if she would return or run.

As she came up to them, they both put on strange, painful expressions on their faces. She was trying to figure that one out when both policemen collapsed to the ground. Two of Han Le's commandos appeared behind the fallen policemen, wiping blood off of their daggers. Laura thought "This is where the going gets rough!".

One of the men pulled a cell phone out of his pants pocket while the other one put his knife away and stepped over the bodies and bowed to Laura. He then took her arm and walked her to the Team building. She turned to thank him but he was gone. She was distressed because they had killed the two policemen, but she had just seen that the commandos were certainly well-trained.

She went in and told Jack what happened. Jack had one of the men go and get Han Le. After the story was repeated, Han bowed out of the room to find out what was going on. He returned within the hour and reassured everyone that there would be no outcry about the missing policemen. They had a bad reputation and there were many places where they could have come to a grisly end. The ex-commandos had sanitized the site and disposed of the bodies so that they would not be found for months, if at all.

Jack called the Team together and it was decided that only the ones who could speak the language and therefore had more of a chance, should risk traveling alone. Mark, Laura, and Gary would partner with a Chinese speaking partner if they had to go anywhere.

Han Le took the opportunity to ask several questions concerning healing that his men had asked him. They wanted to know who healed and how they healed, and even more, why some were healed and others weren't healed.

Jack thought that over for a bit and then got out his copy of the Pocket PC Bible. He referred to Mark 7:32-37 where Jesus healed a dumb and deaf man.

> *32And they bring unto him one that was deaf, and had an impediment in his speech; and they beseech him to put his hand upon him 33And he took him aside from the multitude, and put his fingers into his ears, and he spit, and touched his tongue; 34And looking up to heaven, he sighed, and saith unto him, Ephphatha, that is, Be opened. 35And straightway his ears were opened, and the string of his tongue was loosed, and he spake plain.*

Jack told Han that Jesus had said that his followers would do "greater" works than He did because He was going to the Father but Yahveh's Spirit was coming to live in all believers.

Jack looked at Le and told him, "All we can do is to call for the Presence and healing of Christ, and to pray for Yahveh's Will to be done. Sometimes, Yahveh's way of healing a dying or sick believer is to take them home to live with Him." But Jack recounted several different healings that he had witnessed and actually had been a part of at the time. "The Lord is the one that heals. We can only pray for His healing touch. Why He heals or doesn't is not given to us. He heals for His glory to be seen. He heals to increase faith in the person needing the healing and those around them."

Han Le thought for a few minutes and asked if they would pray for healing for one of his men who had a nervous condition that sometimes would leave him unable to talk or move about. Jack called the Team together and since they had finished "training" their students for the day, they locked up the dojo and went with Han Le to the man's residence.

There were about ten to fifteen people there at the time. The addition of seven more made it rather cramped but still doable. Han Le told Ral Cho that they were all going to pray for Yahveh to heal him of his nervous condition. Ral agreed and sat in a chair in the middle of the room. Since stress was one of the major triggers of his condition, he immediately started mildly shaking.

Jack spoke in Chinese "When we pray for healing, there is nothing we do ourselves other than pray to Yahshua to heal Ral Cho, as Yahshua said at the whipping post "By my stripes you are healed". While we pray, we need to give our full and undivided attention to this one prayer. All of you have been baptized in the Holy Spirit and many of you now speak in a prayer language, or tongues. If you don't have the words, pray in the Spirit." He repeated this to the non-Chinese speaking members, although they already knew it.

Jack prayed for cleansing from their sins through the Blood of the Lamb. He then started the prayer for healing by putting his hand on Ral's shoulder and saying, "Dear Yahshua, we ask for Your holy presence to be with us tonight as we pray for Ral Cho. Master; You know his life is now hidden in Yours and We are interceding for him and asking that You heal this life-long condition of his health, our faith, and Your glory. If there is any demonic activity causing this, we ask that You bind it and cast it into the Abyss to remain forever. If the condition is the result of sin or generational curses, we ask that You forgive him of his sin, tear down the generational curses, tear down the strongholds and free our brother from his bondage. We are all Yours, Father. We ask that Your will be done here on Earth as it is in Heaven."

Several others prayed for Cho including Han Le. Jack noticed the heaviness of the Holy Spirit on the group during the prayer. He also noted that Ral Cho had stopped shaking. They finished the prayer in the Yahshua's Name. Jack asked Cho how he felt. It was like the man was looking everywhere inside of himself for the shaking and couldn't find it. He looked up at Han Le and said, "I felt a wave of very hot heat go from the top of my head to my feet. How I don't feel the shaking, anymore."

Han Le raised his hands and said, "Praise be to Father Yahveh and our Savior Yahshua!"

Ral Cho's healing had an electric affect on the people gathered there. They all started talking and discussing the event.

Jack and the rest of the Team casually made their way out of the house and went back to their sleeping quarters.

About two hours later there came a serious knocking at their door. Mark rolled out and opened the door to see Le and several of the other men outside, "Hey guys, it is one a.m." This was totally lost on the men outside because they didn't speak English.

Jack asked in Chinese what they wanted. They wanted to come in and talk. This seemed to be the norm for these new Christians. They couldn't get enough of God in a normal day.

Laura and Su Li got up and made tea for all of them. Sarah slept through the entire event. Gary finally gave up trying to sleep and joined them after a bit.

Han Le was so serious that Jack almost laughed. That would have been a big social mistake so he controlled his laughter and waited. Han Le locked his eyes on Jack's and said, "The men are all excited by the healing of Ral Cho. They have given me a list of over two hundred people that need prayer for healing. These people are spread out over a three hundred kilometer area. These are relatives, friends, and acquaintances. What I am suggesting is that we go on what you American's call a "road trip" and pray for healing for these people. It will serve us in several ways. First, it will get us away from here and let the local situation calm down. The police are starting to notice things around here and that isn't good."

Han gestured with his hands in his urgency to get Jack's agreement. "Second, this would be a tremendous way to grow the faith and the church in this area. If we do it right, and as commandos we will do it right, then we can appear in one town or village and pray for the believing sick and then disappear for all intents and purposes, until we reappear in another place." He watched Jack to see what he thought of the idea.

Jack had been praying silently while Han was talking and felt that the Holy Spirit was in favor of the "road trip". He looked at the others in the Team and they nodded.

Jack looked at Han and made a stipulation. "Only three men and you are to accompany us. Otherwise it would look like a circus and we could never disappear, anywhere."

Han agreed and suggested that they take a day to plan their route and get supplies. After that, the Chinese went away highly excited.

Laura watched them go and said to her husband. "I wonder if they realize that not everyone is going to be healed the way they want them to be healed."

Jack smiled, "Not our problem, honey. God is behind this part of our China vacation as well as the others. We should look at this trip like when Jesus sent out the twelve disciples. Go where we're welcome and shake the dust off of our feet where we are not."

Gary had been listening to the whole thing. "I would suggest that we limit the number of "healings" per village or we may see this thing snowball out of our control."

Jack slapped him on the shoulder as the Team headed back to sleep. "Again, this is not our problem. The Holy Spirit will tell us who to pray for and when to quit."

Mark smiled, "Since we're going to travel around, work with the locals, and pray for healing, I think I'll call this the "Wheel, Deal, and Heal Tour".

After the laughter they all sought sleep before they would start packing for an extended trip.

CHAPTER THIRTY

As they got ready to start out on their trip, Jack and Laura sat down with Han Le and the three men he had chosen to take with him. These included the two men, Wo Tang and his brother Lo Tang, who had "resolved" the problem for Laura concerning the local police. Han also included Ral Cho as a living example of Yahshua's healing.

Jack expressed the honor the Team felt to be going with them to help other Chinese believers. Then he asked Han how they were going to do this without someone reporting them to the police or the government. There are always those who feel it is their responsibility to report strangers in the village or strange happenings.

Han nodded his agreement. "But, do not worry. We will arrange it so that only the true believers know of our coming, the healings, or where we are. We will be like the mist to anyone that is not directly connected to the Chinese Christian Church. They may hear of us but will never find us."

Jack thought about it a bit. "Then let us have the people staying here pray for us constantly while we are on the trip. You know, have some pray in the mornings, some in the afternoons and others pray through the night. This form of protection will keep us safe."

After the four men had agreed to ask the others to pray, Laura told them about the healings. "We will go where you take us. We don't want to know the names of the towns and villages because if we were asked about it later, we couldn't implicate anyone. Second, I want you four to realize that Yahshua heals who he wants to heal."

Lo Tang asked, "I don't understand that. Can you explain it better for me?"

Laura smiled at him. "I can try. Now, everyone here believes that Yahshua has the power to heal anyone of anything, right? Okay, we also believe that it is His will that all get healed at the proper time, right? Therefore, we know that it is in Yahshua's will that when we pray for healing that he could heal anyone in response to our petition. But it is His timing, not ours. He heals some instantaneously, like Ral Cho. Other people improve slowly over time. We need to explain this to everyone we meet with for healing."

After the discussions, Han Le went back and asked for the prayers while everyone else got ready to go. This would be a walking tour and they had to carry everything they were going to need until they got back. Therefore, there were backpacks for everyone. Finally the six Crossfire Team members and the four Chinese set out to the north for what Han Le called their first appointment

After walking most of the morning and into the afternoon with a short break for lunch, followed by a stroll in the woods to avoid a police patrol, they reached their first stop. It was a medium-sized village with about two hundred people living in it. Han Le led them to a smallish building on the west end of the town. They entered the building and were escorted to a hidden basement room.

As they waited for their first chance to pray for healing, they prayed that the Holy Spirit would identify what they needed to pray for and how they should pray. Jack had explained to the Chinese contingent that they were to be led of the Holy Spirit during the trip and to only pray for the people that the Spirit identified that needed prayer. Also, they would stay until prodded by the Spirit to move on. This would require several of the group to agree on what the Spirit told them to do.

Ral Cho explained that many people in these provinces knew about Jesus but had no real relationship with Him because they could not get any direct information or they were too scared to discuss God for fear of punishment by the leaders. There was a long history of Taoism and other religions that had taught that nature was to be worshipped rather than the one true Elohim.

There was a gentle knock on the door and Lo Tang helped an elderly Chinese woman into the room and to a chair. She had done cooking for others for years to support herself and her children. She had been supported by her grandson since she had lost her sight six years ago. She had been losing her sight for years before that. She just lost her grandson to involuntary military recruitment. Without his support she had no way to live.

The nine member Team began to pray that God would show them what His will was in this case. The Holy Spirit impressed on each of them that they did not need to ask, simply pray for healing and let Yahveh decide. So they prayed and Yahveh restored her sight. In Chinese she cried out, "I can see again! I can see!" She was very grateful and offered to cook for them while they were there. Jack agreed that it would give her a chance to thank them for praying but would also let the other villagers see Yahshua's handiwork.

After word of her healing got around the village, many more people came for prayer and soon each one of the Team was constantly praying for a different person. There were many healings over the three days they were there. Gary was doing deliverance fourteen hours a day and Laura, Sarah, Mark, and sometimes, Jack were sandwiching teaching about the Word and God between praying for people to be healed. Somewhere, Han Le came up with a supply of Chinese language New Testament Bibles. As a person was healed, delivered, and taught, they were asked to bring a Bible or they were given one. When they ran out of people to pray for, the Spirit moved them on to another village only three hours away from the first.

There were several complications during this movement.

CHAPTER THIRTY ONE

As they travelled toward their second village Laura was noting that none of them seemed spent after a hectic three days of fourteen to sixteen hours of work and praying. "It is the work of the Holy Spirit through us and it revives us as we do Yahveh's will. I feel so blessed to help these people. In many cases I detected only a very faint hope of ever finding any solution to their situations. Yet, after they are healed they are full of hope and want to spread it to everyone else."

Mark said, "Yeah, I got that too. But I also felt that their enthusiasm was curbed by the social taboos and the government crackdown on Christianity. They want to tell others but are afraid that it will result in their being reported to the authorities."

Wo Tang, who had been ranging ahead of the group rushed back and told them that there was a large number of men waiting for them over the next hilltop. Han Le wasn't able to determine their intent and wanted to avoid them and go a different path. Gary spoke up, "I sense that the Holy Spirit wants us to confront them. Anyone else get that urging?"

Su Li, Sarah, and Mark all agreed with Gary. So they overruled Han and went straight ahead. When the trail crested the next hill they could see twenty to thirty men standing across the trail a few hundred yards ahead.

When they came close to the men, Jack stepped forward and made a pleasant greeting and inquired as to why they were blocking the path. One man also stepped forward and explained that they had heard the stories about the healings in the first village and they did not believe them. They had decided that the group was not welcome in their town to confuse and trick sick people.

Laura had been praying while the two men were talking and got a word of knowledge from the Spirit. She stepped forward and stood next to Jack. She told Jack what the word was and he repeated it to the man standing there, in Chinese.

The man was apparently concerned that he and the ones with him would lose face and position if this group was able to really heal people. When Jack told him the word that Laura had gotten, the man used that as a reason to start a fight. Yahveh had given Laura the word that the man's father was dying and that he could be healed.

The man used the fact that Laura had given a word of knowledge to imply that Laura was obviously a witch and seer. That set off angry denunciations and suddenly one of the younger men ran at Laura to hit her.

Jack didn't feel led of the Spirit to let his wife be beaten so he stepped between the young man and Laura and used a Judo technique to throw the man to the ground. Suddenly everyone in the village group rushed to attack the outsiders. Most forms of Kung Fu and any other martial art were being employed as well as plain old fist fighting.

Jack, Mark, Sarah, Su Li, and the four ex-commandos were more than a match for the villagers, in fighting capability, which left Laura and Gary at a disadvantage. Jack and Mark tried to keep the fight away from Laura, and Gary wisely stayed close to Laura. Even though the odds were three-to-one to start, it did not take long for the villagers to be defeated.

Unlike the movies about martial arts fighting, when a person is hit or kicked with the proper technique they end up out of the fight. Also, the numerically superior group does not line up and one-by-one attack the other person. They crowd in and try to overwhelm them. Unfortunately for these villagers, the commandos and the Crossfire Team had been in enough combat that they went through two or three attackers before the villagers had any chance to do any real damage. When the last three villagers hit the dirt, Jack called for a halt to the festivities for the time being.

The prayer Team then helped each of the attackers up and asked their forgiveness for having to hurt them. There were many chances for healing prayer right there in the field. By the time everything was done, the villagers decided that they couldn't possibly lose more face than they had already and agreed to allow the Team to come to their village and pray for the sick.

This time there were many people right from the start. Quite a few were relatives brought by the men who had originally attacked them outside of town. The man who had spoken for the combative group brought his father and Yahshua healed him completely. The combined Team of commandos and Crossfire personnel repeated their operations from the first village and were gratified to find many people who did not come for healing, came for teaching. There was a great hunger for this Elohim that would die for them and still lived to heal them.

Four days later the Team moved on to their third town.

CHAPTER THIRTY TWO

Thirty-five days later they had stopped in nine towns or villages. In three of the towns they had not been welcome and had continued on their way. In the others, they spent four to six days providing prayer for healing, deliverance, and discipleship training. Sarah noted that they had exceeded the original two hundred requests by three times, already.

After some discussion, the Team decided to take a break. Han Le knew of a quiet place near a river where they could camp, swim, and generally relax. They found the place to be everything Han said it was and the Lord granted those three days of rest.

On the forth day, Jack was shaken from his sleep by Mark in the dark hours of the early morning. "Jack, get up and get the others going. We're being surrounded by government troops and I don't plan to spend the rest of my life in a Chinese prison."

Jack woke the others in the Crossfire Team and they hurriedly packed what they could and faded into the dark countryside. Mark said that Han Le and the commandos had disappeared after waking him. Mark said that Han told him where the Team should go. But, he was sure that anywhere but where they had been camped, would be better.

After making good time in silence for fifteen minutes, they reached a dry river bed with high banks. Slipping along the arroyo they kept going north until they heard whispers above them, as the government troops moved toward the campsite.

It was quickly apparent that the Chinese did not have any night vision gear or the game would have been over before it started. Mark told them in a hushed whisper that it was a classic encirclement. The government troops knew where they had been and were going to shut off any escape routes. When it became light they would swoop down on the tents and capture, no one. But it wouldn't take them long to find out where they had gone, because the ground was soft and they were leaving a highly visible trail behind them, which would be seen in the daylight.

After two more close brushes with random troops moving toward the river, Su Li got irritated. She slid up next to Sarah and whispered to her for a few seconds. Sarah agreed with her and moved over to whisper to Mark under the bushes where they were hiding. Mark nodded and the two women left the bushes quietly.

Jack could see against the slightly lighter sky above the horizon and watched as Su Li and Sarah singled out a lagging soldier and took him down. They stayed there for a few minutes and then returned to the bushes.

Putting all their heads together they listened as Sarah told them what they had learned. "Su Li has this thing about the government, you know, her parents and Thor. Anyway, she wanted to see what the troops knew, so we asked. Seems that our activities have been reported recently and this little group of ninety soldiers was given the location where we were and were told to "retrieve" us for questioning in the regional headquarters. We have some serious problems just ahead. They have three helicopters that will be here at dawn, or in other words, about an hour. We can hide from them, but, they also have two sets of dogs to track us in the event any of us slip out of their net. Since we have already slipped out of their net they will be angry."

There was a rustle in the bushes and Han Le slipped in next to them. He had two bundles with him. They conferred quietly and then Mark told the Team, "Let's go."

They moved out for a few hundred yards and then made a big arc back to the river, about a mile above their old camp. When they stopped at the riverside, Han Le had them all wade into the water and then he went back a dozen yards and started sprinkling the contents of the bags over the ground. He kept doing it as he backed up to their location. He emptied the bags and wrapped them around a rock which he sank in the river.

They all started wading to the north and eventually came out at a rocky place. They moved more to the southwest as the sky started to lighten in the first signs of the impending dawn. Reaching a cliff, the commandos, followed by the Americans, started climbing the cliff rather than go either way at the base of the wall.

The reason for this strange activity soon became evident. Three-fourths of the way up there was a well-hidden entrance to a cave. Everyone entered it and walked through the dark by holding onto the shoulder of the person in front. It seemed that Han Le knew this cave fairly well since he led and he did it in the dark without running into things.

They started ascending and kept doing that until they reached a level place. Then they were instructed to stand still for a minute. There was a heavy grating sound and fresh air blew out against them. It smelled like rain. Han then guided them forward about thirty feet and there was that grating sound again, but this time it was behind them.

A flashlight came on, virtually blinding all of them until their eyes adjusted to the light. They were in a large, dry cave with all sorts of military supplies stacked to the ceiling.

They walked forward until they could see daylight and the flashlight in Han Le's hand went out. The outside light came from a large opening several feet below the floor of the cave they were in. A large tarp had been pulled aside to let in the fresh air and light. The tarp was the same color as the rocks.

Han Le pulled out a series of camp chairs and everyone sat down for the first time this morning. There was a brilliant flash of light and a clap of thunder from the entrance as a storm rolled in from the west.

During the lull before the storm got there, everyone clearly heard the frenzied yowling of a bunch of dogs. Then the rain began to fall and the sound drowned out the mournful sound of the dogs.

Mark smiled at Han Le. Han raised an eyebrow and grinned. "Yes, Mark, that was red pepper I sprinkled on the ground at the river. The dogs just found it."

Mark laughed and explained it to the others. "The soldiers found that we had left and they tracked us. They had two teams of dogs and they were hot on our trail. Then they ran into the red pepper surprise our friend here left for them. I doubt if any of those dogs will be tracking anything for the next several days."

Han was still grinning as he brought them some cold rations and some warm coffee. He had a tale that he wanted to tell them.

CHAPTER THIRTY THREE

As it turned out, Han Le was an excellent story teller. He had an innate sense of timing and a flare for drama. The only hiccup in the process was that Jack or Su Li had to do a running translation for the people who couldn't speak Chinese.

Han's eyes gleamed in the light of the propane lantern as he started his tale. "This little chase reminded me of a time not too long ago when I had an adventure. I want to tell you about this because you are all warriors and it is a tale worthwhile to share with those, which with you have faced death."

He paused to reflect and perhaps to recollect some of his memories. He smiled and started. "A decade ago China was in a secret war with pirates. What the world never knew was that we were losing the war. The pirates had begun to see success and the word had gotten out that the naval forces of China were incapable of catching and stopping more than twenty percent of the pirates' activity on the seas."

"The problem wasn't technology because we had a great deal of sophisticated search and detection equipment." He smiled at them, "Much of it courtesy of the United States and our intelligence gathering efforts."

This implication was to stolen designs and equipment but everyone there knew that espionage was a two-way street between the super powers.

Han continued, "The problem was the reverse, low-tech. The raiders used small, wooden sampans or junks which were sail powered and were so common as to be indiscernible from the huge fleet of such vehicles that were used by civilians. Having satellite surveillance and side-seeking radar didn't do any good against such craft. The pirates had been originally hunted, almost to extinction and were an inbred group that was highly resistant to penetration by undercover agents. Many tried but failed, usually killed in the most gruesome fashion and displayed as a warning."

"I made an off-hand remark to my superior that we ought to put out our own fleet of decoy ships, the ones that the pirates liked to prey on, to lure them in and destroy them. Thanks to my big mouth, three weeks later I had become the Captain of a small freighter that had more fire-power than a lot of bigger naval ships. The ship had been originally built to sucker in opposing naval vessels and to take them out by surprise. So, in a sense, you could say that it was fulfilling its mission by luring and destroying pirates."

"We had a lot of success in the first six months. We eliminated over forty pirate vessels. There were no survivors to interrogate so we continued to repaint the ship, change the superstructure, add cranes or remove insignia that the pirates might use to identify us as a decoy."

"Unknown by us, because the navy didn't think of us as a surface warship, tensions had escalated between our nation and that of Iraq, over some denial of oil or lack of payment, I'm not really sure which. Maybe both because both sides had their noses out of joint and wanted to show the other how powerful they could be as enemies."

"There had been several run-ins between destroyers from Iraq and various Chinese warships. Shots had been exchanged and damage had been done by both sides. Of course, none of this ever got into the world press because Iraq was even more capable of controlling the news than we were."

Han got up and stretched. He began to slowly pace back and forth in the light of the lantern in the cave. "Having eliminated much of the piracy close into the shore, we had started ranging farther into the ocean in an attempt to catch the ones that were better equipped with larger ships. They normally preyed on yachts and small liners or freighters."

"One gray morning we were watching a suspicious blip on the radar as it closed with our ship. It was making better time than a normal pirate in the rough seas. We were on the edge of a storm and were getting tossed around by the waves. By now, the crew had become accomplished sailors and ignored the weather. It soon became obvious that this particular craft was locked into a collision course with ours. We couldn't see anything because of a general fog in the area."

Sitting down again, Han leaned forward as the emotion of that time grabbed him. "I instructed the crew to prepare for combat. The "Hainiao" which means "Seabird" looked like an unassuming tramp steamer. In actuality, she concealed twenty Ying Ji-82 anti-ship sea-skimming missiles, which were generally comparable to the early models of the French Exocet and the U.S. Harpoon. We also had a quantity of PL-9 surface-to-air missiles which had been derived from IR-homing air-to-air missiles. In addition to nine hardened positions, each containing a heavy machine gun, we had sixty commandos with a great number of rifles, shoulder launched grenades and other weapons. We also had some QW-1 man-portable shoulder launch air defense missiles for close air defense but which also worked like your LAWs, only on a larger scale. The reason we had the anti-aircraft missiles was because many of the more successful pirates had acquired air assets, some of which were quite heavily armed."

"About the time the enemy ship was eight thousand yards away, the sonar operator acquired a contact which indicated a submarine also closing on our position. This threw us all into a quandary. We were fairly sure that the pirates had not progressed to the level of having a submarine and that implied that this attack was more than pirates. Most of us, me included, felt that these were probably American ships acting aggressively toward civilian Chinese shipping."

Han smiled, "Please remember that I wasn't a Christian at that time. We decided to let the surface ship come in close and then determine what to do. The submarine was standing off of our position about three thousand yards and presumably had a firing solution on our ship. We didn't have any anti-submarine weapons and everything here was going to be over by the time any help could arrive."

Mark asked Han through Jack, "Did you try to negotiate with the surface ship? Also, do you think the submarine knew something was fishy when you actively pinged it with sonar, which a tramp steamer would not be likely to have?"

Han shook his head, "We didn't think of that at the time. I knew that the U.S. possessed information concerning the Seabird because of an ongoing spy operation. We figured it had to be the Americans and therefore they already knew what they were facing. We realized that we were probably going to be destroyed and therefore, anything we did would be better than nothing."

"Seeing our dilemma as do-or-die, I devised a radical scheme to give us some time. We sent off the information we had about the approaching ships and their apparent intent to our home base. Then I had the pilot steer us around to the port hard enough that it put their surface ship between us and the submarine. I then ordered the crew to open fire on the surface ship."

"We fired four of the Ying Ji-82 anti-ship missiles at a range of less than 1500 yards. All four missiles struck the ship. The ship blew up in a huge explosion. They had fired on us at the same time but they used guns instead of missiles. Two hits on our superstructure blew away most of the fake mobile housings, but did little real damage to us. As the enemy ship went stern down into the water a brief glimpse was sufficient for us to realize that we had just sunk an Iraqi destroyer, not an American ship. There was no time to figure this out as the submarine was moving to get a shot at us. I continued to attempt to keep the sinking ship between us and the sub but decided that we needed to flee while we had the chance."

"We knew that the Iraqi navy did not have the latest equipment in either submarines or torpedoes and they did not know that we could hit over twenty knots at full steam. So I thought that we could get away toward the Chinese coast and they would not follow us. Unfortunately the storm was upon us by then and our top speed in the waves was more like ten knots. The surface storm didn't change the operational capabilities of the submarine, though they closed with us quickly. We fired delayed fused grenades into the water but it apparently didn't bother the submarine."

"We attempted to zig and zag but it was complicated by the bad weather and the sub closed to within a thousand yards. They fired two torpedoes at us and we managed to turn into their attack path and they went on both sides of us, not hitting us. Unfortunately, this brought us much closer and their next shots were going to be easy. Everyone on board began to see that it was certain that we didn't stand much chance."

"The sonar operator was waiting for the next torpedo runs when I came to his position. He heard torpedoes running but they were different. He looked at me and said, "Two high-speed torpedoes in the water but they are much faster and they are not coming toward us. Suddenly he snatched the headphones off of his ears and his eyes got large. Putting them back on he listened for a few seconds. Then he reported that the torpedoes had struck the Iraqi submarine and sank it."

"At this point I was completely confused. Then the sonar operator said, "I have identified another submarine in the area which did not show up on my screen. It is an American Sea Wolf class nuclear-powered hunter-killer. It is now moving away at high speed from our location. The Iraqi submarine is still sinking and has imploded from the pressure in the deep."

"I had them send a quick summary to our base and headed the ship home through the storm. This would take some interesting writing to produce a coherent report. I didn't know quite how to describe our rescue by the U.S. Navy." Han finished his tale and looked at them for comments.

Mark laughed, "I heard of that little incident while I was with the Navy in the SEALs. The Sea Wolf was designed to be exceptionally quiet; it's very fast and well-armed with advanced sensors and weapons. It is a multi-mission vessel, one mission on which it is normally deployed is to search out and destroy enemy submarines. I remember hearing about it from a Captain who had been the exec aboard the SSN Jimmy Carter, the sub you're talking about. It seems that the Jimmy Carter had been shadowing the Iraqi submarine for a few days. That was just before the end of Iraqi war entitled Enduring Freedom. When the Iraqi sub fired on the Seabird they crossed the line and the Jimmy Carter was authorized to destroy them, which it did. The U.S. was aware of the Seabird's activities and agreed with the efforts to stop the pirates. They weren't going to let the Iraqis sink your ship."

CHAPTER THIRTY FOUR

Han's eyes lit up at the description of the American involvement in the sea battle he had been in over a decade ago. "If you get a chance, tell the officer that we all appreciated their assistance. Please don't tell him I thought I was sinking an American warship at the time. He may not understand my motives."

Mark chuckled, "I think that the Jimmy Carter would have done what it did even if they knew your motives. It was in the best interest of America to eliminate that Iraqi submarine and your ship gave them an excellent reason and a legal right to do it."

Su Li asked Han, "Is that the end of the story?"

Han smiled at the young Chinese woman, "No, not really. After we had sailed away from the encounter with the Iraqis and the American Sea Wolf submarine, we were headed home when we were directed toward a place in the ocean more than a hundred miles north of where we were at the time."

"It seems that several of the pirates had decided that we were picking them off one at a time. So they ganged together for strength in numbers and started hunting Chinese vessels on a grander scale. They had also upped the ante on weapons. They had acquired some French Exocet ship killer missiles and apparently enough information had been put together about the Seabird for a serious hunting trip."

"Our command thought that since they were hunting us, we should let them find us. Command sent a smaller ship out to meet us and resupply our missiles we had expended and give us additional weapons. Because of our success in destroying the Iraqi warship and helping to eliminate the Iraqi submarine they supplied us with forty P800 Russian Cruise missiles.

The P800 cruise missile travelled two and one-half times faster than the speed of sound, owing to its second stage ramjet propulsion. It was designed to be fired from a closed tube launcher and this missile could be employed very easily on the Seabird due to the modular weapon launcher design. In fact, it is so modular that we could also use it on Attack submarines and land based missile sites. It is a smaller descendent of the P-500 Balzat missile dubbed "Carrier Killer", carried aboard the Missile Cruisers of the Russian Navy. Actually, the P800 looked more like the 3M82 Moskit missile carried aboard destroyers in service with both the Russian and Chinese fleets. This would confuse the pirates if they saw them.

Now that we were well armed, we sailed to combat with this nefarious band of cutthroats to bring their era to an end."

"Three days later we were in the area and an aviation asset spotted five of the larger pirate ships sailing out to sea toward where we were trying to bait them. It was growing dark and it would be early dawn before they got to our position, so we kept a close watch but let everyone else get as much sleep as possible. I felt that we were far more than a match for five enemy ships, with less than a fifth of our tonnage. My plan was to get them in range of the P800s and destroy them before they could lock in on us with the Exocets. I went to sleep with visions of victory in my imagination."

Han made a wry face. "The sentry that woke me up at three in the morning dashed my dreams in a hurry. He said, "Captain, please get up quickly. Radar has definite blips for over twenty ships on the horizon. Some of them are as large as us!"

"I hurried to the comm and verified the information. The pirates that the plane had seen were only a small part of the attacking fleet. The pirates were determined to do away with the Seabird. All of their ships were still to the north and west of us and still twenty miles away. I determined that we needed to strike first and had the crew launch twenty of our P800s over the horizon and fire-and-forget cruise missiles that travel at a very high speed. I had several of the missiles targeted at each of the larger ships and one for each of the medium-sized ships."

Han started pacing again. "The results were mixed. The problem with the P800 is that it is so fast that it only gets one shot at the target. Also, some of the medium-sized ships were wooden rather than metal. It seems that some of the missiles tore all the way through these ships and out the other side before exploding. The bigger ships were either destroyed or disabled completely. We had gone bow-on to the enemy and the three Exocets that they did fire in return missed the Seabird by a wide margin."

After the first salvos, we were only facing nine ships and they were all of the smaller to medium size classes. We had eliminated the larger tonnage vessels but it took half our arsenal of P800s to do it. Still, we were sure we were on our way to victory."

"That is when I believe I began to dread radar reports. The radar operator sent word that he now had over thirty new targets and most of these were of the larger class. Where had the pirates gotten such a fleet? Well, it turned out that they had been amassing these ships for several years and brought them all out to destroy the Seabird and send a message to the government not to mess with them, anymore.

We simply did not have the weapons or capability to go toe-to-toe with thirty nine ships. I radioed my base and told them that we would have to flee if we wanted to be on the surface of the sea tomorrow. They told me to stay and fight that help was on its way."

Han shook his head. "Sure it was. I figured that a bill was probably being passed to seek aid for the beleaguered Seabird. Still, orders are orders. The pirates had upped the ante again and were betting all their resources. We readied the missiles and when the range was right we fired off all the remaining P800s. We were prepared to go down fighting. We did take out nine of the larger ships but that still left us hopelessly outnumbered and now, outgunned."

"Then, the radar announced a second wave of ships coming at a higher speed that numbered over twenty. All of these were larger than the ones we were already fighting. We knew that the end was coming for sure. Then the radioman rang up the comm and told us that the new blips were PLA Navy of China ships. Most of them were Type 956E class destroyers. The whole comm center started yelling in surprise and relief. The pirates either turned to face the new threat or tried to escape. It made no difference. Two hours later we were the only ship on the sea other than the destroyers. Every last ship of the pirates had been sunk with all hands. Most were blasted to bits by missiles before anyone had a chance to get off."

"The Admiral in charge of the destroyer fleet was expansive at a state dinner he held that night on his flagship. He told us that the first targets we had destroyed with the expensive P800s were dummy ships towed into range to fool us. Still, he said that we had done a marvelous job in destroying so many of their ships they brought out all their hidden ships so that the navy could get at them. An excellent strategy that had been in the planning for several years. So much for my great input!"

"Anyway, that was a grand adventure. I can tell you that it took several months of being on dry land after that before I forgot that I did not have to walk on a rolling deck."

Everyone laughed and congratulated the ex-commander of the commandos for his lively story and naval prowess. Then it was time to get some sleep on the cots and sleeping bags that had been stored in the cave.

Mark asked Han if they would have to get up in the middle of the night again to flee from the soldiers. Han listened to his question and grinned. "No, we are safe for the moment. The Tang brothers are keeping close tabs on the soldiers and will let us know if they approach this area."

Sarah asked him how they could shadow the soldiers when they had dogs and helicopters.

Han smiled again. "They "liberated" two uniforms and unofficially joined the ranks of the soldiers. Everywhere the army goes, they go. So they will be very close to all the action."

Sarah finished getting into her covers and reached over and held Mark's hand for a minute. "You have to admire their abilities, right?"

Mark smiled, "I'm just glad that they are on our side this time."

CHAPTER THIRTY FIVE

The next morning Han received a message via cell phone from Lo Tang. He listened for a few minutes and acknowledged the information. He hung up and went over to where the Americans were involved in making breakfast out of the stored dry food supplies. He touched Jack on the shoulder and led him to the side.

Han looked fairly serious. "I have heard from Lo Tang this morning. Apparently there is some interest in this area by the army. They will be here in four hours to search the area carefully. My feelings are that we should be away from here before they arrive. How do you feel we should handle this?"

Jack smiled at the older man. "I think we should pray and ask the Master." Han shook his head in irritation. "I keep thinking the old way." He nodded in agreement. Jack passed the word on to the others and then he and Laura walked back to the bunk area and knelt down to pray about the situation.

As they prayed, Jack began to express his love for the Father and became so involved he forgot to focus on their need. Yahveh already knew their questions and provided an answer even while the couple were praying and praising Him.

Mark's secure cell phone chimed and he answered it. It was a burst transmission from General Miles directly into Mark's voicemail box. This was so quick that the Chinese would not be able to track it or Mark's location. "Mark, I don't want you to answer this but be aware that the NSA has deciphered some radio traffic in your area. The local military are attempting to spook you into moving about so that they can get a fix on you via their recon satellites. Stay out of sight if you can, I don't think they have an idea where you are, but I did hear mention of a Christian Team being pursued. When you can do it safely, give me a call." The message ended there. Mark went over to where the Malones were praying and waited until he had Laura's attention. He repeated the gist of what the General said.

Laura smiled and said, "Thank you Father,. Jack, please tell Han about this. "

Mark grinned at his Chinese disguise. It had lost a lot of its effectiveness. "Do you know you are even pretty as a Chinese woman? I was talking to Sarah about that. She thinks it is your pure heart that shines through."

Laura patted him on the arm. "Thanks, Mark, I needed to hear that. I feel like I haven't done anything to my skin in ages. I feel like I'm turning into an old woman out here in the field all of the time."

Mark was thoughtful as Jack came up and hugged Laura. Mark looked at them both, "I'm getting the urge to head back to the states. I think our work here is finished. How do you feel the Spirit is leading you?"

Jack nodded his agreement. "Yeah, I think Han and his people have gotten a good basis on which to build their faith, with the help of all the Christian TV and computer broadcasts. And I don't think we can do much more regardless. Of course, we have to get out of this situation before we can make any moves."

Laura looked up at her husband and realized that he was the same, in a three-piece suit in a company board room, or out here in the middle of China, after two months of living in the field. She also realized that this was one of his strengths that she loved. She could always count on his stability regardless of the situation. "How about we give Zhou a call and see if he can get these soldiers off of our backs?"

Jack and Mark looked at each other with the implication of "why didn't we think of that?" in their eyes. Jack took his cell phone and punched in the number for the Vice Prime Minister.

Jack knew the risk that his phone could be located if he stayed on the line too long. When Zhou answered, Jack quickly told him their situation and asked if he could help. Zhou was also aware of the danger of the call and told Jack he would call him back later.

Everyone waited quietly and caught up on their rest while they waited out the army search and Zhou's call.

It was early afternoon when Jack's phone rang. Zhou said that he had told the army to withdraw their troops from the area and that had been done. There was still the possibility that satellite observation could detect them when they left so they needed to be as stealthy as possible. Zhou asked them to get to his home if possible.

After a brainstorming session, Han made a call to the Tang brothers and early the next morning a truck appeared near the cave entrance. Ten soldiers got out and moved around the area like they were searching it. Wo Tang came into the cave and explained his plan. Eventually seven of the soldiers showed up in the cave. These were all men from the valley who had seen the light and became Christians. They took off their uniform coats and greeted everyone. After a few minutes of fellowship, the Crossfire Team and Han put on the overcoats and left the cave. They returned to the back of the truck which was covered in canvas. The truck moved off and rumbled back toward its base. The Team and Han left the truck under a bridge and got into a van which headed off for Beijing.

CHAPTER THIRTY SIX

As they approached the capital city, Han spoke to them. "My contacts tell me that word of your presence has reached the wrong ears. I believe you are right and it is time you left for your home. We will all miss you." His face showed his regret at the loss as he looked at all six of the Team members. "More than you can realize, but even if it is our loss, we want you to be safe."

The Team had gathered up what belongings they had in two back packs. Jack took one and Gary the other. The Team slid out of a side door of the van and faded into the night. Five blocks later Han had them all stand at a bus stop. It was now after ten in the evening and the bus had quit running to this stop an hour before.

Another truck rumbled up to the stop sign and a man motioned them to climb in the back with him. They did and the truck rolled on its way. A half hour later it climbed a sloping driveway and stopped. Everyone piled out of the back and walked around to the small back door. The door was opened by a smiling Minga. Behind her were the three children and Zhou himself.

After a warm reception, they were escorted into a well furnished room with no windows. Real food and drink were available but the three women opted for a shower first. After getting a whiff of his own self, Jack had to agree with them.

Eventually the Team was cleaned up and fed. With the exception of Han, they were at last able to revert to their normal looks and were sitting in western clothing in soft chairs, talking with the Tangtao family. Jack smiled at Zhou and said, "I thought sure you'd be visiting me first."

Zhou grinned and said in English, "Yes, I did too. But the ways of God mystify us all. Did you know that I am to be made Prime Minister in the next two years?"

Congratulations all around were heaped on the unassuming man. Jack sobered up and asked him how he would be able to do both that job and be a Christian at the same time.

Zhou shook his head, "I don't have a clue. I'm just taking it one day at a time and asking the Spirit of Yahveh to lead me. I was ready to resign before and if that becomes a necessity, I will do it again."

Jack looked at Zhou's family. "Do your wife and children know that you have become a believer?"

Zhou smiled a big smile. "Yes, and after hearing about both their rescue and Laura's battle, and the way Yahshua moved in the valley, they are going to do the same on our second trip to your country. In your conflict with Chun, I lost my only real contact to the church. Shang was one of my best friends and I miss his council."

Jack laughed, "Don't be concerned. You'll see him when you get to the U.S. I understand he has opened a Chinese Christian Church in Denver."

Zhou looked introspective for a few minutes. Then he smiled, "That is good, I now have somewhere to go if I leave government service here."

Sarah asked Zhou how the Team could get out of the country without running into complications, like the fact that they had entered illegally and did not have any papers to explain their presence in China.

Zhou got up and went into his home office. He came back with validated passports and entry visas for the six Team members. He handed each person theirs and told them, "I had some help with this from your General Miles. He seems like an honorable man. I would like to meet him when I visit your country next week."

Mark quipped, "Maybe we should just wait and go with you."

Zhou frowned and shook his head, "I really don't think that would work for any of us." Then he laughed, "I am quite sure that there will be a watch on me the whole first trip. I can probably do some sight-seeing. If it works out, that will be when I visit you in Denver, but I expect even I will have some "minders" with me on the official parts of the trip. I'm not even going to take my wife the first time." He looked at the clock on the mantle over the fireplace. "It is probably time for you to get some sleep. I have you booked on a China Air flight to Australia at ten tomorrow morning."

As they got ready to go to bed in a real bed for the first time in weeks, Sarah looked at Mark. "You know, Zhou is a real class act. He stands to lose everything and be shot after a mock trial if we are discovered in his house."

Mark nodded, "You're right, but I'll bet you dollars to doughnuts that he's very aware of the risks and has planned for them. He didn't get to where he is in the government without being pretty smart."

The next morning there were hugs all around and invitations to visit, given and accepted. The Team said goodbye to Han and told him that he also needed to make a trip to America. He said if he ever did, he could probably not come back. He waved goodbye to them as they got into an airport shuttle bus. Then he walked back into Zhou's house. The two of them had some planning to do which could figure heavily into Han's future.

The trip to the airport, the boarding, and the flight to Australia were uneventful and over fairly quickly.

As a result of Jack's cell phone call to General Miles, they were met at the airport in Perth and were provided an executive jet for the flight to the states. They were also heavily debriefed on the way home. Somewhat irritating, but like Mark said, "It helps to pass the time during the flight."

Eight weeks after they had left for China to rescue the hostages they landed at Denver's International Airport and found the Cadillac SUV that had been left for them that morning in the parking garage. It was an easy fit for the six because they had almost no luggage.

As Jack drove them out of the airport and headed south for the Fortress, lighting flashed and a heavy rainstorm lashed the area. The sky was dark and cloudy as a major storm moved over the Denver area from the mountains.

CHAPTER THIRTY SEVEN

As they travelled south on I-225 through the southwest Denver suburbs, they had to leave the interstate due to construction. Since this was his home grounds Jack used some back streets to get to Dry Creek Road.

The rain came down in sheets and the occasional flashes of lightning lit up the area like a strobe light. Waiting behind another car to enter the major thoroughfare, the Team was quiet. Everyone was tired from their efforts in China and the trip home was catching up with them. Relaxing mentally, Gary Eisenthal suddenly saw a demon. The ugly thing was hovering above the right side of the car in front of them. Gary wondered what was going on when the car in front started to make a left turn and pulled out directly into the path of an oncoming large truck, traveling west in the closer lane. Gary tried to tell Jack to honk the horn but it was too late.

The trucker slammed on his brakes but there was almost no effect in the split seconds before he hit the car broadside, and smashed it across the other three lanes and over the side of the road. Leaving long black skid marks the truck shuddered to a halt a hundred feet down the road on the shoulder.

Jack saw an opening and drove the SUV directly across all four lanes and off the road on the other side. There was a slight embankment and the car had rolled once or twice before it came to rest on its wheels in the mud.

Gary exclaimed, "I just saw a demon blinding the driver of the car so that they couldn't see the oncoming truck!"

Pulling as close as he could to the damaged car. Jack and the others bailed out of the SUV into the rain and slipped and slid over to the car. As Laura got to the car her heart sank. The driver was a young woman, and from the angle of her neck and the open-eyed stare, it was obvious that she had been killed on impact. Looking in the back seat Laura was more dismayed on seeing several small bodies strewn about.

Mark wrenched open the back door on the four-door car and carefully pulled the kids out, one at a time. Sarah held a small girl who looked to be about three years old, who was silent, but staring at Sarah in a wide-eyed fear. Sarah hugged her and stroked her hair. The girl shook and started quietly crying. Jack wiped the rain off of the face of a boy who was about nine years old. He was in shock and couldn't stop staring at the driver's face. He only said one word, "Mommy?"

The other child was another girl about six who was unconscious but breathing slowly and had good color. Su Li cradled her and rocked her back and forth.

Laura was looking at the driver when she felt the urging of the Holy Spirit to pray for her. Opening the door slowly she let the woman's body slide down and Gary pulled her out of the seat belt and onto the ground. Laura got down on her knees in the rain and the mud and started praying for her soul.

There was a strangled cry from the top of embankment and Mark looked up and saw the young truck driver standing there in anguish. He slowly came down the hill and looked at the kids and the woman on the ground. He sat down and just started crying and shaking his head back and forth. Mark went over to him and sat down next to him. Putting his arm around the man, Mark told him quietly that there was nothing that he could have done and that the accident wasn't his fault. But the man just repeated over and over "I killed her, I just killed her".

Laura felt the Holy Spirit's presence and she felt her prayer deepen in intercession for the family. A presence she had felt before came over her and she told Jack and Sarah to give the kids to Su Li and come pray for the driver. As they knelt down and put their hands on the body of the driver they all felt the power of Yahveh. Laura said, "Pray for her life, she wasn't supposed to die today."

Jack felt the power of the Holy Spirit flowing through him. He held the woman's head in his hands and in amazement he watched as her neck straightened by itself and the bones realign. The prayers were fervent and the woman suddenly gasped and started breathing again. The eyes Laura had closed fluttered open and blinked several times. She jerked in a small spasm and then relaxed. Looking up at Jack she said, "What happened?"

Before Jack could answer he saw fear flood her face and she cried, "My babies, where are they?"

Laura put her hand on the woman's shoulder and told her. "Don't worry, they are all right and they're right here."

Struggling, the woman sat up in the mud and saw the kids with Gary and Su Li. The boy was grinning from ear to ear and his eyes were really wide open as he stared at his mother. The three-year old struggled out of Gary's hands and slipped across the mud to her mother and fell into her arms. The six year old was awake now and just sat in Su Li's arms and looked at her mother and little sister.

The truck driver looked at the mother and turned to Mark, "How did..she was...I know she..."

Mark just smiled at him and patted him on the back. The driver shook his head, "I don't understand what just happened. She was dead. I know it. I was in the Marines, I know when someone's dead. But she isn't. I must be losing my mind."

Mark stood up and gave him a hand up. "No, you're not losing your mind. You just saw the supernatural power of God correcting something that wasn't supposed to happen, that's all." Mark delivered this with such conviction and quiet assurance there was no room for doubt. The driver smiled and said, "Oh, thank you God."

Right about then, an EMS Team that had been called by a passerby, slid down the muddy hill with their equipment. They started checking out the woman and the kids. The Crossfire Team gathered together near the truck driver and watched. Four Arapahoe County Sheriff's deputies joined them and started asking questions.

Gary's spirit suddenly went on guard. Looking around he asked the Holy Spirit to show him what the problem was. He was able to discern demonic shapes moving toward the accident scene from two sides. He interrupted the deputies and told the Team to start praying protection for everyone there, NOW!

The Team had been honed by weeks together to work like a well-oiled machine in spiritual matters and immediately ignored everything else to pray in their prayer languages and call down the warrior angels of Yahveh

Almighty. The cops were surprised and taken aback by this bizarre activity. They were somewhat irritated and one of them grabbed Mark's arm to get his attention. This was not a smart move on his part. Mark never missed a beat in his praying but his left hand came up and grabbed the deputy's hand in a massive fist and Mark used a Jui Jitsu technique to remove the deputy's grip. Things looked like they were going to become ugly very quickly when an even more bizarre thing occurred.

A demon named Quanth stepped out of the spiritual dimension into the physical dimension and went for the woman that had been driving the car. Large black-clawed hands grabbed the EMS attendants and threw them five feet away.

Laura's armor flared into golden brilliance and her sword appeared and lit up the landscape in a white glow. She stepped forward and with one backstroke beheaded the demon which dissipated into greasy smoke.

Two more demons made the transition into physical space and advanced on the party near the car. One of the deputies pulled out his sidearm and fired three rounds into the nearest demon. That demon died and disappeared. The other one turned on the deputy. Moving with unreal speed he hopped across the ground toward the young policeman. Mark released the man he was holding and stepped into the path of the demon and side kicked it hard enough it fell to its side and rolled once before coming back onto its feet. It was joined by four more demons. All the deputies were firing into the demonic horde and dispatching several of them. But they were replaced by even more. Laura waded into them and her sword was streaming Holy fire as it slashed through demon bodies. She had to parry several black blades that were being wielded by demons. If they were able to overcome her, it would give them a great advantage. Suddenly, one of the ebony blades hit Laura and penetrated her armor at her right side. She stumbled and fell to one knee but kept battling from that position.

It was a surreal scene with the darkness, the lightning flashes, Laura's armor shining white and gold, flashes of gunfire and hand-to-hand combat between men and demons.

There was a subliminal shift and suddenly Rose, Caleb, and a Heavenly host of angels appeared and waded into the demons. Gary was praying and called down the fire of the Holy Spirit on a group of three demons trying to get the kids in his arms. There was a blinding flare and the demons were gone. None of the others seemed to want to draw that kind of fire so they concentrated on attacking Laura, the angels, and the others.

Cars had stopped on the road and people were staring down into the battle with unbelief. A mobile TV van tried to get close enough to get coverage of the scene.

There were at least thirty demons and ten or twelve angels locked in mortal combat when a large winged angel with a blindingly white robe and a gold belt appeared in the midst of the battle. The demons screamed and fled back into the spiritual realm with the angels hot on their heels. There was suddenly silence everywhere. The large angel stood there and looked around at everyone. But Jack's eyes were locked on his wife as her armor disappeared and he could see the pain and sadness as she looked at him. She closed her eyes and started to fall backward. The angel took one giant step and caught her. He stood up gently cradling Laura in his arms and then vanished.

Sound returned with a crash as darkness suddenly covered everything. Laura's armor and the large angel had been lighting up the whole scene. Mark went over and turned on the headlights on the SUV illuminating the area. Jack was shaking and in fear for Laura as he sank down on his knees and prayed for his wife. He over ruled his worry and all the other emotions and put all of his trust in the Lord and he felt the peace of Yahveh flow over him and he knew everything was all right with Laura. He just didn't know when he would see her again and that concerned him greatly.

There was a great roar of applause and cheering from the crowd. More police cars arrived and the whole area was roped off. The crowd was asked to disperse as mobile light towers were being set up.

Mark came over with Sarah and helped Jack to his feet. Looking him in the eyes Mark told him, "I think she's okay and we'll see her soon." He waved his arm around to indicate the scene of the battle. "But I have to admit, I never read about anything like this in the Bible."

Sarah just hugged Jack and smiled. "Come on; let's see how the family is holding up to all of this."

They walked over to Su Li, Gary, and the little family. Mark squatted down and spoke to the kids. "Have you ever seen an angel before?"

The little girls were wide-eyed and just shook their heads. The boy was grinning and said, "That was sooo awesome! You guys really kicked their butts!" Mark reached over and tousled his hair. "Glad you liked it. How is everyone feeling?"

The woman, whose name was Erin Swode stood up and took one of Jack's hands and one of Su Li's which kind of encompassed everyone in the Team. "I want to thank you for everything you have done for me and my children. I'm still in shock I think. But if you'll tell me that everything that just happened was real and all right then I won't think I'm going mad."

Sarah laughed a quiet laugh, "Don't worry Erin, you're not going mad. All of this was real. It's just not what people see on TV or in everyday life. Are you a Christian?"

She smiled and nodded, "Yes, my husband and I are about to go to Iceland on a mission trip to a village that has asked us to help them find God. This encourages me greatly."

The various police groups came up and asked for information from the Team members and the four deputies. Mark sighed, "It's going to be a long evening!"

As they walked over to a command post, Sarah looked back at the little family sitting on a tarp trying to get some of the mud off of themselves. "She looks pretty good for a person who was dead not too long ago."

Mark just smiled. "Thank Yahveh."

CHAPTER THIRTY EIGHT

Regardless of whom they asked, the police got pretty much the same description of events from each person. The task force commander looked over the reports and shook his head. He had one of the officers bring Jack and Mark over to his desk which was arranged in the back of an SUV with a tarp keeping the continuous rain at bay.

Looking from one to the other he tapped his pen on the stack of reports. "How can I turn these reports into my superiors? Dead people raised back to life by the power of Yahveh, demons, angels, spiritual warfare, and a missing person nobody is worried about. How?"

Understanding the man's problem, Mark said, "Captain, I suggest you edit your version of these reports to summarize the events with the comments, "supposed dead" and people unknown, possibly related to gangs, tried to assault the accident scene and were repulsed by the deputies. You might say that Mrs. Malone was so rattled that she apparently left for home before you had a chance to talk to her and that you will have an officer talk to her later."

The Captain stared at Mark, "Obviously this isn't the first time something like this has happened to you guys." He then nodded his head. "Okay, I can do that. I will also tell the men involved that this whole affair is classified and they are not to discuss it with anyone, especially the excitable press."

As they walked back to the SUV Mark saw Jack looking skyward with a touch of sadness. There were no words that he could say that would make things better, so he wisely remained silent. The trip to the Fortress was quieter than the one before the accident. Everyone was pretty well spent and concerned about Laura.

After negotiating the security measures they took the elevator to the living room. As they exited the elevator, Jack let out a big sigh and laughed. Sitting on one of the couches was Laura looking calm and pretty. He strode over to her and as she stood up he embraced her and kissed her neck. She laughed and kissed him back. Everyone crowded around them and waited until Jack sat her down again. Then they all tried to talk at one time. Jack held up his hands and motioned everyone to sit down. Then he asked Laura the question everyone wanted answered. "Honey, what happened to you?"

Laura grinned, "I went to Heaven and met Jesus."

There was complete silence in the room. Jack smiled back, "More words, Laura, we need more words."

There was a new composure evident in Laura's demeanor. A serenity and calmness that had developed since they last saw her and her angelic protector disappear into the night sky. She looked at each one of the others with humor in her eyes. "Okay, you know that I was wounded by one of the demons, right?" She arched one of her eyebrows as she waited for confirmation from everyone. Then she continued, "It felt like a heavy blow to start with but quickly began to feel like a cold numbness that was spreading from the wound throughout my body. When the archangel caught me I was falling into a deep black pit that was full of pain." A flash of that pain showed in her eyes as she remembered it.

Clearing the memory she smiled again and kept talking, "I woke up in a place I don't have the language to describe. The closest I can tell you is that everything was perfect and I was bubbling over with an exuberant joy. I felt such a deep peace that there was no end to it." As she talked the others felt some of the joy and peace she was describing.

She tipped her head to one side and said, "Then I saw Yahshua. He was standing a few feet away and smiling at me. He was beautiful, but the most commanding thing I saw was His eyes. Overwhelming love and acceptance just flowed out of his eyes." They could hear the awe in her voice.

Su Li asked her, "What did the Lord look like?"

Laura smiled at the young woman. "I think He would look different to everyone who looked at Him. I saw a man, roughly six feet tall, darkly Caucasian with curly brown hair and a gleaming white outfit. I don't remember what He had on his feet. In fact, the gown or robe went all the way to the ground and I don't think I saw His feet. But the power and love He radiated was immense, way off of any scale I had. He came over to me as I was sitting on the ground, which I can't remember if it was grass or what it was. He put out His hand and helped me up. When I touched His hand I felt, something like eternity flow through me. It wasn't electricity or heat; it was as if time flowed out of Him and through me. As he released me I saw the nail holes."

Laura continued, "He asked me how I felt and I told Him I felt wonderful and full of joy and so glad to see Him. He smiled at me and told me that He had "removed" the wound I had taken and that He was proud of me for my willingness to fight for people who couldn't defend themselves."

She looked inward for a few seconds. "You know, I felt completely at ease talking to the Son of God. It must have been His peace. I told Him that I had been both angry and afraid of the demons. He nodded and told me that true bravery is advancing, even though one is afraid. He reached out His right hand and touched me on the forehead and told me that I would not be afraid any more but, I was now capable of fighting the enemy at a new level of combat. Then, to my complete amazement, He embraced me and told me to tell each of you that He loved each of us and He was proud that we were humble enough to go to the aid of strangers and even battle to keep them safe from the enemy. He told me that we had given the enemy a great defeat by being obedient and willing. I closed my eyes and hugged Him back and then found myself sitting here on the sofa as you walked into the room."

Jack took the hands of Sarah and Su Li who were sitting on either side of him. The others joined hands as Jack prayed their thanks to a loving Yahveh for the safe return of Laura. Afterward, the others headed to their rooms to get cleaned up and Jack and Laura sat in the living room holding hands and smiling at each other.

Jack looked down and then back at Laura. "I was never afraid for you through this whole thing but I was sad that we weren't together. Now I'm glad that you had a chance to meet the Lord and even more glad that you are back. I missed you."

Laura patted his hand and said softly. "I know."

CHAPTER THIRTY NINE

Things settled down into the normal Fortress routine for the next three days. On the morning of the fourth day Mark called a meeting of the Core Team in the War Room.

In addition to Mark, Sarah, Jack, Laura, Su Li, and Gary, were Sensei Jim Grady and the ex-Chinese investigator Charlie Wu. Mark sat back in his high-back executive desk chair and started the summary of the China trip

Jack got a phone call relayed in from the military troops outside the Fortress. He excused himself and left for a few minutes. He came back in and motioned to Mark to suspend the action report for a minute. He stood there lost in thought for a few minutes and then looked up and spoke to the group. "I just finished talking to the local resident agent for the FBI. Their Colorado office has been named point for an extremely imminent and serious terrorist event against the City of Denver. Gary Rhodes called us because he has worked with Laura and me before. Agent Rhodes believes that the people involved are part of the group that attacked us in Washington."

Mark frowned, "You mean Chun's men?"

Jack nodded, "In a sense. The men Chun used to attack us and then died in the plane crash, turned out to be an amalgam. Two were Chun's personal assassins and the rest were part of an embedded espionage group. This group provides their services to all foreign countries that want wet work done in the United States. They are called the American Liberation Association and they are very well funded, supplied, and professional. They solicit business through their own web site both here and overseas."

Laura looked at Jack but spoke to Mark, "I can't believe that the FBI hasn't linked through to the CIA via Homeland Security to locate and eliminate these people!"

Mark smiled, "I'm sure they have but obviously there is something else going on here." He looked back at Jack.

Jack continued, "What I do know is that they urgently need to meet with us to discuss what part we could play in uncovering and eliminating the ALA. There is an FBI Team headed out here as we speak."

Jack spoke to Charlie Wu. "Charlie, will you check them out?" Charlie nodded and got busy with his computer keyboard at his position. He would make sure that it really was the FBI and, who was supposed to be coming. Their common enemies could have intercepted the phone calls and attempted to substitute their own people to gain access to the Fortress. In several minutes time, Charlie had pictures of the four men that were headed their way. He also requested and received bioscan identifications for each of the men. This would be confirmed at the first gate before they ever got into the tunnel.

Mark frowned for a moment as he thought about the implications. Then he asked Jack, "Why us? They have the manpower and the budget to do this type of operation, why include the Crossfire Team?"

Jack described the rest of the information that Gary Rhodes had given him. "It seems that the investigation has run into trouble from the spiritual world. Gary feels that there is an uncanny similarity in the increase of evil this operation has gained recently, to the increase accomplished by Don Miland's operation here in Denver. It would be some sort of a familiar spirit. Gary believes that the power behind this group is the same demon that was behind Don Miland."

Sarah, Su Li, and Gary were looking slightly lost since they had not been a part of the Team at that time. Jack frowned at the memories and attempted to bring them up to date. "Don Miland was a small time prostitution and gambling hood that had aspirations of greater things. He was invited to take on a silent partner who offered him a lot. Don Miland suddenly became the most powerful street gang boss in Colorado. Competition gave him their operations, fled the scene, or died. Whatever he wanted to do succeeded beyond his wildest dreams. The only catch was that his silent partner was a demon that had entered this world with the express purpose to gain control of the crucifixion nail. Several months later, Yahveh involved Laura and me in the defense of the nail, resulting in my stewardship of it."

Jack shook his head. "Don Miland had an inside operative in the Denver Police Department named John Dalman. Dalman set us up, making it look like we had killed two Denver Policemen when he had actually done it himself. Eventually, Mark and Jim joined us and we took the battle to Don Miland at his manor, south of Denver, one night."

Jack got up and stretched to relieve the tension the memories brought back. Then he made sure he had everyone's attention. "In the basement of that building, the demon attempted to kill three of us and Carol Nolan, the CBI mole the Don had discovered and had been torturing. Jesus spoke to the demon and forced him to leave, taking only the spirit of Don Miland in place of us. I think that really irritated the demon. This could be round two in his desire to acquire the nail. Be warned, he is totally evil and will use anybody or anything to get what he wants. I'm sure by now he is well aware of our capabilities and who we are at present. We need to pray for protection and for the total elimination of this particularly foul spirit this time!"

Most of the faces showed agreement or veiled anger, with the notable exception of Laura. Her face was almost serene in its peace. Jack noted that she was a totally different person than the one that faced John Dalman in the Chicago alley many months ago.

CHAPTER FORTY

Resident Agent Rhodes was duly impressed by the Fortress and its defenses. He and the three agents that accompanied him were finally seated in the living room in the midst of the Crossfire Team.

Gary took out several documents from a briefcase and tapped the top one. He talked directly to Jack. "I've got incontestable evidence that proves that the ALA has been given the assignment to destroy the City of Denver and that they have managed to smuggle a briefcase nuclear weapon into the State of Colorado to accomplish the mission." He was very serious as he looked around at the Team. "I believe that they were able to accomplish the import of this weapon through the assistance of the spiritual forces allied with them. It was only a lucky break that we found out about it yesterday and can move to try to prevent the detonation of the weapon. Our problem is that we have lost the signature of the nuclear material, completely. My superiors think I have become unhinged somewhat, because I am sure that the weapon is on its way to Denver and is being shielded by this demonic force to prevent our intercepting it." He sat back and waited for Jack or his group to respond.

Mark asked him, "Gary, I have seen the DOD and NSA track as little as ten ounces of U235 across three continents without ever losing it. The typical briefcase nuke has three pounds of fissionable material and needs a minimum of twenty feet of ferroconcrete or six feet of lead to hide the signature from the satellites. What do they attribute the missing signature to?"

Martin Chin, one of the other agents fielded that one. "The head shed thinks that the info and the previous signatures were false and the whole thing is a red herring to make us look at Denver, when the actual threat is somewhere else, like Washington D.C. We have some pretty positive indicators and informants suggesting that Washington is a target."

Mark looked back at Gary Rhodes. "But, you're sure it's going to be Denver?"

Gary simply nodded his agreement. He didn't feel that it needed to be proven again.

Jack saw the look Laura gave him. "When is the expected attack due to take place?"

Gary said, "Day after tomorrow. There is both a Bronco's game and a huge rally downtown to support the war on terror and the troops overseas. The expected attendance for both events is over three hundred thousand people. Our best guess is that the detonation would do the most damage around one p.m. What we know, they know. So I expect that we have less than forty eight hours to stop it." He looked around at the Team, "If I am wrong about this I will lose my career and still be glad that it didn't happen. If it does happen, I'll probably be downtown at that time and it won't matter for me. What can we do to get past the demonic coverage?"

Jack explained that the battle would be God's and they needed to pray for direction and protection. The FBI agents were somewhat taken aback as the Team simply bowed they heads and some of them got down on their knees, to seek God. Jack smiled at the four men. "It's all right if you want to pray, too."

As Laura prayed and drew close to God in humble adoration, she felt the presence of Yahveh's Holy Spirit and in her mind she saw a light approaching in the darkness. It was her friend the angel Rose that came out of the light and grew in her mind. Rose was alternately blindingly white and glowing gold in color. She came close to Laura and smiled at her. "I am happy that the Most High has touched you and clarified your ministry for you, Laura." The white dimmed as the gold color became dominant. "The enemy has death and destruction planned for the people of Denver. It is up to you and your Teammates to stop this. The demon you face is named "Mortaldeath" and your husband faced him before. He is a territorial spirit and much more powerful than a normal demon. But, he is on his last assignment and if you can break his power he will be finished forever. Mortaldeath will be banished to the Abyss until judgment day. Mortaldeath is aware of your new status and in his pride, will attempt to have a direct confrontation with you. The light from your sword will destroy his ability to control humans or affect events. The Lord is confident in your ability to stop him." She began to fade in Laura's mind picture. Rose added one more comment as she disappeared. "Look for Roger Prince to find the demon." Laura opened her eyes and waited until Jack looked at her.

Jack asked the assembled cast what God had told them. Most of the Crossfire Team had felt assurance but no details. Agent Chin looked somewhat perplexed. "I've never felt such a Presence of God before. I clearly heard two names though. "Mortaldeath" and "Roger Prince", He looked at Jack and asked what that meant.

Laura answered for Jack. "What you heard was confirmation of the information God gave me. "Mortaldeath is a territorial spirit and we can find him if we can locate this Roger Prince."

Charlie Wu was busy with his laptop computer and before the agents could use their cell phones he spoke up. "The FBI and CIA databases list Roger Aaron Prince as a mob enforcer who has recently dropped out of sight and is possibly working for a foreign terrorist group, possibly the ALA. He was last seen in the Colorado city of Pueblo and is a known killer. There are two warrants out on him. Both warrants are for murder. He's five-foot eleven inches tall, one-hundred, seventy pounds, thick brown hair, brown eyes and a pale complexion. He has a three-inch scar on the left side of his neck. He prefers sports cars and has been known to steal them when he can. He affects turtleneck sweaters, usually gray, along with gray slacks. He is fond of Italian shoes and carries a Glock nine-millimeter automatic in a back holster."

Gary Rhodes looked for a second at Charlie. "How did you get into our data base? It's supposed to be secure."

Charlie smiled at him. "The operative word would be "supposed". I was trained on cyber intelligence in China and pretty much have access to anything I want to get into. Don't worry, I won't tell anyone else about it." He sat back and watched the agent.

Gary shook his head. Looking at Jack he asked. "If we survive this next period, and I'm still working for the

Bureau, could we hire Charlie's services to help "spook-proof" our computer system?"

Jack smiled, "We'll see, but we have to find this bomb before thousands of people are killed." He looked at Laura, "Where do we start?"

She pointed at Gary Rhodes, "We need to locate this Roger Prince. Once we know where he is, we'll probably find the demon and possibly, that will be where the bomb is, also. Gary, how quickly can your group find this guy?"

Gary shook his head. "What you see here is all that the Bureau will give me to follow up, what they believe is a "red herring". It won't be enough."

Laura pulled out her cell phone and punched in a preset number. Getting a response she said, "I need to speak to him if possible. This is an Alpha Ultra situation." She waited for a minute and then started talking again. "Mr. President? I'm sorry to intrude on your staff meeting but we need you to kick some backsides at Homeland Security and the FBI for us. Yahveh has assured us that if we don't stop some terrorists in the next two days a nuclear weapon will be detonated in downtown Denver with the loss of life to be in the hundreds of thousands. Yes, sir. Please pray and confirm this with the Father, Sir. Yes Sir, I am positive of this. No doubt whatsoever. The resident agent for the FBI is with us but wonderland won't believe him or give him any assistance because they "believe" that is not a real situation. Yahveh says it is a terribly real situation. Yes sir, thank you."

Laura hung up and looked at Gary. The President is going to make a phone call and you will have all the resources you need within the hour."

The FBI agents looked at each other and wondered just exactly who they were dealing with inside this mountain.

Five minutes later, Gary Rhodes' cell phone chirped. He answered it and listened for several seconds. He then passed on the information on Roger Prince and the timeline involved. He wanted to work outward from downtown Denver in all directions seeking this man, but concentrate the efforts to the south toward Pueblo. He hung up and stared at Laura for a few seconds. "That was the head of Homeland Security himself. He will have as many agents in the area, in the next six hours, as is possible. He is also going to coordinate the search with the other agencies and classify the search, both Top Secret and Top Priority. The implication here is that we will find this man in the next twelve hours if he is to be found."

Jack looked at Mark. "Gary can take care of the governmental response. How should the Crossfire Team prepare for our confrontation with this group? I expect that Laura will be the point person for demon defense work but we will probably have the rest of the "professional killers" of the ALA running interference for this operation."

CHAPTER FORTY-ONE

Mortaldeath considered the forces arrayed against his human enemies. Puny as they were against him, they could negate his carefully planned operation. He called two minor demons to him and assigned them the task of creating confusion in the ranks of his opponents. They were to make the various levels of their security organizations jealous of each other and plant misleading information to throw the groups off track.

He considered his chosen tools for the destruction of the city. They thought they were only bringing the device to the city for others to sacrifice themselves, setting it off at a later date. Actually, they would die as soon as they were in position, tomorrow. They had believed him when he had prompted them through their greed that they would be safe. They were stupid, like all mortals. It would be satisfying to eliminate them and their tiny egos at the same time.

The involvement of the Crossfire Team was predictable and he could keep them hunting false leads until it was too late. It would be satisfying to get them in the area of the explosion, if possible. He would have to consider the dangers of luring them to the city which would put them in proximity to his sending the weapon into the downtown area.

The irony of the blast occurring during a major anti-terror demonstration wasn't lost on the demon. He wanted to take out as many people as possible with the detonation. The football game at the Denver Broncos Stadium would be packed and he was glad to destroy that many more people. The other major surprise for the humans would be the building where the explosion would take place. Mortaldeath had spent a great deal of demonic energy arranging for the delivery of the special elements to that building. He had to postpone the explosion three different times just so it would bring everything together properly. That didn't matter now. Everything was in readiness.

Mortaldeath had been made painfully aware by his master that this mission was not just fun and destruction. The crucifixion nail was a parallel demand. The demon thought about the origin of the nail and realized that the thought unnerved him. The demonic realm had been completely defeated by Christ at that time and if this artifact retained any of the power of that time, it could be very dangerous to him.

CHAPTER FORTY-TWO

As more than eighty FBI/NSA/HLS agents spread out from Denver in search of Roger Prince, the Crossfire Team each employed their unique abilities to help search out the extents and the dimensions of the threat.

Jim Grady pushed his network of informants as hard as he could for any information concerning Roger Prince, terrorist activities, or rumors of doomsday for Denver. He was getting a smattering of questionable rumors, at best.

Mark and Sarah used their investigative contacts to search for the same things. Mark concentrated on their inputs from U.S. groups while Sarah concentrated on information from groups outside the U.S. Nothing of any real substance had been forthcoming as the twenty-four hour mark passed.

Su Li worked with Gary Eisenthal quartering the city and the southern approaches with a specially equipped helicopter that could detect the smallest sign of organized radiation. Background and naturally occurring sources were ignored by the electronics. Gary was along because he felt that he might be able to sense the demonic involvement that Mortaldeath would generate.

Charlie Wu and his wife, Linda, spent their time on the computers attempting to find anything relating to the ALA and this operation.

Carol Nolan had been seconded by the Colorado Bureau of Investigation to the Crossfire Team as liaison and used the War Room's electronic database and communications network as a clearing house for all incoming information concerning the ALA, demonic activities detected in the area, and investigative inputs.

Jack and Laura coordinated the various operations and continually prayed for Yahveh's help to prevent this atrocity. They also sought Yahveh's direction for their efforts against the powers of darkness.

Fourteen hours before the probable attack time, a possible break came from Carol. She called Jack into the War Room and explained her concern. As Jack and Laura sat down she slid a paper over to him. "I don't know if this has any bearing on what we're doing but it just seems odd and I believe that the Holy Spirit drew my attention to it."

Jack looked at the information and asked the Lord if this was important. He got a definite "yes". It seems that there had been an unusually large shipment of Cesium-137 supplied as part of a laboratory and sterilization equipment order sent to Denver last week. The local police and the CBI had been properly notified and provided security for the shipment, which is being held in special vaults in a building downtown."

Laura shook her head. "What is Cesium-137 and why it is important to this investigation."

Jack looked across at Carol and the definite knowledge of the danger was obviously recognized by both of them. Carol turned to Laura and said, "Cesium-137 is a beta and gamma emitter with a half-life of thirty years. It comprises a small percentage of total fission products of a nuclear explosion. It's a primary long-term gamma emitter hazard from fallout, and remains a hazard for centuries. If that nuke goes off near this stuff, the death toll will be much higher and be spread much wider. Besides that, Denver will be uninhabitable for hundreds of years."

Carol added, "I pulled up this article about the stuff. In September of 1987, scavengers dismantled a metal canister from a radiotherapy machine at an abandoned Cancer Clinic in Goiania, Brazil. Five days later a junkyard worker pried open the lead canister to reveal a pretty blue, glowing dust. The dust was radioactive Cesium-137. In the following days, hundreds of Goianian citizens were exposed to the radioactive substance. It was a nuclear disaster second only to Chernobyl, and it was caused by only a few ounces of radioactive Cesium-137. We've got to be talking about a hundred pounds in this case."

Jack turned to Carol, "See if you can find out who requested this much of this stuff and why."

Laura asked, "How much of it is normally required?"

Carol said, "About one-half ounce to two ounces would be necessary for most applications and there couldn't be but five or six users here."

Jack frowned, "So why did they ship a hundred pounds of the stuff to Denver last week?"

Carol shook her head and got started tracking the shipment and the recipients.

It took her less than two hours to contact all the users in the area. She called Jack back into the War Room. "There has been no request made by any known user of Cesium-137 anywhere in the State of Colorado. The alleged recipient on the bill of lading is an empty business suite."

Jack nodded and dialed a number on his cell phone. After it rang once, Mark answered. Jack explained the problem and Mark said he would take care of it.

Mark called the Army Acquisition Pollution Prevention Support Office, or AAPPSO, headquartered in the US Army Materiel Command, in Alexandria, Virginia. AAPPSO had the responsibility for pollution prevention. They were the best ones to handle something this big and this dangerous in such a short time.

Explaining the problem and the potential for a disaster, "General" Connelly placed a "Top Secret" handle on the operation to remove the Cesium in the next five hours. The entire operation would be handled very discretely so as to not alert the enemy. Mark warned the Operations Officer that there could be look-outs posted near or in the building to prevent the removal or to call in additional forces. The Officer noted the information and said they would carefully sweep the area first to prevent anyone from seeing them remove it.

Linda Wu walked into the War Room and sat down. It was hard to realize that this small, quiet Chinese woman had been one of the top security agents for China just two years ago before Jesus came into her life. Her beauty hid a terrifically sharp mind and keen insight into the combative nature of humanity. She smiled and looked at the piece of paper in her hands. "Although Charlie and I have not found anything that relates directly to the ALA or to this project in our search, we have found an interesting fact that could mean something."

She handed the paper to Laura who scanned it and passed it on to Jack. Linda summed it up. "Last year, Chinese intelligence determined that the ALA had stolen a Russian Tochka missile and launcher and had gotten it out of the country, destination unknown."

Laura asked her, "What is the Tochka missile?"

Linda tipped her head to one side and considered the information. Then she gave a short summary of the possibilities. "The SS-21 Scarab, which is also known in Russia as the Tochka, is a single-stage, short-range, tactical-ballistic missile, which is transported and fired from a 6x6 wheeled transporter erector launcher. Because it uses an extremely accurate inertial guidance system, during transport the missile is enclosed with the warhead in a temperature-controlled casing. That is why the transporter is so important."

Linda looked at Carol as she continued. "The Scarab has a maximum range of 120 km or about 75 miles. The basic warhead is a high-explosive fragmentation but the SS-21 can also carry the AA60 tactical nuclear warhead. The unit that was stolen was equipped with a nuclear warhead. The missile is launched vertically and reaches its maximum range in about two and one-half minutes. The AA60 warhead provides a 10-kiloton bomb which, in downtown Denver, would kill some 100,000 civilians and irradiate 700,000 more and flatten everything in a half-mile diameter"

Linda sat back in her chair. "As far as the Israeli, U.S., or Chinese intelligence services are aware, the ALA has not used this weapon nor have they sold it. It is highly unlikely they would scrap or abandon such a pricey weapon once they had their hands on it."

She pulled another piece of paper out of her pocket. "Yesterday, I ran across a strange item in the Daily Reporter-Herald newspaper serving Loveland, Colorado. I was searching for any odd happenings in the area and this caught my eye. The article is not very accurate but the photo is interesting. Listen. "Last night, around 1 a.m., Bill Burney and his family were going home off Highway 287, south of the city, and they had just turned west toward Bert's Corner when they were almost run off of the road by an Army tank or something. Bill's son, Harold had been videotaping the countryside and got a shot of the huge vehicle that he sent us. It is a whopper. This paper called the Army department and they said that they didn't have any tanks roaming around at night. So if you see this one, you'd better get out of the way, because according to Bill it didn't stop and didn't honk either."

Linda put the paper down and produced a copy of the picture. "It's a little grainy due to the low light conditions but that definitely is a Russian 9T238 missile transporter trailer. Loveland is not that far away from Denver. This may not have any bearing on our present problem but I think it is stretching credibility too far to have a report of the ALA having stolen a nuclear missile and the appearance of the 9T238 transport trailer just north of Denver, which is supposedly going to be attacked by a nuclear bomb provided by the ALA. See what I mean?"

Jack nodded and gave the report to Carol to include in the threat matrix. "Carol, see if you can determine any possible launching sites for this thing. They would have to keep it out of sight from the public, which means it could be inside a building. Have Mark and his military experts help you."

As the three women discussed the implications, Jack got a definite mental picture showing a certain place and the area it was in. It was nowhere he had ever been before, so it wasn't a memory. He considered the thought could be from the Holy Spirit and determined that he would check it out before wasting the other people's valuable time on what could be a wild goose chase.

CHAPTER FORTY-THREE

Telling Laura that he wanted to research a thought, Jack took his SUV and traveled to the subdivision south of I-76 near Foothills Park. There was a definite beauty to the view. He could see almost north to Wyoming and twenty miles south of the city of Denver. The city itself was spread out below the subdivision in a vast panorama.

Trying to determine why God had led him to this place he slowly drove around the area. Nothing seemed to be important or even interesting in light of the impending disaster. On the north side of the development he saw something that snagged his attention. A large home was set back from the street by almost two acres of poorly tended lawn and had three large outbuildings on the property. The thing that interested him was the out-of-place NO TRESPASSING sign on the gate, with the security wall surrounding the place.

Driving on, he found an open acreage a block away from the gate. Parking the SUV he started to call in his intention but again he had the feeling that this was probably nothing and everyone was so focused he would upset their operations.

Taking a .45 caliber Para Ordinance automatic out of the weapons hold in the vehicle he checked the load and verified that there was a round in the chamber. Jack especially liked the small gun for its heavy caliber rounds and its ability to store ten rounds in an easily concealed automatic. He clipped an inside-the-pants holster on his right side and cocked the automatic. He put it in the holster under his windbreaker.

Exiting the SUV he walked through the vacant lot until he reached the back of the target home site. He waited for several minutes watching for any sign he had been detected and then scaled a small tree and climbed out on a limb and dropped lightly onto the secured grounds.

Jack had the random thought that he was breaking the law. Even if it was for a higher purpose, he was still doing something illegal by entering their property. Still, if it was important enough for Yahveh to lead him here, then it probably would result in something that would justify his misdeed. He decided to check on the larger outbuilding first. Keeping to cover as much as possible, he reached the back of the building and slowly edged around to the far side which wouldn't be visible from the house itself.

He located the door and it was secured with a padlock. Moving farther to the front he found a window. It was partially covered over with a blind on the inside, but there was a gap at the bottom. Peering into the darkened interior, he spotted a very large vehicle that was covered with a huge tarp. He couldn't be sure, but it had the right dimensions to be the missing Russian missile launcher.

Checking around, he didn't see anyone. He slid to the front of the building and checked the house. Still, there was nobody in sight. Something was wrong here. This highly professional bunch of assassins, who were being backed by a major demon, wouldn't have just parked a nuclear missile and its launcher and forgot to protect it. The ALA would have to be pretty careless to do something like that.

Drawing his pistol, Jack darted from the side of the building and jumped into the bushes ten feet away. Hunkered down he strained his hearing and eyes to detect anything. Nothing out of the ordinary came to him. He carefully pulled his cell phone out and hit the speed dial for the Fortress when something heavy struck his head from behind. Both the phone and the gun fell from his hands as he fell into a sudden darkness.

Jack had a serious dream about flying that disappeared as he regained consciousness. He felt very sluggish and disoriented which he realized was from the blow to his head. Resting quietly with his eyes closed he inventoried his body for damage. Other than a roaring headache and the sluggish feeling, nothing seemed to be out of order. Jack prayed for coverage for his wound in the blood of Yahshua and felt the disorientation lessen.

Smelling dust rather than dirt and hearing silence rather than sounds of nature, he was fairly certain that he wasn't in the bush anymore. He opened his eyes slowly and tried to look around. He couldn't move his head at all. He realized that his head was held in position by a metal brace and two leather straps. Trying to move his hands and feet told him that they were equally immobilized. All he could see was a slight glow in a Stygian darkness. Praying that God would enlighten him as to what had happened brought conviction of his having assumed it was Yahveh that brought him out to this place. Obviously it was some other source. Jack repented of presumption and asked the Lord for cleansing and forgiveness. He felt the peace in his spirit that he had been forgiven.

Realizing how greatly he had been duped, Jack did not waste any of his time on self-recrimination or beating himself up for being bagged so easily. He prayed for wisdom and protection from the Father in this situation. He realized that he had been led to the real headquarters of the ALA for this attack. Why? He thought he knew but would wait to find out. Carefully checking his condition through kinetic pressures, he concluded that he was dressed in his underwear, slacks, and shirt. He didn't have on his shoes, jacket, or anything in his pockets. It wasn't surprising that they had taken his gun and his cell phone along with his wrist watch and sunglasses. He was tied to a plank or structure and completely immobile. He could move his eyes from side to side and wiggle his fingers and toes. But, that was the extent of his freedom.

Using a technique he had learned in his Martial Arts instruction he quieted his heart rate and calmed his mind to allow him rest while he waited for whatever was coming next. He wasn't worried about dying because he knew that God was with him and there was the fact that they hadn't already killed him. It probably meant that they wanted something from him.

Jack prayed for the full armor of Yahveh and for warrior angels to protect him from the demonic forces involved in this operation.

He had been waiting for over an hour when there was a change. The darkness lightened slightly and a person came into his view. After a second of consideration Jack realized that this wasn't a normal person. A remembered feeling of unworthiness and filthy crawling struck him and attempted to make him cower. But, this wasn't the brand-new Christian that met this demon in Don Miland's basement. Jack said, "I rebuke you and your attempts to belittle me in the name of Yahshua, Messiah of Nazareth, who came in the flesh."

This evidently rattled the demon. Jack suddenly found he couldn't speak at all. Mortaldeath moved closer to him and gently raked his claws down Jack's right arm. He didn't draw blood but it was obvious he could have with very little effort. The demon spoke in a very low register that almost sounded like a rumble. "You will not speak that name again! If you attempt to, I will strike your head from your body, do you understand me?"

Jack found he could speak again. "I understand." He wanted to see what this foul being wanted with him.

The demon was incredibly ugly to the normal human senses. His face was sunken in with a large hook nose and evil eyes that were set in a skin that seemed to be old, scarred and seamed leather. His body was misshapen and bent. It looked to be very powerful for all the distortions but it stank like putrid, long-dead meat. He actually had fangs and triangular teeth. They were mostly black and jagged.

The demon stepped back and looked at Jack. "Where have you hidden the crucifixion nail this time?"

Jack stared back and answered him. "If you'll answer my question, I'll answer yours."

The demon seemed amused by the human's defiance. "What is your question?"

Jack asked him, "Why and how did you enter our dimension with all its inherent dangers for your kind?"

The demon seemed to consider the question for a bit. "Because I could and because I needed to become physically involved on your level to acquire what my Father wants. Now, where is the nail?"

Jack tried to shake his head which didn't work. "I told you that I will answer your question when you answer mine. You haven't answered my question, yet. How did you enter this dimension?"

Mortaldeath frowned, "Don't try to tell me what you will do or not do. You are the captive and I will tell you what is to be done!" This last was shouted into Jack's face.

Jack took the fear that tried to rise up and gave it to Yahveh. Acting unaffected by the anger of the demon, he simply said, "If you don't want to tell me, then I don't want to tell you about the nail."

The demon reached up and slowly drew his claws down Jack's right arm. This time all four claws drew blood. The pain was severe but Jack used a mental technique to ignore it and stared at the demon without blinking.

The demon stepped back and studied the human. This one wasn't reacting properly to pain or threats. "You couldn't understand the physics involved in interdimensional shifting, even if I told you what happened. Just know that I asked permission to enter this dimension and it was granted me to do so. I then "willed" myself to move from the spiritual plane, as you humans call it, to this one. Does that answer your question?"

Jack thought about that for a few minutes. "Yes, I guess it will have to do. The answer to your question is this. It is locked in a secure safe that is protected from spiritual as well as physical attacks. Even you cannot open it without the proper "permission". It will be completely melted before any force can be applied to the safe it is in. It is located in our headquarters in southwestern Denver. Beyond that, I can't give you any more information."

The demon thought about that for a few minutes. Then, without any noticeable message, three men walked around the platform Jack was tied to. Mortaldeath said to the men, "Soften him up but don't do any real damage. I need him alive and cooperating. Any injury done to him will result in a visit to my world for the transgressor." The demon left the area in front of Jack and the three men starting in by tearing his pants and shirt off of him. They then began to whip Jack with slender rods. This was an exceptionally painful Oriental torture and these men were experts at their trade. Jack took the pain as long as he could and then sought relief in unconsciousness.

CHAPTER FORTY-FOUR

The search for Roger Prince ended suddenly. The FBI followed up on a possible sighting of Roger Prince in Colorado Springs. The agents involved determined that it was Prince and that he and others were holed up in a private home in the mountains, behind the city itself. The news was flashed to all involved parties and multiple levels of response locked down the area of the home and surrounded the dwelling. Considering the potential for disaster and the mindset of the people involved, the various police and federal agencies quietly evacuated the people in the surrounding two-mile area.

By the time the four-person Crossfire Team arrived, the elite anti-nuclear SWAT Team was poised to enter the home. Things went quickly off-schedule as one of the ALA members walked out of the house to go somewhere. He stopped and looked around and realized that there were no neighbors, kids, dogs, or any kind of activity. Sensing trouble, he started to turn around to sound the alarm when a silenced shot from an FBI sniper ended his career of murder at that point. The SWAT Team immediately advanced to enter the home quickly in the event someone inside had seen the takedown.

Simultaneously crashing through three doors and four different windows, the SWAT Team quickly took control of the building and there was only one shot heard. The leader of the SWAT Team came out and reported on their success. The only casualty of the strike had been the subject of the search, Roger Prince. He had attempted to arm the weapon or detonate it and the raider closest to him had to shoot him to prevent it.

The nuclear disarmament group opened up the casing around what they figured was the briefcase nuclear bomb and every detector from handheld to satellite confirmed that they had the right package. Checking it over they determined that it wasn't active and they immediately removed the weapon for transport to the nuclear facility at Rocky Flats to dismantle and destroy it.

Outside the house, Gary looked at Mark, Sarah, and Su Li. "I don't like this. There is something wrong with this whole capture."

Su Li nodded her agreement. Mark shook his head, "Gary, it was a righteous bust. Yahveh told us to look for Roger Prince. They found him and the bomb. We just caught them off-guard."

Gary was still shaking his head as the troops around them celebrated their success.

Sarah said, "I think I know what the problem is but why don't you let us know why you're saying it's wrong?"

Gary Eisenthal looked at Mark. "It was too easy." He saw Mark start to shake his head and rushed on. "Not in the physical! In the spiritual! Where is Mortaldeath? Where is the warfare? I don't detect any type of activity to warn them to stop us, to interfere in any way. This is not the main attack; it's a red herring to make us stop looking for the real threat."

Mark stopped protesting and frowned. Looking up at Gary Eisenthal, he smiled wanly. "You know. You tend to make too much darn sense every now and then." He went off to find Gary Rhodes of the FBI.

Sarah looked at Gary Eisenthal. "You know, Mark is right about one thing. The Father said to find this Roger Prince guy. So, there must be something here that will give us what we need to find the real threat, right?"

Gary nodded. "I'd say that is right on. Yahveh doesn't make mistakes and he's never surprised. He had us chase this guy so that we could find our way to the real bad threat."

Mark came back with Gary Rhodes in tow. Gary was not a happy camper. He looked at Gary Eisenthal with consternation. "What's wrong? We found the guy that Yahveh told us to look for and we got the bomb. My boss just called to congratulate us on our good work in saving Denver and is closing this case. Why are you now telling me that this isn't right?"

Mark put his hand on Gary Rhode's shoulder. "Gary, remember when we were going against Don Miland? Remember all the problems we encountered? You told me that the whole criminal world was going to him and that you couldn't get a line on anything he was doing? It was like fighting against nature itself, wasn't it? That was because of the influence of this same demon, Mortaldeath. This whole thing here simply fell into place and went off without a snag. Not one of our people or a single civilian was hurt or really inconvenienced. Nobody had equipment malfunctions; no communications were lost or interfered with in any way. If Mortaldeath was involved, would we have located Prince or the bomb so easily and taken it without a problem?"

Impressed with the logic Gary Rhodes nonetheless, wasn't convinced. "What if this demon had decided to drop the whole thing and left?"

Gary Eisenthal said, "A demon's whole thing is to kill, rob, and destroy. There is no reason in the universe that a demon would leave an operation that could easily kill thousands and destroy billions of dollars worth of city. No way."

Gary Rhodes shook his head. "You are probably right. But there is no way I can convince my superiors to keep this operation going now that they believe that we've got the bomb and the bad guys. No way. And remember, we did get the bomb."

Mark looked at Sarah with a knowing look. "The Scarab has to be the real threat. This was to throw us off the trail or derail the investigation completely, which it seems to have done."

Sarah nodded and wondered where Jack was, again. She tried his cell phone without success.

CHAPTER FORTY-FIVE

While the FBI and other federal agents interrogated the people arrested in the house, forensic Teams went through the building in exacting detail looking for any leads to the mastermind behind the attack and the method of acquisition of the nuclear bomb. Scientists were confused by the light-weight shielding that had apparently kept the nuclear signature from being detected. They had taken that back to a federal laboratory for analysis.

Su Li had gone back to the Fortress and returned with Laura. Mark and Su Li toured the area around the house and talked with returning neighbors. Gary Eisenthal and Laura went through the house, room by room, attempting to sense anything in the spirit.

As Gary had explained to Laura, there had to be something here, or God would not have told them about Roger Prince. The FBI would still have gotten the word and searched for him,. But, why the Crossfire Team?

As they reconvened on the front lawn, Laura shook her head. "I sensed nothing but some faint signs of Indian spirits still involved in the ground itself. Did anyone else come up with anything?" When nobody had anything to add she suggested they return to the Fortress and try to follow up on what the agents were able to get out of the ALA personnel or the results of the forensic Team.

That afternoon there was a lot of satisfaction in Washington about the capture of the bomb and troops. Tomorrow was the weekend and they could rest securely in the knowledge of another threat nipped in the bud.

At the Fortress in Colorado, the sense of urgency was getting worse for everyone. The big parade and demonstrations were only nine hours away and they didn't have a clue as to where the missile trailer could be set up or, if that was even the real threat.

Mark, Sarah, and Laura were discussing the possibilities. Mark said, "If they are going to launch that battlefield short-range missile, there is only a small band of space they could do it from. He drew on the computer screen in front of him. The image was reproduced on each person's screen in front of them at their positions.

His first circle was at the maximum range of 75 miles and the inner circle was at ten miles to keep them from suffering from the blast themselves. This still left a band 65 miles wide all the way around Denver's downtown.

After eliminating many of the areas of the band due to physical impossibility and things like military bases, airports, and other things, still left hundreds of square miles of flat land and mountainous terrain to be searched. Something the few members of the Crossfire Team and the single FBI agent could not do in the remaining few hours before the predicted attack.

Laura called Mark out of the meeting and expressed her concern over Jack's absence. "I'm worried about him, Mark. He left this morning to research a lead and I haven't been able to contact him since then. There was an interrupted call from his cell phone around two p.m. Attempts to locate him have failed and this isn't like him at all. Will you see what you can do?"

Mark hugged her and told her not to worry, that they'd find him. He called Charlie Wu and told him to track Jack while he worked on trying to refine the location of the possible missile launch.

Charlie thought for a few minutes and then took the elevator to the garage. The only vehicle missing was the Malone's Cadillac SUV. Returning to his desk he called the On-Star people and requested a GPS track on that vehicle. He got the coordinates in less than two minutes. He called Mark and told him the location. Mark relayed the information to Laura who, in turn, called Sarah for reinforcements. The rest of the Team was too involved in attempting to track the possible location of the Russian missile launcher to distract them.

Twenty minutes later Sarah told Laura to report to the helicopter base. Once she got there she ran to the heavily armed stealth helicopter that already had its rotors spinning. Climbing on board, Laura put on her headset and talked to Sarah. By then the lift had the chopper up to the launch point and Major White had pulled pitch and the armored chopper lifted quickly off of the pad and headed west-northwest at a high rate of speed. The sun had set behind the mountains four hours ago and there was less than five hours until the deadline.

Laura asked Sarah for an update on Jack. Sarah pulled a map out of her thigh pocket and pointed to an area just west of Denver. "That's where we found the SUV. Satellite surveillance of the area indicates that Jack's unique identifier button is located in the main building of this property. Running a quick check on the ownership of the property shows that it is owned by a front company that is allied with the ALA. I think Jack has fallen into their hands and we're going to go get him. I've already gotten an electronic counterterrorism warrant from the Federal Judge and notified all of the local authorities that this is a sanctioned effort. The local police have begun evacuating everyone in the neighborhood. The last Keyhole satellite pass was less than eight minutes ago and we could detect over forty-five heat signatures of people on the property."

Laura looked at the people in the helicopter. There was Gary Eisenthal, Sarah, and herself. Even with the power of the helicopter's armaments, forty-five combatants could be a little much for the four of them. She frowned and looked at Sarah with the question. Sarah smiled and pointed out the window in the side hatch of the chopper. Laura looked and saw two blacked out troop helicopters keeping pace with them. Sarah told her, "I thought things were getting a little dicey so I called up the SOG."

That more than evened up the odds. Laura, as was her way, started praying for the success of their mission and for Jack. As she prayed she felt the presence of the Holy Spirit and in her mind's eye, she saw herself standing in the dark in her armor with her sword drawn and pointed at a large black cloud of evil. Coming out of the vision she knew she would be facing the demon by herself, soon.

CHAPTER FORTY-SIX

The bucket of cold water slammed into his face and body and jolted Jack back to a world of pain and suffering. He prayed that God would give him the strength to endure the torture and he felt a small measure of control. He opened his eyes and saw the three men waiting to start whipping him, again. He braced himself for more punishment when the three men threw down their whips and ran past him and disappeared.

Taking stock of his condition he realized that the pain was mainly welts and small cuts over most of his torso and legs. The overall pain level was high and it kept distracting his mind so that it was hard to concentrate. He began asking God to give him the ability to block out the pain sensors and to help him concentrate on his predicament.

He had determined that he was still hung on some kind of platform and had no ability to move his hands, feet, or his head. He started praying for Yahveh's help to escape the situation.

Upstairs in the large house, Mortaldeath was rallying the troops. There was a force headed their way to interfere with their operations. He wanted the ALA members there to stop the main force but to allow a certain member to get through to the chamber where they were torturing Mr. Malone.

These were the top troops of the ALA. All were combat tested and ready to defend their base. Their training was good and their positions were hardened to defend against an attack of a police SWAT Team. They armed themselves and rushed to their positions.

In the attack helicopter, Mike White watched the predator scan of the activity at the target site. He called Sarah and explained that it was obvious that the enemy knew they were coming. He then called the other two helicopters and routed them to drop troops at locations away from the apparent kill zones. He would take the fight to the troops before the ground troops ever made contact. Coming in quickly to the location, he targeted four groups of blips and released four Hellfire missiles with their own tracking capabilities. This was a good example of "fire-and-forget" targeting. Mike White knew he could forget about the twenty troops at the impact points because they weren't going to exist in the next few seconds.

The four large explosions briefly lit up the compound like daylight in the dark. His night vision FLIR system identified eight more troops moving to intercept the SOG troopers. He triggered a sustained burst from the two twenty millimeter cannons under the front end of the chopper. The incoming rounds totally devastated the entire area where the eight men had been. The signs faded quickly, that there was any life at that point. The SOG men and women were advancing from both flanks as Mark set the combat chopper down and let Laura and Sarah leap to the ground. He rapidly rose back to a position where he could provide additional fire support as needed.

Laura and Sarah were both armed with CAR-15/M203A3 carbines and their backup pistols. They had body armor and night vision capability. They moved toward the front of the house and Sarah said, "Knock knock"; as she triggered a 40-mm. grenade that removed the front doors and part of the wall. Laura sent a second round into the opening but this one was buckshot. That cleared the way. One group of the SOG joined them at that point and they entered the building and spread out looking for Jack or the enemy.

Laura felt an urging to go to the basement and quickly checked the spirit that gave her that leading. It wasn't of the Lord. She hit her broadcast button. "Be advised that the enemy is attempting to lead us to the basement area. So, let's take them up on their invitation, but be alert for deadfalls and traps."

Two of the SOG troopers found the entrance to the basement in the kitchen and called the rest of the ground floor force to that location. At the moment there was a pitched battle going on the second floor and the landing of the living room. The ALA troopers were in the firefight of their life against the SOG forces and were slowly being shot down and killed. They had prepared for a highly professional SWAT Team attack but had never expected a full military invasion. They had lost most of their troops in the opening seconds of the battle and this was a rearguard action that had most of them bottled up on the second floor of the house. A shuddering explosion blew a part of the second floor out into the front yard as a SOG trooper eliminated a hard spot with a 40mm grenade.

Parts of the ceiling fell on to the troops gathered in the dark in the kitchen. Laura shook the debris off of her head and shoulders and led the way down the stairs into the basement. As the troops spread out to search and destroy, Laura and Sarah intuitively knew which room was the right one.

Opening the door, Laura and Sarah entered the room quickly and went to either side of the opening. In a flash of light, their weapons were ripped out of their hands and the door was slammed shut. Sarah pulled a light flare out of her hip pocket and triggered it. Throwing it forward it suddenly illuminated the room with a bright white light. The tableau it revealed was shocking. The demon Mortaldeath was standing near Jack with his sword drawn and at Jack's throat. Jack looked like he was bleeding from his entire body and blood covered the floor around him. He was tied hand, foot, and head to a board on a platform that held him upright. Laura derailed her emotions at the sight of the love of her life in such vile straits and concentrated on praying for Yahveh to empower her to remove the threat of the demon.

Sarah moved to the side of the action and watched for additional surprises. She had seen Laura in action before and wasn't worried about that aspect. But there were other possibilities and her training wouldn't let her ignore those possibilities.

Mortaldeath rumbled a bass voice and chuckle at the same time. "Well, well, his woman comes to rescue him. Let me tell you that he is as good as dead right now unless you do as I tell you."

Laura moved closer to the demon, "Just what do you want, you unspeakable filth?"

Mortaldeath's anger flared. "I want the nail and I want your solemn promise that you will give it to me or I will gladly cut his throat and then destroy you."

Laura walked around to the demon's right side. This caused the demon a problem since he held his sword in his right hand and he couldn't defend himself from Laura and still keep it at Jack's throat. Choosing the safest path he turned to confront Laura.

He exerted the power he had and both Laura and Sarah were paralyzed. Laura's expression never changed. She kept praying in her prayer language in a mounting righteous anger. Jack watched as small gold flickers appeared around Laura and began to brighten and form an outline of her armor. Mortaldeath backed up away from Laura and kept trying to keep her from functioning with all his power. Sarah saw some shadows forming but couldn't move.

Jack had been forgotten as the demon laughed and told them, "It doesn't matter how this battle ends, I have already completed the assignment to destroy the city and bring thousands of unsaved souls into my Father's hands. The missile has been launched and there's nothing you can do to stop that now!" He laughed a maniacal laugh at the thought of the death and destruction to Yahveh's people.

As Laura's armor began to come into sight, Mortaldeath focused his power on her and Sarah was released from her frozen state. In one smooth motion she drew and raised her automatic. She triggered it three times and the three men rushing at them were slammed backward and to the ground. Even though they had body armor on it didn't stop the .45 caliber Hydroshock rounds that impacted each man in the forehead. Sarah was very good at her trade. Later, she found out that these were the three men that had tortured Jack with the whips.

Ignoring the loss of his three troops as inconsequential, the demon raised his large black sword in preparation to do battle with Laura. He was a principality-level demon and knew he had more than enough power to overcome her.

Jack prayed out loud, "Father Yahveh, I ask you to burn this demon with the Fire of the Holy Spirit and destroy him completely in the name, and by the blood of Yahshua." This was a very fervent prayer.

There was a flutter in the room that drew everybody's attention. As a symbol of Yahveh's Spirit, a small white dove appeared above Laura and flew toward the demon. The righteousness of Yahveh slammed into everyone in the room. If the conviction of their sinful condition compared to the Holiness of Yahveh was intense for the three Christians, Yahveh's righteousness was pure poison for the demon. Mortaldeath barely had time to scream "Noooo!" as the dove sang a note of music. A blast of fire flew out from under the dove's wings that instantly volatilized the demon and blew out a good portion of the back wall at the same time. The noise accompanying the fiery blast was like being caught in the same room with a bomb. The blast also destroyed the flare and sudden darkness clamped down. Jack wanted to pray his thankfulness to a faithful Yahveh but he was so convicted of his sinful condition he was ashamed and knew how miserable his little prayer sounded next to the Holiness of the Lord. It came to him in a flash how much God forgave him every day and still loved him. His pain faded into a sorrow that seemed to be endless.

A second later another flare was triggered by Sarah and both women rushed to Jack and released his restraints. Jack lost consciousness again as his brutalized body fell forward into Laura's arms.

Sarah was suffering the same conviction as Jack but her training wouldn't let her sit on the floor and cry about it. She went to the door and forced it open. Two of the SOG women warriors were waiting to see what came out of the room. When they saw it was Sarah they lowered their weapons. Sarah told them to help Laura get Jack upstairs and out to the helicopter. She raced up the stairs and noticed the quietness. Captain Wollard told her that the site was theirs and that the enemy had died to the last man. None of them requested any quarter and none was given.

Sarah looked out the window at a quietly sleeping city with the exception of the local neighbors. It could have been something about the noise of four Hellfire missiles and a couple of chain guns that disturbed them. She looked at Laura, "The demon said the missile had been launched, but I don't see anything happening."

Laura was cleaning the blood off of her uniform and spared a glance at her friend. "Come on Sarah, you know that a demon lies don't you?"

Sarah was a little embarrassed to have overlooked that fact. "But, he seemed so happy about it."

Laura nodded, "I'm sure he wanted to be happy because we haven't been able to stop it as yet."

The SOG medic had given Jack a painkiller and covered his body in an antiseptic gel and bandages before they carried him to the chopper on a stretcher. They were going to take him directly to the Presbyterian/St. Luke's Medical Center on East 19th Street. The heavily-armed chopper flew along with them as security on the trip. Laura was updated as she stayed with Jack. The SOG had finished inspecting the grounds and turned the whole situation over to the local and state police. They had found where the missile launcher had been in one of the outbuildings but it had apparently left earlier that evening.

Jack had regained consciousness and asked Laura if they had gotten the missile launcher. She shook her head as the emotions of his beating, the conviction of the Yahveh's Spirit, and the post-combat jitters all flooded her at the same time. She let the tears flow as she prayed to an Elohim that suddenly seemed far too lofty to hear her prayer. She still prayed for his grace and mercy for Jack. Jack reached up with a bandaged hand and touched her cheek. "It'll be fine honey. I talked to an angel about it. Thanks for bailing me out back there. I let them use my pride again to suck me into their trap. It will not happen again."

Laura was glad to see the anger and determination in his eyes. She again felt the Presence of the Holy Spirit and wondered why He could stand to be around her. Her spirit knew the truth and gave her peace as the troop chopper was vectored directly to the top of the medical center to off-load Jack for the Emergency Room.

Major Mike White got permission from the medical center to refuel from their supply and flew out to the refueling pad on the property. As he landed he noticed the shock on the faces of the people at the refueling pad. He chuckled as he realized that his aggressive-looking combat chopper with its obviously used cannons and empty missile racks was a major change from the normal Life Flight choppers they were used to seeing at the refueling station. He left the chopper rotating as he hopped out to help them refuel the craft. Ten minutes later he was airborne with full tanks and joined up with the troopship as it left the top of the medical center for the journey back to the Fortress. Mike watched the hospital disappear and worried for them all because if that missile struck downtown, this place was going to be heavily damaged or completely destroyed.

CHAPTER FORTY-SEVEN

Forty minutes until H-Hour.

Mark was exasperated. He and the other Team members had done everything they could to find the missile launcher without success. He pulled the information about the missile and the launcher up on his screen again and read it looking for anything that would help them. This was his own research on the missile and something didn't align with the information that Linda Wu had given them. He called her and asked her to bring her data back again.

Linda walked in with the original papers and asked Mark what she could do. Mark showed her his information and told her something wasn't the same as what she had given them. Could she figure out what it was?

Linda scanned to two documents and nodded. "The difference is that the normal Scarab missile is equipped with inertial guidance. The one they got away with had been modified to use a new version of the American laser guided bomb's guidance systems. It had been experimental and that was why it wasn't locked down as tightly as normal."

Mark thought for a minute and had a thunderbolt of an idea. He said, "Who's available?"

Linda hit a key combination and scanned the personnel list. "Only Carol and myself. Everyone else is on the raid or out seeking the missile launcher."

Mark thought for a second, "Where are Su Li and Gary Eisenthal?"

Linda said, "They're south of downtown in Su Li's chopper and looking for likely launch sites. Why?"

Mark jumped out of his chair and grabbed his communications gear and rushed out the door. Linda sat there for a second and then called Sarah on the comm link.

The sun rose high into the sky during the operation and the trip to the hospital. It was almost noon as the helicopters headed back to the Fortress when Sarah took the call from Linda. "Yes Linda, what do you need?" Linda told her about Mark's sudden departure and wondered if she could find out what it was all about.

Sarah said she would see what was going on. There were only minutes left until the expected launch and detonation time. She called Mark and he responded with a curt, "Hi Hon, can't talk now. I think I know how to derail this attack and I'm headed downtown right now. Get into the Fortress. If this doesn't work, you'll be safe from the effects. Love you. I'll see you later," and he hung up.

As the choppers reached the platforms for the Fortress, she felt a heartache starting about her one true love heading into the ground zero area, but knew if there was anybody that could take care of themselves, it was Mark.

Mark had called Su Li and told her to move up to the middle of the city because they could be useful. He then called for satellite support using his "General Connelly" persona.

When the control officer came on the line, Mark described what he needed and the fact that he needed it in the next ten minutes. Racing on the freeway he swerved around slower traffic and took the off-ramp to West 6th Avenue toward downtown. Five minutes later he arrived and still didn't know where to go. Pulling to the curb he recontacted the control officer and explained his urgency. "This is an Ultra request because I'm trying to stop a terrorist attack against Denver using a nuclear weapon. Do you have anything for me?"

The control officer stayed calm and professional. "Yes we do, General Connelly. The building you're looking for is located on the southwest corner of Lincoln Street and East 8th Street. Good Luck, Sir."

Mark dropped the cell phone into his pocket and tore through traffic to the intersection. He saw the tall building on the southwest corner and slammed his car to a halt at the curb in a no-parking zone. Racing into the lobby of the building he told the security officer to call the FBI and get Gary Rhodes down here as quickly as possible. Commandeering an elevator, he called Su Li and asked her where she was.

Su Li was orbiting the site of the now empty Cesium-137 building. Mark looked at his watch. Less than three minutes to go. He prayed that Yahveh would grant him favor in his endeavor. Exiting onto the top floor he raced to the stairwell door and entered. A locked gate stood in his way to the roof. Drawing his pistol he fired one round and the lock exploded. Mark threw the gate open and charged up the two flights of stairs to the roof exit.

As he stepped out onto the roof he saw that the impact time was only two minutes away. That meant that the missile was already in the air.

CHAPTER FORTY-EIGHT

The dread in Mark's heart grew with every step he took across the tarred roof surface. He was running as fast as he could but knew he might be too late to stop the total and final destruction of hundreds of thousands of innocent people. The thought that he would also die didn't even cross his mind. As he ran, he held his .45 caliber automatic in both hands in a Weaver grip.

Coming around the last ventilation tower he saw the two men standing at the edge of the roof. The satellite had been right on the spot, finding a building with only a few people on the top. Mark's worse fears were confirmed when he saw the laser identifier in one man's hands. It was pointed into the downtown area at the building that had once held the Cesium-137. The other man was negligent in his duties to protect the spotter because he too was looking up to see if he could see the missile in flight. They both knew that the explosion would kill them and therefore they weren't afraid of dying.

As Mark pelted across the rooftop toward them, the guard heard him and swung around with his AK-47 assault rifle. Mark fired a double-tap of 230-grain Hydro-Shock bullets that struck the man in the chest. The body-armor he wore stopped the bullets from penetrating into his body but the force of the rounds slammed him backward and over the edge of the ten story building. The body armor didn't do anything to protect him when he hit the ground.

The spotter tried to keep the laser identifier on the building because he knew that the missile was already in the air and coming at supersonic speed. The seeker head on the missile would lock onto the laser spot and draw the missile to that spot.

Mark lowered his aim and fired three rounds. The first shot missed but the second two took out the right leg of the spotter. As his leg was knocked out from under him, he fell back onto the roof in shock and pain and dropped the laser ID unit. Mark's next two shots ended his pain forever.

Mark dropped his gun and grabbed the laser ID unit and fanatically looked for anything that would be within the scanning range of the missile's seeker head but wouldn't kill people. There was nothing anywhere within the range of the identification unit that he could use to misdirect the missile. It would still impact in the downtown area if it couldn't find the laser marking because it would follow its last known trajectory until it either hit something or saw the laser spot.

Mark could almost feel the rapidly approaching missile as he prayed that Yahveh would make his hair-brained idea work. He had learned to pray for Yahveh's help in the name of Yahshua. Mark acted on the thought without debating the costs.

Keying his throat mike he called Su Li.

Su Li was almost directly over the building that had held the Cesium when Mark called. Mark told her, "Su Li, we've only got one chance to keep the missile from hitting the city. Climb as quickly as you can to one thousand feet, relative. No, make that twelve hundred feet and hover! Do it now!"

Su Li fed the full power of the engine to the rotors and the helicopter went up like an express elevator. Gary Eisenthal felt like he was being mashed down into the copilot's seat by the g-forces of the climb.

As she approached the altitude she backed off on the pitch of the blades and the climb stopped. Su Li knew what Mark was planning and she willingly joined him in the effort. Gary wasn't tuned into the military mindset and didn't have a clue.

Mark fixed the laser identifier on the front of the distant helicopter and triggered the unit. It hummed as it poured out a solid laser mark on the helicopter. Mark continued to pray for perfect timing. When he felt the urging of the Holy Spirit he simultaneously shut off the identifier's laser beam and told Su Li to drop altitude immediately.

Su Li reversed the pitch and since the rotor acts as the wing to hold the chopper in the air, removing that wing, in fact making it push downward, really causes a fast fall.

Su Li knew that Mark had cut it close when she saw the missile as it flashed over the helicopter with no more than twenty feet clearance. She stabilized the chopper after bucking the supersonic shock wave from the missile, checked Mark's GPS location, and headed west toward the building that Mark was standing on.

Mark prayed his thanks to God for making it all work out. He watched as the missile flew over the city and out into the sparsely populated eastern flatlands. Counting the seconds after the missile had passed the chopper he reached 140 seconds when the missile struck the earth. Covering his eyes from the flash, he prayed that whoever lived near the strike zone wasn't home today. He saw the helicopter approaching as Su Li called him on the radio. As the chopper settled to a hover above the roof, Mark stared to the west where there was a large cloud resembling a mushroom formed above the earth. The shock wave had been minimal and was ignored by most of the people celebrating at the game or demonstrating in the downtown area. They never knew how close they had all come to meeting Yahshua that day.

CHAPTER FORTY-NINE

Mark called Gary Rhodes and gave him a quick outline of the events and explained the rerouting of the missile to its new ground zero. Gary Rhodes, in turn, got in touch with the nuclear response Team and also tasked his people who would get the local authorities to barricade the area and to determine the damage and loss of life.

The missile had struck the Colorado plains about two miles north of Rock Creek and twelve miles north of Hoyt, Colorado. Again, the Lord's hand moved to lessen the effect of the enemy's thrust against humanity. The missile had fallen to ground in the bottom of a rock quarry. As it finished its flight, it had entered an old mine opening that contained most of the light, heat, and blast effects. The area around the quarry was vaporized for almost six hundred yards and the shock was still sufficient to cause many buildings in Hoyt to collapse.

The loss of life came to twenty-three people. Twenty of them died in the collapse of the buildings in and around Hoyt. The other three were actually at the quarry and their bodies were never found. The damages caused by the explosion were estimated to be in the range of two hundred million dollars. The radiation was expended mostly deep inside the mine.

The cruel nuclear attack shook up the nations much like the September 11, 2001 attack on the World Trade Center buildings and the Pentagon. The President authorized all efforts to be utilized in finding and eliminating the ALA until it no longer existed, anywhere in the world.

The crew that had launched the missile had escaped before anyone could find the launch site. The missile launcher was found in a field twelve miles from the house where Jack had been captured. More than half of the ALA's soldiers had died in the battle to protect Mortaldeath.

Most of the Crossfire Team retreated to the Fortress to rest and recuperate. Mark had Su Li take him to the hospital where he joined Sarah and Laura at Jack's bedside.

Jack was in stable condition but looked like he had been run over by a truck. The torturers were very skilled at producing the maximum pain with the least amount of actual physical damage. That usually came in the next session if the first one did not produce the type of results they wanted.

Jack's wounds were covered in bandages and he was full of pain killers but still lucid enough to talk to his Teammates and kiss Laura. He told her that he was in an unconscious state for a good part of the past few hours and began to understand what they had to do to make their lives approvable to Yahveh as servants. Seeing the sad look on her face he joked, "Don't worry honey, this is right up your alley. It's all about love. She smiled a weak smile and held his hand tightly.

Early the next morning, Jack checked himself out and gingerly rode back to the Fortress.

Two weeks later Jack was feeling much better physically after a good deal of rest, healing prayer, and specialized whirlpool therapy. That was when they had an unexpected visit from the President, himself. Facing the Team who were standing in a line in the living room of the Fortress, he expressed his gratitude and that of a thankful nation for the efforts of the members of the Team in stopping the nuclear strike against Denver.

"By virtue of the authority vested in me as President of the United States, it is hereby ordered that the Presidential Medal of Freedom is awarded to each member of the Crossfire Team for their service and bravery." He walked down the line and handed each person his, or her, medal and shook their hands. "I'm sorry I can't do this at the White House with all the honors and public admiration. But, since you requested me to keep you out of the limelight, this will have to do." He finished handing the medals out with Jack's. Stepping backward, the President brought his right hand up in a salute. Everyone returned the salute and then stood there like they were waiting for someone else to do something.

Gary Rhodes spoke up. "I want to tell you that my superiors in the FBI and Homeland Security ate a large helping of crow pie and asked us to forgive them for not listening to us, after they found the first bomb. There have been some serious re-arrangements of personnel after this fiasco with Mortaldeath. Two of the managing directors have been replaced with very talented men who are also Christians, and who will consider the possibility of spiritual warfare being involved rather than scoffing at it.

Jack laughed at the thought of the FBI checking to see if there was any hint of a spiritual angle to a case. It probably violated someone's idea of separation of church and state. Who knew? Maybe after this little mess, that arrangement could actually happen. He walked over to Laura and hugged her, gently.

His body was healing up quickly but was still tender and occasionally sore. It was his spiritual condition that really needed help. He stared at his beautiful wife and soberly asked her if she would like to take a short vacation.

Laura smiled at the thought. "Last time we tried that we ended up in Israel fighting terrorists, remember?"

Jack nodded and waved Mark and Sarah over to them. He said, "Look guys, I need another week to get back into shape and I know that there is nothing on the burners right now. What do you say to a one-week stand-down for the whole Team and the four of us take a little rest and relaxation?"

Mark thought about that. This series of adventures with the Malones had a non-stop quality to it that could use some serious time-off. "Okay, let's come up with a destination that suits all of us, won't involve us in any action, and will be excessively fun." Jack looked at his best friend and answered, "Something like that."

They called the rest of the Team over and gave them the next week off. In less than two minutes the four of them were the only ones left in the living room. Jack took a deep breath and said, "I know that we've all been running at the ragged edge for quite a while, but I want to suggest a week of prayer and reassessment for the four of us."

That concept really made everyone think for a few seconds. Mark hadn't been in the basement with Mortaldeath when the Holy Spirit appeared and wasn't under the heavy conviction the other three were. He looked at Jack and asked, "I'm not sure I understand the line of reasoning here."

Sarah spoke up at that point. She explained the feelings they had experienced and told him that she had an instant understanding of how sinful her life still was. "I've got to get closer to the Father or I won't be able function at all. I thought I was in pretty tight with Him, what with the way he has used me. I was wrong. I am closer than a lot of people but I have such a terribly long way to go I can't wait to get started."

Laura saw the confusion on Mark's face and reached over and took his hand. "Mark, Yahshua wants you to love him before anything else in the universe. He already loves you that way. The difference is our unrepentant sin burden that we don't even know we have. It is an individual thing between each person and Yahveh God. What Jack is suggesting is that we take a break and concentrate on learning what God wants us to eliminate in our lives. I know you feel that you're pretty free from sin. But, I thought that also until recently. What you need to do is spend time in prayer with the Father and ask Him to show you what He wants you to confess as sin and turn from it. It won't be finished in this week but it will show Him that you are serious about becoming a spotless bride for Him."

Mark realized that what she was saying was all too true. His pride in his abilities had handicapped him too long in working with God. He agreed to spend the next week seeking the Father's direction in cleansing his life.

Jack said, "Let's leave our cell phones, pagers, and GPS trackers here and get Mark White to take us to an exclusive hotel I know about in upstate New York, where we can have the solitude and discrete service we need. This may be our biggest battle yet.

CHAPTER FIFTY

Seven days later, Jack stood at the window of their room and looked out at the peaceful forest spread out before him. His thoughts reflected his efforts over the last week. He could sense the Father much more clearly now. He thought of all the things which he had to confess as sin and repent of and walk away from, forever.

He knew now that this would be a long effort. It was sort of like peeling an onion. God was only giving him a few things at a time to see if he would be obedient to turn away from each one. Any refusal would be rebellion and that would be where he was stuck until he finally let it go. He had never known how riddled his life was with things that he hadn't even known were offensive to Yahveh. Once God had exposed them to Jack it was painfully obvious and he was eager to avoid them for evermore. He hadn't had to think twice about any of the things he needed to get rid of. Things that had been instilled in him since birth that was just wrong in Yahveh's sight. Idolatry, lust, greed, gluttony, the list seemed to go on and on. But Jack wasn't going to stop cleaning up his life for God for anything.

Not only did he have to repent sins in his life but the cost of the required sacrifice was staggering. Yahveh didn't want his best stuff, He wanted it all. Jack reached a point during the week where he finally knew in his heart that nothing he had was his. It never had been his. It was all Yahveh's and He could require Jack to give it all away at any time. Jack now understood that none of the things on this earth were worth anything anyway. He truly loved Yahshua more than his own life. He gladly accepted the role of steward or caretaker of Yahveh's things which he had incorrectly assumed were his before. It became clearer as he stayed in communion with the Father over the week. Nothing in this world was of any consequence in the long run. It all belonged to Yahveh, anyway. He felt better than he had ever felt. Sure, he had millions of dollars. But he knew that the bulk of it was to bless others, not him or

Laura. Yahveh was his provision and nothing could take that away from him anymore.

Jack reflected on the love he felt from the creator of the universe. That was worth more than any amount of money, possessions, or power. He felt the presence of the Holy Spirit and knew that he was still a long way from being what God wanted him to be, but he was closer and on the right path.

Laura came up beside him and put her arm through his as they looked out on the forest. She had gone through the same things and no longer felt ashamed to be in the presence of the Father through His Holy Spirit. She realized that Jack had been right about it being all about love. Love for the Master, love for her fellow man, even her enemies. The future was brighter than she had ever expected it to be. They were moving up, glory to glory with God. She leaned her head on Jack's shoulder and felt the all encompassing peace and joy of God wash over them both.

The Crossfire Team will return in **"Texas Crossfire"**.

If this story has awakened your spirit or moved you to seek the love of Christ and His power for your life, whether you've never accepted Jesus as your savior or you've fallen away, repeat the following prayer and begin a most wonderful journey into eternal life with Him today.

Father God in heaven, As You said in Your Holy Word, (Romans 10:9) that if we confess the Lord our God and believe in our hearts that God raised Jesus from the dead, we shall be saved. (This is a sample prayer when asking Jesus into your heart. You can pray this in your own words.)

Salvation Prayer

Dear God in heaven, I come to you in the name of Jesus. I confess to You that I am a sinner, and I am sorry for my sins and the life that I have lived; I need your forgiveness.

I believe that your only begotten Son Jesus Christ shed His precious blood on the cross at Calvary and died for my sins, and I am now willing to turn from my sin.

Right now I confess Jesus as the Lord of my life and my soul. With my heart, I truly believe that your spirit raised Jesus from the dead. This very moment I accept Jesus Christ as my own personal Savior and according to His Word, right now I am saved.

I thank you Jesus, for your unlimited grace which has saved me from my sins. I thank you Jesus that your grace that never leads to license, but rather it always leads to repentance. Therefore Lord Jesus, transform my life so that I may bring glory and honor to you alone and not to myself.

Thank you Lord Jesus, for dying for me at Calvary and giving me eternal life.

Amen.

If you just said this prayer and you meant it with all your heart, we believe that you are now saved and have been born again.

You may ask, "Now that I am saved, what do I do next?" First of all you need to get into a spirit-filled, bible-based church, and study God's Word. Once you have found a church home, you will want to become water-baptized. By accepting Christ you are baptized in the spirit, but it is through water-baptism that you show your obedience to the Lord. Water baptism is a symbol of your salvation from the dead. You were dead but now you live, for the Lord Jesus Christ has redeemed you for a price! The price was His death on the cross. May God Bless You!

www.ingramcontent.com/pod-product-compliance
Lightning Source LLC
Chambersburg PA
CBHW071332250626
47159CB00004B/1572